Michael
Without
Apology

Michael Without Apology

A Novel

Catherine Ryan Hyde

LAKE UNION
PUBLISHING

Published by Lake Union Publishing, Seattle

www.apub.com

Amazon, the Amazon logo, and Lake Union Publishing are trademarks of Amazon.com, Inc., or its affiliates.

EU product safety contact:
Amazon Media EU S. à r.l.
38, avenue John F. Kennedy, L-1855 Luxembourg
amazonpublishing-gpsr@amazon.com

ISBN-13: 9781662522307 (hardcover)
ISBN-13: 9781662522291 (paperback)
ISBN-13: 9781662522314 (digital)

Cover design by Shasti O'Leary Soudant
Cover image: © Lynn Whitt, © Peter Greenway / ArcAngel;
© kongkiat chairat / Shutterstock

Printed in the United States of America

First edition

MICHAEL,
AGE NINETEEN

Chapter One

I'm Going to Have to Call You Back

Michael was walking through the quad, cutting across grass—anxious to get to his film-workshop class even though he was too early—when his phone rang in his pocket.

Even before he slipped it out and looked, he figured it was a pretty good bet that it was his mother.

He slipped it out and looked. It was his mother.

"Mom," he said, picking up the call.

"How was your first day, honey?"

"Seriously?"

He almost bumped into a gaggle of students moving in his direction because his mother was distracting him. But he looked up and jumped aside at the last minute. They didn't seem to notice.

"Isn't that a pretty normal question?" his mother asked. "Aren't mothers all over the world calling their children to hear about their first day of college?"

"Yeah, *at the end of the day*. It's . . ." He glanced at his watch. "Not even two in the afternoon."

"Okay, then. How was your first *morning*?"

Michael sighed.

"It was fine," he said. "I guess. I had two math classes. But the one I'm most looking forward to is my film workshop, and I'm almost there, so . . ."

"I'm doing that helicopter thing again, aren't I?"

"Little bit, Mom. But I'll take it as a sign that you care. Six six oh four."

"Six what?"

"Oh. Sorry. I guess I was talking to myself. That's the room number I'm looking for. Six six oh four."

Michael looked up to see a white stone building, two stories, with its stairway outdoors. All of the rooms seemed to open into the outdoor air. There were no enclosed hallways that Michael could see.

"Must be around the other side," he said, only half paying attention to the recipient of his words.

He walked around the side of the building, and there it was.

It was at the top of a flight of outdoor stairs with stone railings. Michael climbed the stairs and stuck his head into the room. It was an amphitheater room, with seats sloping down auditorium-style and the professor at the bottom. He was sitting at his desk, reading some papers that lay in front of him. His head was down, and he wore a black beret. At that moment the beret was most of what Michael could see of him. On the blackboard behind him was written the name "Mr. Robert Dunning."

Michael glanced at his watch a second time.

He was early. Embarrassingly early. Nearly fifteen minutes.

He decided to slip away again, sit in the shade of some nice tree, and finish the conversation with his mother.

Before he could, Robert Dunning looked up and saw him standing in the open doorway.

Michael froze when he saw the professor's face. Almost literally, from the feel of it. Little electric ice crystals flitted around in his gut, cutting as they squirmed, and the rush of adrenaline made his head feel almost dizzy.

Robert Dunning was a scarred man. Burn scars, from the look of it, though Michael was still far away.

"Mom, I'm going to have to call you back," he said, and ended the call.

Michael walked down to the front row, slipping the phone into his pocket. He found a seat more or less front and center and sat, wondering what to do next.

He glanced up at the professor as subtly as possible.

The entirety of Robert Dunning's face seemed to have been burned, but the scarring was especially severe around his mouth. His lips looked stretched and inflexible. The edges of his nostrils had a melted appearance, and his ears seemed welded to the sides of his head, with no real independence or definition. His hands were burned as well, with two of his fingers shortened and ill-defined. Those two fingers had no fingernails.

"Hello," Dunning said.

"Hi."

"Robert Dunning."

"Michael Woodbine."

"You're very prompt, Michael Woodbine. More than prompt, in fact."

"I know," Michael said. "I'm sorry."

Dunning looked directly into Michael's face and held his gaze. Under normal circumstances Michael found eye contact challenging, but in this case he had no choice. The older man simply hooked him and held him.

Dunning had eyes an unusual color of dark—almost navy—blue.

"Try not to go through life being sorry," he said.

"Okay," Michael said. "Sorry. I mean . . . not sorry. I meant . . . thanks. For that advice."

"It's unsolicited advice. And you know what they say about advice. They say one should only offer it in a life-and-death situation, or when asked for it. And I'm afraid I break that rule too often, because, you see, even though you wouldn't die without that advice, I think one misses out on a lot of life in the process of feeling so apologetic. So in that sense it's life-threatening. It doesn't threaten to end your life, but it does diminish it. You'll forgive me if that was more than you wanted to know."

"No. It's good advice. Actually."

"It wasn't a criticism or a judgment."

"It kind of was, but it's okay. I can hear that I have more stuff to learn."

"No, it actually isn't a criticism."

"But if *you* can go through *your* life without apologizing for things you don't really need to be sorry for, doesn't that make you a better person?"

"It does not," Dunning said. "It makes me a happier person. More relaxed. But not better. It's not a guide to my character, which is the only fair platform on which to judge me. Bear in mind that I'm fifty-nine years old. I've had more practice than you. Being a person takes practice."

"I've noticed that," Michael said.

Robert Dunning looked up and past him, and Michael turned to see that a young woman had entered the room. He felt relieved. Even though he was drawn to the energy of this man, it was also intense and exhausting to be so directly seen.

———

"My name is Robert Dunning," the professor said, standing before the class. He began to pace back and forth in front of his desk as he spoke. "I prefer to be called Mr. Dunning. Professor Dunning is all right, but not necessary. Robert is not all right. We are not 'buds.'"

Someone entered the room late, and a bit noisily, and Dunning broke off his talk to address the young man.

"Come in. Hurry up now. And do it quietly, please. We start this class on time. We start this class at two fifteen p.m., regardless of who is or is not here. Come in whenever you must, but the class waits for no one. If you arrive at two twenty, you will have missed five minutes of instruction, and so forth and so on. But I ask that you take pains not to disturb the students who managed to get here on time."

He paused in his pacing and waited for the young man to take a seat, causing all eyes to turn to the student.

That'll get him here on time, Michael thought. *Or at least it would work for me.*

"Now," Dunning said. "Where was I?"

He had a deep, booming voice that fairly dripped with confidence and authority. With every word Dunning had spoken—both directly to him and to the class at large—Michael had struggled to decide whether he was more drawn to the professor or more intimidated by him. And he still had not decided.

"As I said, my name is Robert Dunning, and I have scarring on my face and hands. Actually I have scarring all over my body, but you see the face and hands, so that's what we'll talk about."

He allowed a pause, in both his words and his pacing, which struck Michael as being quite purposeful. It seemed to be designed to throw his students back on their heels.

"You didn't think we'd talk about it, did you? You're all looking at it, but you all figured we wouldn't speak of it. Why not? It's not a secret. It's not a scandal. It's not a moral failing on my part. It just *is.*"

Dunning scanned the room carefully, seeming to stop briefly as he locked gazes with every student, or at least every one who would look directly into his eyes. Most turned their attention quickly down to their desks.

"Go ahead and look," Dunning said. "This is your chance. All of you. This is where I stand in front of you and say 'This is me. Get used to it.' And that's what you do. That's your job. To get used to it. Literally. Find your way to that place of familiarity."

Michael felt a tingling sensation move through his brain. An urgent voice in the back of his head said, *Wait. You can do that? Why didn't I know you could do that?*

Dunning stood looking over the class a moment longer, and one girl in the front row seemed to fill with pressure and then explode.

"I'm sorry!" she said, her voice breathy. "I didn't mean to stare."

Michael wasn't sure what caused her to take Dunning's comments so personally, since he was speaking to everyone equally, but he could relate to her.

"You have nothing to be sorry about. Not a one of you does. Just go ahead and look. I'm not required to be sorry for being scarred, and you're not required to be sorry for noticing. It's not a moral failing on your part, either. It's just being human. We recoil from injury in others not because we're uncaring or judgmental but because we've been genetically programmed to recoil from injury as a whole. It's part of our self-preservation instinct. So stop being ashamed for either one of us. Now, go ahead and get the staring part over, and when you're ready to start learning about filmmaking, let me know."

He stood with his hands clasped together in front of himself and waited in silence.

A minute or two ticked by, and the class began to shift uncomfortably in its collective seat.

Finally it was Michael who raised his hand.

"I want to learn about filmmaking," he said. "I'm ready."

Dunning broke his statue-like pose and pointed at Michael enthusiastically.

"Excellent! I like a person who isn't afraid to be the first to speak up. Now. Here's the most important thing I have to say to you people about film—today, and for the length of this course. If you're only going to take one thing away from my instruction, let it be this: You have to have something to say. Tattoo that on your forehead if it's the only way to remember it. *You have to have something to say.*"

He paused briefly, as if to let that sink in.

"I know you want to learn about various cameras, and lighting, and sound equipment. And video editing. And I promise that will all be covered. But what do you get if you know all that, but you don't know what you want to say?"

He waited, but no one dared to guess.

"Nothing," he said. "You get nothing. Film is a form of communication. The filmmaker, like the painter or the writer, has a vision. He or she sees something inside her head, and has a driving need to share that vision with as much of the world as can be made to pay attention. But what if the world looks inside your head and sees the sad truth that there's nothing in there? Then you have unequivocally failed in spite of your technical skills. Therefore . . . your second assignment for this class will be to make a film of your own, and almost your entire grade will depend on it. Your first assignment will be to know with every fiber of your being what you have to say using said film as a vehicle. I'm assuming that's very clear."

He waited, but no one said a word.

"I will take your silence to mean that it's very clear," he said.

———

Class had been over for three or four minutes when Dunning looked up from his phone and noticed that Michael was still sitting in the front row of his classroom.

Michael had been wrestling with himself over leaving, but he had not left. He could not leave. Somehow, in some way he could not explain to himself, he had been living in a new world since meeting this man, and he couldn't bear to go back to the old one.

His deepest fear was that the professor would ask him why he hadn't left, and he would have to attempt to explain this sudden change in . . . well, everything.

"You're still here," Dunning said.

He seemed to place no particular judgment on the sentence. It was just a neutral observation as far as Michael could tell.

"Seems that way," he said.

"You don't have anyplace more important to be?"

"I'm not sure there *is* anyplace more important to be."

Dunning tilted his head slightly, as if it would give him a better look into Michael's psyche. But he offered no answer.

"Maybe I could just stay and monitor your next class," Michael said.

"I don't have a next class. I'm done for the day. I was just catching up on some texts to my wife before I started driving."

"Oh," Michael said. "Okay."

He tried not to sound disappointed. He failed miserably, and he knew it.

They both rose, and stood considering each other for a moment.

"I'm having trouble figuring you out," Dunning said.

"Ask me anything. I don't mind."

"What's your angle?"

"Excuse me?"

"You seem to want to latch on to me for some reason. I'm old, and not especially attractive, so I'll rule out any romantic motives. It seems to have something to do with my scarring, though I'm not even sure why I say that. Generally when someone is drawn to me it's someone with injury-related body issues similar to mine. But look at you. You're a very handsome young man. Why, you could be a leading man in the film world. Every now and then an uninjured person will latch on to me as if I were some kind of special project. As if they can assure themselves of their high moral character by overlooking my appearance. I hope it's nothing like that. I don't do well at being anyone's special project. I'm not suited to that role at all."

"No," Michael said. "It's nothing like that."

"What, then?"

That was the moment when Michael knew what he had to do. What he *would* do. It was a thing unimaginable in the frame of his life before stepping into that room, but it had suddenly turned unavoidable. But in that moment, he stalled before doing it.

He simply stood in front of the man for a time. Maybe a minute. Maybe three. He could feel himself leaning forward ever so slightly, defiantly and with effort, as if facing a headwind. The more time passed, the harder it was not to cry.

Worse yet, Dunning noticed. Michael could see him notice.

Then, in motions that felt dreamlike, as if someone else were making them, he pulled his shirttails out of his jeans and unbuttoned his shirt. When it fell open, it only revealed a white undershirt. Michael always wore a white undershirt. Just in case. Just as an added layer of emotional protection.

He grabbed the hem of it and pulled it up above his collarbone.

For a moment, their roles lay reversed. The professor stared at Michael, and it was his job to get used to it.

"It all comes together now," Dunning said. "I could use a cup of coffee. Would you like a cup of coffee?"

"Absolutely I would."

"Button your shirt, Michael Woodbine, and we'll go get some coffees and talk."

"You don't drink coffee?" Dunning asked.

They sat in a coffee shop in the student union. Michael was drinking orange juice because he actually hated coffee. Dunning was drinking a double espresso.

"Not so much, no," Michael said.

"Then I guess when you said you wanted to go out for coffee you were speaking more figuratively."

"I wanted to talk to you some more."

"Yes, I got that part."

They had secured a table near the window, and Michael was distracted by watching the people walking by—the way they missed a step when their eyes landed on Dunning.

"Do you know yet what you want to say in film?" Dunning asked him.

"Not really," Michael said, averting his eyes.

"I'm surprised. I would have thought you knew. You seem so driven. I thought you had a very definite something to say and it's what drove you into my class, and into filmmaking. Why do you want to make films, then?"

"My lifelong dream was always to be an actor."

"We have a decent drama department."

"I can't be an actor."

"No good at it?"

"I'm good enough."

"What's the problem, then? You certainly have the face for it."

"You know what the problem is. Sooner or later I'd be asked to do a nude scene, or even just a shirtless one."

Dunning sighed deeply.

"You're in a unique situation," he said. "Well, no. Not unique. I try to be exact in my language, and that was inexact. A relatively unusual situation, I should have said. Or maybe I should simply say it's a very different situation than mine."

"Because I can just keep my shirt on, you mean?"

"Yes, that. I sense you think that was a bit of luck on your part, but I'm not so sure you're correct."

"I . . ." Michael was unsure of how to unpack what he'd just been told. "I definitely don't feel lucky about any of it, but yeah. I think I like it better this way than the other way around. Why? Do you think it's better your way?"

"I don't know if it's better," Dunning said. "I just know you have the option to hide this one aspect of your whole self to feel safe and avoid discomfort. I haven't lived out both roles, so I have no right to place a judgment on the two situations, except to say that what we both face is wrong, because nobody should be made to feel unsafe for being himself. Maybe one is more wrong than the other. I'm not trying to judge. But I don't think it's lucky, the way it worked out for you. Luck*ier*, in certain moments, maybe. But not lucky. You're feeling compelled to betray yourself in return for a sense of emotional safety. The world should ask that of no one. You've been passing for uninjured, Michael. Granted, I don't blame you in the least. It's an easy short-term solution to your situation, and I don't say that critically. But you're selling away a piece of yourself in return."

"What am I selling away?" Michael asked, even though he knew in his heart and gut it was true.

A woman leading a three- or four-year-old boy by the hand passed near the window. The little boy put on the brakes when he saw Dunning, his face briefly alarmed. Dunning smiled and waved. The mother tugged on her son's arm and all but dragged him away. Before they lost sight of each other, the boy smiled and waved in return.

"In a few months it will be time for spring break," Dunning said. "College boys all over the country will crowd onto Florida beaches to blow off steam from their first semester. They'll party in nothing but swim trunks. They'll party in not even that much. They'll hook up with college girls for meaningless flings. It's a tradition. Will you be doing any of that with them?"

"Well, I never did before," Michael said. He had attempted to toss it off as half joking, but it fell flat. "No," he said. "You're right. I won't."

"And you're still unclear on what you've sold away? Even when we add back in giving up your dream of being an actor? Look, I'm not trying to give you a hard time. I get it. I'm just trying to place a thought in the back of your mind. Like a seed. Who knows? Maybe it will take root and grow in that dark, moist space. Here's the thought: Your life will be your own when you can do what I did today. Stand in front of whatever small segment of the world you find yourself facing and say 'Here I am. Get used to it.' That's when you'll truly be free."

"Maybe that's what I should be saying in my film. 'Here I am. Get used to it.' Too bad I'm not quite there yet. Now that I've met you I could almost do the 'Here I am' part. I'm not sure I could instruct anyone to get used to it."

"Act as if," Dunning said. "Another piece of unsolicited advice. Also known as 'Fake it till you make it' by those who prefer their advice to rhyme. It would appear that stating a thing over and over again, whether you believe it or not, tends to wear down the psyche after a while. The mind picks up on the repetition and starts to believe it. But it's not my job to tell you what you have to say."

"I brought it up, though."

"You did indeed," Dunning said, and drained the last of the espresso from his cup. "Which might be telling. Just sleep on it. And now, though I've enjoyed our conversation, I should probably get home to my wife."

MICHAEL,
AGE SEVEN

Chapter Two

A One-Way Ticket to Atatürk International

"I want to go in the water," Michael said.

"I'm just not up to taking you down there," his mom said with a sigh.

She had been detached and distant all evening. Even more so than usual.

They sat together on a blanket in the sand, in the dusk of evening, waiting for the fireworks show to begin. Listening to the sounds of the surf, and the crowd, and more than one competing boom box.

"I'll take him," Michael's father said.

Michael jumped to his feet.

"Where's Thomas?" his mother asked.

"No idea," his father said.

"How can you not know?"

"Well, you don't know either. He's eleven. He's old enough to know where he is. He probably had to go pee or something."

"Did he say he was leaving?"

"I don't know, Livie. I thought you were watching him."

"I'll stay here and wait for him. You two go swim."

Michael's father crouched down and invited Michael to climb onto his back. Then they trotted to the edge of the surf.

It was something like riding a horse. Except Michael never had, so it was more like how he imagined riding a horse might feel. He had ridden a pony once when he was five. But the pony was sleepy and calm, and obviously couldn't wait for the ride to be over, stalling in the shade whenever his handler's attention drifted away. Michael's father was a racehorse that day. He was on fire.

He barreled into the surf with Michael on his back, and just kept going.

Saltwater splashed and sprayed into Michael's face as he ran. Wave after wave threatened to break right into them and knock them back. Maybe even hold them under. But every time his father jumped up and managed to crest over the top of it, until finally he was swimming instead of running.

Michael could feel the energy of the man against his chest and legs, and he seemed to be fairly buzzing with it. The normally slow and slightly lazy father Michael had always known was now Superman.

For a few moments it was exhilarating. Then it quickly jumped the line into frightening.

And long after it jumped, his father just kept swimming out to sea.

"Why are we going so far out?" Michael shouted into his ear.

"You wanted to go in the water, right?"

"Yeah, but not so far from shore. I feel like we're about to show up in China."

"Why such a scaredy-cat? You don't trust me?"

"No, I do."

The truth was, normally he did. Mostly. But he seemed to be riding on the back of an entirely different father that evening. And he had no idea where this new person might take him.

Still his father swam.

"Can we go back?" Michael asked, his voice panicky.

"Why do you want to go back?"

"I just do. Please?"

Still his father swam.

"Please!" Michael screamed into his father's ear. "I want to go back!"

His father stopped swimming away from shore. For a moment he treaded water in the cold ocean as Michael clung desperately to his neck, feeling the waves swell and recede.

Then he turned and swam for the beach, and Michael breathed for what felt like the first time in a long time. Longer than would literally have been possible, he knew.

When they reached the shallow water Michael found himself unceremoniously dropped onto the ocean floor, where he fell over and got sand in his swim trunks and saltwater in his eyes.

He scrambled to his feet and ran after his father all the way back to their blanket.

Thomas was there with his mother.

"Oh good, you found him," his father said.

"He wandered back on his own. That was a fast swim."

"Don't look at *me*. I would've stayed in a lot longer, but Michael right away started screaming he wanted to go back."

"Yeah, well, that's Michael for you," his mother said.

Michael pulled on his T-shirt and shivered, wet and cold, in the evening breeze.

"You boys wait right here," she said. "Your dad and I will be right back. Don't get into any trouble."

Then, for the fourth time since they had arrived that afternoon, they headed back in the direction of the parking lot.

This time they were gone for a weirdly long time.

———

"Let's go do something interesting," Thomas said.

It immediately struck Michael as a bad idea. It hit a note inside him that vibrated in fear, like a tuning fork. Not because of the words themselves but because he knew his older brother well. He knew what kinds of mischief Thomas classified under the category of "interesting."

19

"We should wait for Mom and Dad."

"If we wait for them to get back, they'll make sure everything we do is boring."

"The fireworks'll be interesting," Michael said. "I think they're going to start any minute now."

"They're not, moron. They're not going to start until it's much darker. Don't you know anything?"

"Why do Mom and Dad keep going back to the car?" Michael asked, glancing nervously over his shoulder for what felt like the hundredth time.

"You really *don't* know anything," Thomas said, "do you? Come on. Walk with me. You're about to do something brave."

Thomas jumped to his feet, but Michael stayed deeply rooted to the blanket, not liking the sound of what had been proposed. Not liking it one bit.

"Why do I have to do something brave?" he asked his brother.

"You want to live in America, don't you?"

"I already live in America."

"You want to keep living here? Or you want to get sent away?"

Michael looked up at his older brother. The sun had set in a spot behind Thomas's shoulder, and the backdrop to his brother was a quickly darkening red sky. Thomas's long, shaggy hair was uncombed and flying wildly in the light wind.

"Where would I get sent? And who would send me?"

Michael knew from the hard knocks of experience that not everything his brother Thomas said was true. Not by a wide margin. But this sounded serious. It sounded like something one could not afford to ignore unless they were absolutely certain.

Thomas reached down and grabbed him by the shoulder of his T-shirt, stretching the fabric out of shape as he pulled Michael to his feet.

"Come on, dummy."

They began walking through the crowd at the edge of the water, Michael attempting to straighten out his stretched shirt.

"It's like this," Thomas said. "America is the land of the brave. Right?"

Actually, Michael knew the song by heart. Words and music both. So he knew it was not exactly the land of the brave. It was the land of the *free*. The *home* of the brave. He didn't correct his brother.

"So?"

"So if you want to stay here you have to do something brave."

Michael stopped walking suddenly, his feet firmly planted in the sand.

"Why just me?"

"Not just you. Everybody."

"Well then, why don't *you* do something brave?"

"I already did. When I was seven. Now it's your turn."

He grabbed Michael again by the stretched-out shoulder of his T-shirt and tugged him along.

As they walked, Michael saw they were getting closer to the cordoned-off area where the professional fireworks guys were going to put on the Fourth of July show. It was surrounded by wooden sawhorses with signs that clearly read "KEEP OUT."

A fire truck was parked on the sand nearby, its three firefighters huddled together, talking and laughing.

"How will they know I did it so they know not to send me away?"

"I'll tell them for you. There's paperwork. I'll do the paperwork."

"What do I have to do?" Michael asked, feeling something pound inside his head.

"You have to sneak in there and steal one of the fireworks thingies. Like one of those rockets. See how those rockets are sitting near the back? Near the wooden things that block it all off? And everybody has their backs turned to those. We'll take it and go down the beach as far as we need to till there's nobody around. And we'll set it off."

Michael stopped again.

Fear was making his face feel tingly and hot. It made him feel as though he were only just barely in control of his bladder. When he spoke, his voice sounded distant and slightly foreign, as though it might belong to someone else entirely.

"Everybody will see it and then they'll know we set it off."

"The minute we set it off we'll run away."

"What if I don't do it?" Michael asked, sure he didn't want to do it.

"Then you have to leave the country."

"Would you and Mom and Dad leave with me?"

"Oh hell no. We want to live *here*. You'd have to go alone."

"Who would I live with, then?"

"Nobody, I guess. They just fly you someplace. Someplace that's not America. France, or Istanbul. Someplace like that. And then that's it. They just put you off the plane and you're on your own from there."

Michael only stood a moment, noticing the way the world no longer held still. It seemed to spin around his head in a way he found most unsettling.

"You want to stay," Thomas said. "Right?"

"Sure I do."

"Then come on."

———

They lay on their bellies in the sand for a long time, just watching the movements of the men—the firefighters and the two guys who knew how to set off fireworks. Most of the couples and families had set up blankets much farther away from the action. Other than Thomas and Michael, no other beachgoers seemed to dare come that close. And yet no one seemed to be paying any attention to them.

Thomas leaned close and whispered in his ear.

"When I say go, just do it. Go fast. Don't stop for anything. Just grab one and then run like the wind."

For one brief instant Michael was almost prepared to say no to his brother. He even went so far as to open his mouth to say the word. But then he pictured himself standing all alone on the tarmac at an airport in Istanbul. He closed his mouth again.

He didn't even know what language they spoke there.

A second or two later the three firemen turned and walked toward their fire truck together.

"Go go go!" Thomas whisper-shouted in his ear.

Michael crawled like lightning through the loose sand and under a sawhorse, his blood pounding wildly in his ears. He wrapped his hand around the heavy, imposing tube of a rocket and pulled it up from its rack-like holder. Then he crawled straight backward to where Thomas waited.

They stood. They spun. They ran.

They ran faster than Michael had known he could run.

Just before they rose up over a bluff and out of sight of the crowded beach, Michael dared a glance back over his shoulder. One of the firefighters was standing very still near his truck, facing them. It was almost dark, so it was hard to be sure, but he seemed to be watching them run away.

"He saw us!" Michael said.

"Nobody saw you take it. I was watching."

"He saw us running away."

"Well then, run faster, dummy."

They dropped down over the bluff to a more deserted stretch of beach and just kept running. Michael was still aware of the weight of the rocket in his hand. It felt daring and dangerous.

His chest burned, his side developed a painful stitch, and he could barely breathe, but he kept up with his brother through the sheer power of adrenaline.

They scrambled up and across another bluff. It was thickly covered with those puffy plants his mother called ice plant, which made it hard to navigate without tripping. Then they dropped down onto a second beach that was utterly deserted.

"Here," Thomas said.

They stopped running.

Michael fell onto his side in the sand and panted.

"You can't set it off," he said, his words barely intelligible.

"Sure I can."

"You need fire."

Thomas reached into his pocket and held up a bright-yellow disposable plastic lighter.

"Where'd you get that?"

"From Dad."

"Dad doesn't smoke."

"Yeah he does."

"I never saw him smoke a cigarette."

"Well, not that kind of cigarette," Thomas said.

Michael scrambled to his feet—all the better to get out of the way fast when needed—and watched Thomas plant the rocket firmly in the sand near their feet. Then his brother stood back for a brief moment, still holding that bright-yellow lighter.

A movement caught Michael's eye, and he looked up and past his brother and saw the firefighter standing on the bluff above them, in a tangle of the ice-plant ground cover, looking down. Looking right at them. He was silhouetted by the western edge of the sky, still fairly light, and Michael could see him surprisingly well.

Those two things Michael would always remember. Some of that night would become a blur. The majority of it would be lost forever. But for the rest of his life Michael would be able to see the bright-yellow plastic lighter and the firefighter on the bluff when he closed his eyes.

If he dared to try.

Everything that happened after that happened with blinding speed, and it all revolved around Michael making two key mistakes. One, he thought Thomas had also seen the firefighter. Two, since he figured Thomas had seen the firefighter, Michael assumed Thomas knew better than to light the fuse.

Quickly, and without thinking, Michael threw his body over the rocket to hide the evidence of what they had done. He knocked it over and half buried it in the sand with his weight, all in one movement.

It was only when he felt the sizzling fire of the lit fuse burn his belly that he knew just how monumental a mistake he had made. But it was too late to correct it. It was too late even to register it in his brain.

In less time than it would have taken for a signal to travel from a brain to a muscle, Michael's world exploded. Literally.

The pain was entirely unlike anything he had experienced before. It was unlike anything he had even imagined existed in the world to be experienced. It felt as though a strong giant made of white-hot fire had stuck its fingers between Michael's ribs and roughly, angrily torn him wide open.

But it only lasted for a second or two.

The blast threw him up into the air, and he landed sprawled in the soft sand. He felt sand in his eyes and mouth, but not much else. He had fallen into such a deep state of shock as to be incapable of experiencing much of anything. In fact, he had fallen into such a deep state of shock that, in his seven-year-old consciousness, the condition could easily be mistaken for having died.

He heard his own voice very clearly.

It said, "Oh no, I'm dead."

But he didn't think he had actually spoken. He didn't think he could actually speak. Still, the words rang crystal clear in his head, and they were in his own voice.

And he believed them.

In the distant world that Michael thought he had left behind, he heard the first pops and booms of the public fireworks show starting. They sounded like something that lived in a completely different dimension from him.

Anything else that might have happened that night happened after Michael had surrendered consciousness for what would prove to be a very long time.

Chapter Three

Where's the Reset Button, Jeffrey?

Michael opened his eyes.

He was lying on his back in what felt like a bed, but it was not *his* bed, and it seemed to support him in too upright a position. Everything he saw was white, which did nothing to dampen the impression that he was dead.

It filled him with a sense of terror and dread, and yet those feelings seemed distant, as though happening to someone else—someone who was nearby but who was not him.

The pain in his torso was dull and yet fierce at the same time.

It seemed unfair. If you're going to have your life ripped away, at least the pain should go with it.

Then he noticed a black TV suspended high on the wall, its screen blank and dark. It was the only nonwhite object he could see without moving his head, which he was afraid to do.

A face appeared suddenly in his line of vision.

It surprised him. Before he'd died, he would have made some kind of startled jump over such a sudden development. But his body seemed not to move that way anymore. Or any other way, really.

She looked about fifty, the woman leaning over him. She was dressed all in white. She had bright-red hair and laugh lines around her eyes, and when she spoke her voice carried some kind of pleasant, lilting accent. But Michael didn't know enough about accents to know what kind it was. He just knew he liked it.

"Look at you, darlin'," she said. "You opened your eyes."

Michael moved his mouth slowly and carefully, afraid to see if his words even worked.

He heard himself say, "Am I dead?" His voice sounded croaky and weak. Really not like himself at all.

"Oh no, darlin', no. You're not dead. You came awful darn close, though. Awful close. Closer than anybody likes to see for a little guy your age. Why, it's only just in the last couple of days that your doctor started entertaining the idea that you maybe planned to stay with us. He just changed your condition from critical to serious yesterday."

Michael felt his forehead furrow in confusion. It felt encouraging, because it was the first time any part of his body had moved.

"How long have I been here?"

"Nine days, darlin'."

He wanted to ask how such a thing was possible without his knowledge, but asking felt like more than he had the energy to do.

"How's your pain, Michael?"

"It hurts."

"I'm not too surprised to hear that, all things considered. I'll just bump your pain-medicine drip a little bit till you tell me you're pretty comfortable."

Michael moved his eyes slightly to follow her motions. He saw a hanging bag with a tube trailing down from it. But he couldn't see where the tube went without moving his head, so he didn't try.

A kind of comfortable warmth spread through him, starting in one arm, and the pain moved further away. Or maybe the pain held its ground and Michael moved further away.

"Where're my mom and dad?" he heard himself ask, as if from a great distance.

At first he heard no answer.

27

Then the woman said, "Now we're getting into things outside my department, darlin'. But I'll get you your answer."

He watched her pick up . . . something. He didn't know what it was, but it had a cord on one end and a red button on the other. She pressed the button and then set it down again.

Just a few seconds later she looked up and past him.

"Oh, Lina," she said. "Good. Call Dr. Banerjee, please, and tell him his youngest patient is awake and asking after his parents. And also, because of that second thing and all . . . please call that lady from CPS and tell her, too."

"What lady from CPS?" a young-sounding, distant voice said.

"She left her card at the nurses' station."

"Oh. Okay. I'll figure it out."

The red-haired woman turned her gaze down onto Michael again, and she looked almost . . . loving. Almost motherly.

"We'll get you some answers, darlin'. We'll get you what you need to know. You don't deserve not to know. You don't deserve any of this. You shouldn't be here at all. If anything, that brother of yours—well. Don't get me started."

Michael felt his eyebrows lift.

"You know my brother?"

"I never met him personally, darlin', no. And it's a good thing for him I didn't, because I'd want to give him the spanking of a lifetime and I don't know as I could resist the temptation. I only know he broke down crying and told the police the truth about how he tricked you into doing it."

But Michael had no memories of his brother tricking him. He didn't even know the nature of the "it" he had done.

"Wait . . ." he said. His eyes drifted closed for a moment, and he seemed unable to stop them. He forced them open again. "There were police? Why were there police?"

"Well, honey, there's always police when a minor child gets hurt as bad as you did. Even if it seems like an accident. Kids your age aren't supposed to get into accidents this bad, because somebody's supposed to be looking after them. Oh, things can happen, I know. But it's like a car crash. Maybe nothing could've been done to prevent it, but the police are still gonna want to know for sure. Maybe somebody was texting on their phone or had a lot to drink. Anyway, I've said entirely too much already. I'm way over the line and out of my department. You just try to get some rest, darlin'. The people who can give you your answers'll come around and see you by and by."

———

Michael pulled himself up from a state of semiconsciousness—how much later he didn't know—to see a man standing over him. The man wore a white lab coat. He had brown skin and gray hair and smiling, friendly eyes. He was staring at Michael intently.

"Hello there," he said when Michael connected with his gaze. "My name is Dr. Banerjee. How do you feel today? How is your pain?"

The doctor also had a pleasant and lilting accent, but this one Michael knew. Dr. Banerjee was an Indian man. Michael had a friend from school whose parents had moved to this country from India. *That* accent he could identify.

"It's bad, until that lady comes by and does something with the hanging bag. Then it's kind of . . . still there and still bad, but it's like I can't feel it so much."

"I'm afraid that might be the best we can do for you under the circumstances. Can you tell me your name?"

"You don't know my name? The nurse knows my name."

The doctor smiled, but Michael wasn't sure why.

"I do know your name, actually. It's here on your chart. I just want to be sure *you* know it."

"Who doesn't know their own name?"

He was feeling sleepy and dull, and disconnected from the world, and his words slurred together as though he were drunk.

"You'd be surprised," the doctor said. "After a severe trauma like this one, people can have memory issues."

"But it wasn't my head that got hurt."

"But you lost a lot of blood, and that can cause issues in your brain as well. So . . . do you know it?"

"My name? Michael Costa."

"And what about your parents' names? Do you remember that too?"

"Miles and Olivia Costa."

"And do you know what month it is, Michael?"

Michael tried to press his brain into action, but he seemed not to have a way to access it anymore. It seemed to live behind a closed door now, like those doors that said "Authorized Personnel Only." Suddenly he was no longer a person authorized to go inside.

While he was waiting for an answer, Dr. Banerjee gently held Michael's eyes open, one at a time, and shined a light into each one.

"I'll give you a hint," he said. "It's the same month as it was when you came in. The same month as your accident."

Michael stared at the imaginary closed door to his own mind for a few more seconds. Then he shrugged ever so slightly. Shoulders only, and not much of *that*.

"Okay. That's okay. Do you know what year it is?"

But by that time Michael was tired. Too tired even to try.

He shrugged again.

"It's okay," the doctor said. "It's not a test."

"It's *sort of* a test. You're testing my brain, right?"

"It's not a test where you need to feel bad about how you do. How many fingers am I holding up?"

"Three."

"Good."

"Where're my mom and dad? When can I go home?"

The doctor briefly connected with Michael's eyes. Then he averted his gaze, directing it down toward the floor. Michael knew that gesture. It was what grown-ups did when you asked a question and they knew

30

you wouldn't like the answer and felt bad even having to be the one to tell you.

"There's a woman coming to see you in an hour or two. Her name is Ms. Keller. She'll answer all those questions about your parents. As far as when you can be discharged . . . honestly, I don't know yet. But not anytime soon, I'm afraid. You have another surgery coming up tomorrow or the next day. We need to take some layers of skin from your thighs and graft them onto your torso. We have to be very careful about infection until you're much more healed. To be completely honest with you, you should plan on being here for a few more weeks."

He waited, in case Michael had something to say. But what could you say to the idea of weeks more, the only part Michael truly understood? It was devastating. Then again, everything was devastation, though he didn't use that word in his mind because he didn't know it. But he felt it. His life had fallen into devastation. Michael had a sense that the news dropped onto all the other terrible news in his life but couldn't force the pile of awfulness down any lower. The awfulness had bottomed out.

"I'm sorry," Dr. Banerjee said. "I'll let you get some rest now."

For a minute or two Michael only stared after him.

Then he started to cry.

He didn't know how long he'd been crying when the voice startled him. He couldn't judge.

It was male, the voice, and sounded young. Not as young as Michael, but young. It clearly came from inside the room, but not from anyone Michael could see.

"You okay over there?" it said.

"Who *is* that? Who's there?"

"It's just me," the voice said. "Jeffrey."

Michael watched as the curtain to the right of his bed twitched slightly. Then he saw two heavily bandaged hands appear at one edge of it. They were clearly incapable of grasping anything, but the person attached to them managed to catch the edge of the curtain between his wrists and tug it back.

On the other side was a second bed. Settling on the edge of the bed was this Jeffrey person.

He looked to be a little older than Michael's brother, Thomas. Maybe twelve, Michael guessed. Maybe even thirteen. He was wearing a hospital gown, like the one Michael wore. He had tons of curly blond hair that fell all around his face as he leaned forward, and he smiled in a way that made Michael feel warmer.

"Hey," he said.

The word had a friendly sound.

"Hey," Michael said back.

Then they just regarded each other for a moment.

Jeffrey had long, thin bare legs that swung back and forth slightly as they dangled off the side of the hospital bed. His feet were bare, his toes long and graceful.

"Have you been here the whole time?" Michael asked. "I didn't know there was anybody over there."

"No, I just came in this morning. I have to have another surgery. They just put me in this room a couple of hours ago. I was here on the Fourth of July. Now I'm back."

As soon as Jeffrey said it—that date—Michael remembered. A lot.

He remembered too much.

The bright-yellow lighter. The firefighter looking down from the bluff, silhouetted by sunset.

And then, even though he tried to stop the flow, he remembered what it felt like to explode.

"I was here on the Fourth of July, too," he said, leaning away from the bad memories and into the comfort of having something in common with . . . well, anybody, really.

"Fireworks got you?" Jeffrey asked.

"Yeah. You?"

"Fireworks. Yeah."

They sat in silence for a long time.

They could have spoken, Michael thought. If they'd wanted to. At least, that was how it felt to him. They weren't withholding, or afraid to have a conversation. It felt more as though nothing needed to be said.

Then Jeffrey said, "I'm trying to think what I want to tell you. Like . . . what I wish somebody had told me. And I think I know what it is. Have you looked yet?"

"At what?"

"Have you seen what you look like under the bandages?"

"Not yet," Michael said, feeling a creeping sense of unease overtake him.

"Sooner or later they'll come by to change the dressings. Maybe they already did, but sooner or later they'll do it while you're awake. Anyway, here's what I think I want to tell you. Don't look."

"Ever?"

"Well, no. I don't mean *ever*."

"Good, because that would be weird. Like, never look at the middle of yourself for the whole rest of your life."

"But these things are better when they've had some time to heal," Jeffrey said. "At least, I sure hope they are. Even if it's not a whole bunch better, it's bound to be *some* better. And now is not a good time, anyway. You're in a strange place, and you don't know where your parents are."

"How did you know that about my parents?"

"I heard you talking to your doctor. I wasn't trying to listen in. I just couldn't help it. I guess I'm just saying wait till you're in a safe place and you have people you know around you. When you're feeling better about things. You know what I mean, right?"

"I think so."

For a moment Michael only nursed that disturbing sense of dread. He had known he hurt. He had known it was awful to be in a hospital alone, and that what had happened to him was frightening and bad. But he had not yet considered that life held more unpleasant surprises in store for him. He had not thought about how his body would look now, or how it would feel to him to see it for the first time.

He had not considered that, even in the light of his unexpected survival, everything had changed.

"Did you look at your hands?" he asked Jeffrey.

"Yeah. I did. And now I wish I hadn't."

They sat without talking for a minute or two. Michael noticed that, even through the sea of dressings on Jeffrey's hands, it was clear that he did not still have all of his fingers.

It made Michael feel a little sick inside, as though he were suffering on Jeffrey's behalf.

"It was just, like . . . a second," Michael said.

"What was?"

"My accident. With the fireworks. It was like I did a wrong thing, but only for a second." And now it was dawning on him that the effects of that one-second accident would last. Maybe even forever. "It just seems weird. You know. To have to . . . *keep* what happened. You know what I mean?"

"Maybe. I'm not sure."

"Like, it just seems wrong that I can't undo it. Just walk up to that second and do something different. Just choose a different thing to do. Somehow. I mean . . . I don't want to sound stupid. I know you can't. I just wonder *why* you can't. It doesn't seem fair."

"Time only goes one way," Jeffrey said. "What's done can't be undone."

"I know. I know it *is* that way. I just wish it wasn't."

"You and me both," Jeffrey said. He lay back down on the bed, on top of the covers, and stared at the ceiling for a few seconds. "Like a reset button," he said.

"Yeah, like that."

"Like on a video game. The game says you're dead. It says 'game over.' But then you can just reset it and start again."

"At least we're not dead," Michael said.

"But I don't think we can ever reset this."

"No," Michael said. "I don't think so either."

———

Despite what the doctor had said, Ms. Keller did not come to see Michael in an hour or two. She came the following morning.

Michael's eyes shot open, and he blinked into the light, and there she was.

She was small and neatly dressed, and she seemed to be one of those people who liked everything just so. Her hair, her clothes. The world. He would not have summed it up in those words, but he had known people like her before.

He turned his head carefully to see if Jeffrey was awake, but the other bed was neatly made and empty.

"What happened to Jeffrey?" he asked Ms. Keller.

"I don't know," she said. "I don't even know who that is."

She had a voice like the rest of her. Just so.

"I really, really want to know, though."

"I could ask the nurse."

"Please," he said.

She turned and left the room.

A minute or two later she was back with that nice motherly redheaded nurse in tow.

"Jeffrey had his surgery yesterday afternoon, darlin'," the nurse said, "and then he got to go home."

"Oh," Michael said, trying to disguise his disappointment. "That's good. I mean, for him."

Ms. Keller stepped up to his bed again.

Michael shot a desperate look toward the nurse—because he at least knew her—and he begged her with his eyes not to go away. She must have understood that language, because she hung in the doorway and waited.

"My name is Ms. Keller," the new woman said, even though he already knew that. "I'm your caseworker. That means it's my job to make sure you're taken care of, and that you have everything you need. I know you've been asking about your parents. The reason they haven't come to see you—well . . . let's just say they have some troubles that are keeping them away."

"What does that even mean?" Michael asked. "Nothing should keep them away."

"They literally can't be here."

"Why not?" Michael was growing agitated now, and his upset was tightening his belly and chest. It was excruciatingly painful, but he didn't know how to make it stop. "What kind of trouble? What does that mean? Tell me."

"Soon we'll have you in a foster home and your foster family can explain a lot more."

"Tell him," the nurse whispered into the caseworker's ear. But she sounded mad, and it came out loud for a whisper, and Michael heard it just fine.

The caseworker and the nurse exchanged a long stare that Michael thought looked like a fight. Then they both walked out into the hall outside his room. But Michael could hear most of what they said, even though he thought he probably wasn't supposed to.

"It's a tough truth for a child his age."

"As opposed to what'll be going on in his head if he doesn't know? As opposed to thinking they're just not bothering to be here? Tell him, or I will."

"I don't think you have a right to—"

"Tell him they're in jail," the nurse said. "So he doesn't think they don't care."

For a moment everything was very, very quiet. Quieter than Michael thought an area could get just by subtracting all the sounds.

Then they both walked back in.

"Why are they in jail?" he asked.

The caseworker shot an angry glance toward the nurse, like saying *This is all your fault* but without any sound.

"Well, I'm sorry you overheard that," Ms. Keller said. "I didn't mean for you to. But now . . . I don't know. Well. Your parents have been charged with child endangerment. That means for not making sure you were safe."

"Why? It wasn't their fault. They didn't tell me to do it. We snuck away. It wasn't their fault."

Michael didn't know whose fault it was, or if they had snuck away. He didn't remember. But in defense of his parents, he said it all the same.

"There were other factors," she said, "that the judge felt *made* it their fault. We don't know yet how long they'll be in jail."

"But when they get out they'll take me back, right?"

"We hope so. But not right away. We'll need some time to be sure they're in a good position to keep you safe. Until then you'll be in a foster home with a very nice couple. Their names are Mr. and Mrs. Woodbine—Charles and Judy Woodbine—and they're going to come in tomorrow to meet you."

"Is that where Thomas is?"

"No. You and your brother will be in different foster homes. The judge thought it would be better that way."

Michael's gut had not unclenched, and he could not unclench it with that woman talking to him, and the pain was unbearable. It was making him cry—big hot tears that leaked out no matter how hard he tried to clamp down on them and hold them in. At least, he thought it was the pain making him cry. It was certainly one factor.

"Stop talking to me," he said. "It hurts. I need more of that stuff for pain. Can you talk to me later? It hurts too much now."

The nurse came and took the small caseworker by both shoulders and steered her out of the room. Then she came back and adjusted Michael's pain-medication drip.

"You all right now, darlin'?" she asked.

He only nodded.

He had never asked her name, and he felt guilty for that now.

He waited a moment for the pain meds to ease into his blood. It relaxed him, which relieved about half of the pain very quickly.

"Tell me the truth," he said, his voice barely over a whisper. "You're the only one who tells me the truth."

"The police found something illegal in their car. And in their systems. And they'd been drinking a lot. A *lot*. That's why they got charged."

Michael opened his mouth to speak, but the drugs were completely knocking him down by then. He wanted to be upset, but he couldn't break through the haze to feel what was right there to be felt.

"Why can't I go to the same house as Thomas?" he managed, with great effort, to say.

"They think he's a bad influence on you, because he almost got you killed."

"Oh."

He drifted for a minute or two, halfway to dropping into a coma-like sleep.

"Thank you for telling me the truth," he whispered.

Then he was down for most of the rest of the day.

MICHAEL,
AGE NINETEEN

Chapter Four

You Might Not Think It's Happy, But It's Me

"I'm going to be making a student film," Michael told them over dinner. "For my film-workshop class."

"About what, honey?" his mom asked.

Michael found himself hesitant to tell her. So, for a moment, he didn't answer.

They were eating sloppy joes, wearing their napkins like bibs. His father was working hard at eating neatly, and it seemed to be absorbing all his attention.

"Like a movie with a story?" his mother asked. "Like a love story with actors playing the parts?"

"No, like a documentary. And I was really, really hoping you'd be willing to buy me a camera. Or to lend me the money to buy one, or give me some work I could do to earn the money to buy one. You get extra credit for using something better than your phone. The school has six video cameras for the people who can't afford one of their own—or maybe they belong to Mr. Dunning, I'm not sure—but there's going to be a lot of competition for those. It'll be a lot easier to film on your own schedule if you have a camera that's yours."

"What would a thing like that cost?" his father asked.

It was a pretty basic question, and one Michael knew he should have been prepared to answer. He should have gathered detailed numbers before he ever raised the subject.

He wanted to look immediately on the internet, but there was a strict "no phones" rule at his family's dinner table.

"I'll find out," he said.

"We can at least lend him the money," his mom said, "can't we, Charley?"

"I'll tell you when I know how much money we're talking about."

She turned her attention back onto Michael. It made him feel slightly uneasy, because he knew she was going to ask about the content of his film.

"Tell us about this documentary."

"I still have to work it out in my head," he said.

"But you must at least know what it's going to be about."

"I think so."

He didn't say more for some time. Then he realized he was going to feel this discomfort until he went ahead and spit it out.

"It's going to be about scars," he said. "About people with scars."

In his peripheral vision he saw her head come up. She seemed to be staring at him, but he purposely didn't turn his head to look.

"That doesn't seem like a very happy subject," she said.

"Not all documentaries are happy."

"But yours could be."

"And another thing," he said suddenly, feeling a flash of something like anger. "When you say scars are something we shouldn't be talking about because they're not happy enough, you're talking about me. How do you think that makes me feel?"

It was a direct and fairly brave thing to say, and it was generally unlike him to say so much. He expected some kind of explosive or defensive reaction from her, but she seemed to just absorb his thoughts and move on.

"I just think we can focus on the better parts of whatever life's dealt us. You know what I mean?"

He opened his mouth to say that she was suggesting he acknowledge only part of himself.

His father quickly capped the conversation before he could respond.

"Judy," he said, "leave the poor boy alone. It's his film, not yours, and it'll be about whatever he wants it to be about. It's not a film by Judy Woodbine. I'm sure when he's done he'll lend you his camera and you can make one of your own, and it can be as happy as you want it to be."

Michael opened his mouth to thank his father for rescuing him. But he didn't want to hurt his mother's feelings, or make her think they were siding against her.

So he only said, "I'll get some prices on cameras and let you know."

———

He found his father a few minutes after dinner. He was in his den, smoking a pipe and reading the evening paper. His mother didn't think well of his smoking it anywhere else in the house.

It all had a certain nineteen-fifties-sitcom feel to Michael, but that was his family.

"Hey," Michael said, and sat down on the ottoman next to his father's sock feet.

His father set down the paper.

"They start at around sixty-five dollars," Michael said. "And they go up to around two hundred and fifty or more. But for, like, a hundred and twenty-five dollars you can get one plenty good enough for what I have in mind."

"It's amazing."

"What is?"

"The way this new technology comes out and it costs an arm and a leg, and then you turn around and you can get it for the price of a good dinner. Especially since a good dinner keeps getting more expensive." He ran his hand in a downward stroking motion along his dark beard, as if smoothing it into place. It had been shot through with gray just a few months earlier, so Michael figured he must have started coloring it. "Tell you what. I'll give you a hundred and twenty-five dollars, and half of it will be a loan and half of it will be a gift. How's that sound?"

"It sounds great. Thank you. That's very nice."

"We'll find you some paid work you can do, or you can pay it a little at a time out of your allowance. Up to you. And listen. You know your mother means well, right?"

Michael was a little taken aback by the question. It was unusual for his father to break ranks with his mother in private conversation, out of her earshot.

"Um . . . yeah. Yeah. Of course I do."

"She just wants to protect you."

"I know that."

"But she's a little slow to get it. You know. That you're a man now. She's a good woman even if maybe she tries too hard sometimes. I think in some ways she still sees you as that wounded seven-year-old boy who needed so much help from us. She made a commitment to keep you safe the way she figured you should have been safe all along, and now she can't quite set it down again. Anyway. You make the film *you* want to make. Don't think about what she wants. Put it out of your mind."

"I don't want to upset her, though."

"But that's not a proper way to go through life, holding off doing the things you want to do because it might upset someone else. First of all, it never works. Somebody else'll be upset that you *didn't* do it. And you'll get to the point where you really can't do *anything*, because there's no such animal as a thing that nobody could possibly object to. After a while you get to be just like those damned politicians. They try so hard to be all things to all people that they end up being nothing to anybody. You're better off being you. Half the people you know'll applaud you for it and the other half'll be pissed off. If the people applauding you are the people you like and respect, then you'll know you got it right."

"That's good advice," Michael said.

"Don't sound so surprised."

"We should talk like this more often."

"Yeah, we should." He patted Michael firmly on the shoulder, then picked up his paper again. When he puffed on his pipe, Michael smelled a cherry aroma in the tobacco. "Buy your camera. Make your film. If your mother has complaints she can take it up with me."

"Thanks, Dad."

He rose to his feet and looked down on his father for a few seconds.

"My new film professor . . ." he began.

The rest didn't seem to want to come out.

"What about him?"

"He's scarred too."

"Oh. Okay. What kind of scars?"

"Burns."

"I see."

"I was talking to him today, and I think that's what put the idea in my head about the film. He's a good person to talk to. Because . . . you know."

His father peered up at him over the top of his paper. He didn't wear glasses, but maybe he should have. He tended to hold his reading material close.

"Well, sure. We all like to talk to somebody who's been there."

"I don't know how to explain the effect it had on me. Meeting him. It changed everything. Like all my life I just assumed I should hide my scars, and then I met someone who just . . . doesn't. Well, he can't. But more importantly, he doesn't. He tells people to look. He invites them to talk about it. He won't be ashamed of it, and he won't let anybody else be ashamed because of their reaction to it. It changed me, Dad. I don't know how to explain it any better than that, but it just changed everything."

He knew he was getting quite loud and animated as he spoke, but not how to stop.

His father seemed to chew that over for a moment. His face was a bit concerned, but Michael wasn't sure why.

"Just don't let him upstage me," his father said after a time. "Don't forget your old dad."

"No, I won't. Of course I won't. Thanks."

He turned to go.

Before he could get to the den door his father said, "Aren't you forgetting something?"

He turned back to see his father counting money out of his wallet.

"Thanks, Dad," he said, and took the wad of cash. "My film professor never gave me a hundred and twenty-five dollars. That's how I'll remember you're still the dad."

———

Michael sat in front of Dunning's desk again after class, watching him tap away at his phone.

In time the teacher looked up and into Michael's eyes.

"Ah," he said. "Mr. Woodbine again."

"Am I being a pest?"

"Not at all. Just let me finish this text."

His thumbs tapped for a few more seconds. Then he set down the phone and gave Michael his full attention.

"I'm going to do that film," Michael said. "The one we talked about. I'm going to make a documentary about people with scars, and I'm going to call it *Here I Am*. You know. Like we were talking about. I halfway wanted to call it *Here I Am—Get Used to It*, but it just feels a little too 'in your face' for where I am with all of this right now."

"Understood," Dunning said. He was fixing Michael with that look again. Pinning him to the wall with that fishhook of a gaze. There was just no wiggling off that gaze. "And I think it's an excellent plan. Did you just want me to know about it, or is there also something I can do to help with the endeavor?"

"Well," Michael said, "since you brought it up. I want it to be about more people than just me. You know. Every story is different. But I'm just not all that sure where I'd find people who might agree to be in the film. Especially since I can't afford to pay them."

"Hmm," Dunning said. "May I think on that for a time?"

"Of course."

Dunning stood. He gathered up his papers and closed them into his leather briefcase. Then he walked up the aisle of his classroom toward the door.

Michael watched him go.

When Dunning was almost to the door he stopped and turned back to Michael, who was still glued to his chair.

"*I* might be available if approached correctly," he said.

Then he turned back to the door, and he was gone.

Michael froze for a moment, then sprinted after him.

"Wait," he called, but Dunning was apparently already too far away to hear.

Michael ran up the aisle and out into the bright afternoon, then down the stairs. He caught up with Dunning on the quad.

"Wait," he said again, slightly breathless.

"Walk and talk," Dunning said.

Michael fell into step beside him.

They walked through the dappled shade together, the hot breeze feeling good on Michael's face.

"What would be the correct approach?" he asked the professor.

"Well . . . you'd have to *ask*."

"But . . . you made it sound like there was a special *way* I had to ask."

"It's just an expression, Michael."

"Oh."

They walked in silence for a few seconds. Maybe more.

"Thing is," Michael began, "I should tell you something about the film before you say yes or no. Because once I tell you this, you might not want to have any part of the whole thing. It's going to involve . . . some . . . nudity."

Dunning stopped. In fact, he stopped so fast that Michael had to work hard to stop with him. His momentum wanted to keep him moving forward alone. It was a sensation almost like tripping.

"Define 'some.'"

"I'm not saying people can't leave their underwear on. Or wear swim trunks or something like that. It's not a film about people's private parts, so there's no need to go there. *I'm* not going to leave my underwear on, though. Just, for myself . . . for my own personal decision . . . I don't want to seem to be holding back. That's why I'll take off everything. I thought I'd just use my hands. Like . . ."

He demonstrated cupping his hands in front of his genitals for privacy.

"Ah. So the filmmaker will be taking off his clothes as well."

"Yeah. Of course I will. I'm not going to ask anybody to do a thing I wouldn't even do myself."

"Always a good guideline as you go through life. But if the goal is just to show the world your scars, you could leave your pants on."

"No. Not really. I have these big patches of scarring on my thighs where they took skin to graft onto my chest and stomach."

"I see."

They walked again. And, for a moment, did not speak.

"How many others are you hoping to get?"

"At least five or six total. Maybe seven."

"And there must be more to this film than just a striptease."

"Yeah. Of course. I thought each person could tell the viewer a little about their life. About what happened, but more about how it is now. What it's like to walk through the world with a body that's . . . different. And then at the end they can show their body as a way of saying they're not ashamed and they don't apologize."

"That actually sounds promising," Dunning said. And he sounded like he meant it. He sounded almost . . . impressed. Or maybe not even almost.

They walked in silence for a few beats. Michael didn't know what Dunning was thinking about his own participation, and he was afraid to ask.

"Let me get my wife's thoughts on the subject, and I'll give you an answer tomorrow."

"Okay," Michael said. "Thanks."

He stopped walking. Dunning did not.

When he was about ten paces away, Dunning directed some words over his shoulder.

"Put something up on the bulletin board in the student union. And think about some kind of personal ad in the local independent paper."

"Wait," he called. "Personal ad? In what category?"

"There you'll have to get creative," Dunning called back, without stopping.

Then he turned a corner, and he was gone.

———

Before he left campus that day, Michael wrote out a handmade sign on a sheet of notebook paper. It said: "Need volunteers for a student documentary film. Do you have a lot of worry and stress about your body and your appearance? Call Michael."

He wrote his cell phone number vertically on ten little strips at the bottom of the page, then cut the paper between them so they could be torn off easily. Then he wondered if that was a mistake. Did anyone physically take a number on a piece of paper anymore, or did people just photograph the contact info or enter it into their phones?

He pinned the notice onto one of the bulletin boards in the student union.

Then he realized he'd left a light jacket in Mr. Dunning's room.

He went back for it.

Knowing it was probably pointless, and too soon, he stuck his head into the student union to see if any of the little phone-number slips were gone.

They were all gone.

Chapter Five

This Is Going in an Unexpected Direction

The phone woke Michael at 7:16 the following morning.

He stared at it through squinted eyes before answering. It was an unknown number.

"Hello?" he said, sounding like he was still ninety percent asleep.

"Oh, I'm sorry," the voice said. It was a man, and he sounded very old. *Very* old. "Did I wake you up?"

"I'm . . . not sure. Hang on a minute." Michael sat up in bed. Blinked furiously. Rubbed his eyes. "Okay, I'm here. I think."

"My name is Rex Aronfeld."

"Okay."

"I'm calling about this student film of yours."

"Oh. Good."

Michael blinked out the window, squinting into the morning light. There were starlings in the tree outside—lots of them, making lots of chaotic starling racket. He wondered how he had slept through all of it.

"My neighbor brought me home your number. Nice young lady. We had just been talking about issues like that. You know. Appearance and such. She brought me a little slip of paper with your number on it. She said it might be right up my alley, so to speak."

"Okay. Great. Do you mind telling me a little about yourself?"

Michael's mother stuck her head into his room and shot him a questioning look.

"Who is that calling so early?"

He covered the phone mic with his hand. "Nothing. Just . . . it's for my film. Now, please . . . if you could just . . ."

She sighed and slipped out again.

"I used to be an athlete," Rex Aronfeld said. "But more than just an athlete, actually. An Olympian, which I daresay is the highest pinnacle an athlete can achieve. I competed as a gymnast in the 1936 Olympics in Germany. Berlin, 1936. You know what that means, right? That was the Summer Olympics in Nazi Germany. Hitler's Germany. Very controversial. I took the silver medal for the US, and I had to shake Hitler's hand. It's the shame of my life, really, and of course now I wish I'd spit in his face instead. And I'm Jewish, too, but all of my family was in the US. We had no family or friends in Germany. We didn't know then what we know now, or in any case not all of what we know now. I was only fifteen years old."

"Wow. That's quite a history."

"But I know, I know. I'm getting off track. Sorry. Anyway, my body was something I was very, very proud of. Of course. Why wouldn't I feel pride? It was almost perfect, if there's indeed any such thing as perfection. I didn't mean to, but I guess I started to define myself by it. Like I *was* my body. Everything I loved to do, everything I was proud of, everything I was receiving accolades for, it was all something that came to me because of my body. It was my whole world."

He paused, and Michael wasn't sure if he should interject.

But in time he did.

"Then . . . did something happen?"

The man surprised Michael by laughing. Loudly, and for longer than Michael would have imagined he might.

"Yes, of course something happened, my young friend. That was eighty-eight years ago. *Eighty-eight years* happened."

"Then you're . . . wait. I can do math in my head, it's just that it's early."

"I'm a hundred and three years old."

"Wow."

"Ever seen a hundred-and-three-year-old body?"

"No."

"Most people haven't. Nurses see them. And spouses see them, I suppose. But . . . no, actually, even most spouses don't see them. For that, both people would have to live to be a hundred and three, and how often does that happen? My wife died when I was only seventy. Mostly nurses. Other than that, most people haven't, and they would be quick to tell you they wouldn't care to."

"And you'd be willing to show it to the camera?"

"Oh yeah. Heck yeah. I used to walk around naked all the time. I mean, not in public. I'm not a pervert. At home, and around my male friends. I felt no shame. I don't do it now, but I should. Why shouldn't I? I've just lived longer than most people. I shouldn't have to be ashamed of that. Is that something you could use?"

For a beat or two, Michael didn't answer. It wasn't exactly what he'd been picturing. But there was no reason to limit the film to scars, when he stopped to think about it. After all, feeling uncomfortable with your own appearance certainly didn't limit itself to any one situation.

And it sounded like a compelling story. Common, but somehow unexpected at the same time, and full of uncommon twists.

"Yeah," Michael said. "I think so. I think that could be really interesting. Can we talk in person?"

"If you could come here, we could. I don't drive anymore. I don't get around the way I used to."

Michael entered the man's address into his phone as Rex dictated.

"I'll call you when I'm doing interviews," he said. "Oh. And by the way. Maybe I should have mentioned this up front, but I can't afford to pay people for doing this."

"Yeah, that was clear from the 'volunteer' part," Rex said. "I'm not trying to get your money. It's just something I'm not hearing people talking enough about. Me, I want to talk about it. That's just the way I am. And by the way, don't slow-walk getting me on film, son. I'm a hundred and three, after all."

———

Michael got what he thought was his second call as he was driving to school. But he quickly discovered that it was actually his third. As he ever so briefly looked at his phone to pick up the call, he saw a voicemail he had missed. Another unknown number.

He was more or less stopped anyway—sitting in his car on the freeway in heavy traffic, his surroundings looking like a big parking lot.

"Hello?" he said out into the car in general, speaking as he was to his hands-free Bluetooth system.

"Hey. Are you Michael?"

It was a man again, but younger this time. Not young. Just younger. Then again, everybody Michael had ever spoken to in his life was younger than Rex Aronfeld.

"Yeah. That's me. Is this about the film?"

"Right," the man said. "The film."

Then the line went silent for a time.

The car in front of Michael rolled forward a few feet, and he followed suit.

"It's just a volunteer thing," the man said. "Right?"

"Right. I'm sorry. I don't have the money to pay anybody."

"No, that's okay. It's not about money. I have a job, and I do okay. I work as a janitor at the college, so it's not like I was looking at this for extra cash. That's not what it's about. That's not why I'm calling. Just—nobody ever asked me that before."

"Wait, I'm lost. Asked you what?"

"What you asked on that flyer. If I have a lot of worry and stress about my body and my appearance. I do. And I've always known I do, but somehow it's just coming up for me more lately—like, how much the whole thing has tanked my life, especially my personal life. I just find myself focusing on it more and more, and it's making me so damned uncomfortable. And I just figured, if that's what you're looking to showcase, I feel like I'd like to get in on that."

Another pause. Another rolling forward in traffic, but only a few feet.

"Do you mind if I ask . . ."

"Sure. Of course. I guess you have to. But it might not sound like much to you. To somebody else. But for me it's sort of a big deal. I'm just unusually skinny."

"Skinny?"

"Right."

Michael opened his mouth and almost asked if this was a joke. But part of him knew it wasn't. He could hear it in the man's voice. And he felt deeply grateful that he hadn't said anything so thoughtless, especially to someone who appeared to be baring his soul, simply because he'd spoken before thinking.

"Don't most people want to be skinny?" he asked instead.

"No. Most people want to be slim. I'm not slim. I'm skinny. I'm like a hundred and sixteen pounds."

"That's not so bad."

"I'm six foot three. Maybe if I were a woman it would be different. Maybe it's better to be stick-thin when you're a woman. People would think you look like a model, maybe. Which I realize is completely unfair. I'm not saying it like it's okay that it *is* that way, but it's just what the world throws at us, you know? And everybody loses. But with a man, it's different. It's not so much about being as slim as possible, it's about being strong. Weight is power. Strength is power. Half the guys I meet could *bench-press* a hundred and sixteen pounds. They could pick me up and throw me across the room. It's a really weird feeling."

Another pause, during which traffic did not budge.

"I eat and I eat, but I don't gain, and I get really tired of people telling me I'm so lucky because I can eat as much as I want of whatever I want. It's not lucky, because I can't change my situation no matter what I do, and if they were me they would see that. You have no idea how often people say that to me."

Michael opened his mouth to comment on people's tendency to say just the wrong thing. But the man—whose name Michael didn't know—was still talking.

"I used to try to ask girls out. I mean, years ago, when I was in high school. They always said no. They didn't say it's because I'm so skinny, but I always figured that's why. Maybe I didn't have a good personality. Maybe I asked wrong, I don't know. But probably not. I'm just not a good-looking guy, you know? It's just the truth. It's just how it is. After a while I stopped asking. And now I'm pretty much alone. I mean, I have poker buddies and all. But as far as, you know . . . intimate relationships and like that . . . Anyway, I'd like to be in your film, if you'd have me."

"It would be a great contribution. I mean, this is all so new. I'm still trying to find the direction I need to go with this, but it feels like something I'd want to use. Thank you for sharing it. I'll hold on to your number and call you when it's time for interviews."

"Just an interview, yeah. That's all I ask."

"Before you hang up . . . would you be willing to take off your clothes in front of the camera? I mean . . . doesn't have to be *all of* them. Not like full frontal or anything."

"I guess, yeah. I mean, if I could keep my shorts on. It's to make an important point, right? So I guess it's worth it."

"Sure. You could."

"Just call me, then, okay? Freddie is my name."

The line went dead, and the traffic moved slightly.

When it stopped again, Michael pressed "play" on the voicemail.

"Michael," the recording said. "My name is Tanya, and I saw your ad—or flyer, or whatever—and I want to talk to you about my belly. That might sound weird, but . . . it's like I've been going back and forth about this. Not about your film, I mean, but just about my problem in general. On the one hand, I think it's normal. It's like lots of other women's bellies, especially after a few kids. I have five kids, and the last three came all at the same time, triplets, so my belly is just . . . I don't know. You'd have to see it, I guess. Stretch marks, of course, but also just too much skin, and it's kind of puckery, and I keep telling myself there's nothing wrong with that, and there isn't. But turn on the TV. Open a magazine. Look at what they're telling us our bellies are supposed to look like. It's just starting to bother me a lot. Anyway, call me. If that sounds like something you can use."

Michael eased off the freeway at his exit just as the call ended.

"This is taking an unexpected turn," he said out loud to his phone.

———

"This is taking an unexpected turn," he said to Dunning.

It was a little before 9:15, and Michael was running the distinct risk of being late to math by stopping to see Dunning in his classroom. But of course he was doing it anyway.

"Mr. Woodbine," Dunning said. "It's nine fifteen in the morning."

"Right. I know."

"You're pushing your habit of 'promptness plus' to a whole new level this morning. What exactly is taking an unexpected turn? Your film?"

"Yeah. That."

"In what direction is it turning?"

Dunning was standing behind his desk, leaning on it with his thighs, his hands in his pockets, watching his first class filter in. Fortunately for Michael, everybody had chosen to sit in the back so far.

"I thought it would be so hard to find people, but it's not. They're coming in, like, a wave. I've already gotten three calls in much less than a day. But they just weren't what I expected. They're people who think they're not fine, but I think they're fine."

"I could say much the same of you, Michael. You think you're not fine, but I think you are."

"But they're all people who have bodies that are pretty ordinary. They're not scarred or disfigured at all. The things they're worried about are things I'd be happy to have."

"No," Dunning said. "You wouldn't. We always think that about other people. We see them from the outside and think if we had their problems we'd be happy. But if we had their problems we wouldn't be on the outside of them anymore, and we'd likely feel the way they feel."

"If they were me they would see that," Michael remembered Freddie saying.

"What did you say in your ads?" Dunning asked, snapping him back into the moment. "Did you ask for people with scars?"

"I just said, 'Do you have a lot of worry and stress about your body and your appearance?'"

"Michael," Dunning said. "That's pretty much *everybody*."

For several seconds Michael only blinked too much.

"Not possible," he said. "Lots of people like the way they look."

"Quite a few people have managed to fit fairly well with the standard of beauty put out by our society, yes. Most of them have had to work hard for it. But there's a huge problem with that standard, and it affects even the people who manage to attain it: One of its most stringent requirements is youth. Therefore it comes with a built-in guarantee that even if you have it, you can't keep it."

"Funny you should mention that, because one of the calls was from a man who liked his body a whole lot when he was a fifteen-year-old athlete, but now he's a hundred and three."

"It's always a case of diminishing returns. You can pretty much divide people into two categories: those who never will feel attractive by that near-impossible standard, and those who have given up a lot to achieve it but feel it slipping away. So 'worry and stress about body and appearance'? That's just about everybody. You're learning an important lesson here, Michael. More people are afraid to go to the beach than you realized."

Michael only stood a moment, trying to press his brain into action. Trying to figure out what to ask next.

"I don't know what to do now," he said after a time. "Do I go the direction I meant to go, or do I follow the turn this thing has taken? I mean, the way I worded it, I knew not everybody who responded would be scarred. But I thought it would all be big stuff. Or at least stuff that seemed big to me. The rest of this I didn't see coming."

"Well, if you're asking my advice," Dunning said, "which we all know is one of the two circumstances in which I'm supposed to give it, I'd say follow the direction in which the universe is pushing you. In my experience you can never go far wrong by following the direction in which the universe is pushing you."

MICHAEL,
AGE EIGHT

Chapter Six

The Real Why

"We want to adopt you," Mrs. Woodbine—his foster mother—said.

It was sudden, the words tumbling out all at once, as if she had held them in under pressure for too long.

They had taken Michael out for ice cream. And they usually didn't do that—they usually preferred he avoid most sweets—so he should have known that there was something going on.

He was eating two scoops of rocky road out of a paper bowl, and he stopped with the plastic spoon halfway to his mouth. For the first time in his life, he wasn't sure he felt hungry even for ice cream.

"But . . ." he began.

Then he simply couldn't bring himself to finish.

"We know all the 'buts,'" Mr. Woodbine said. "And we honestly do understand. We know you have parents. And we know you were hoping to go back with them. And that's why we wanted to talk to you—hear from you—before we make any official moves."

"We just love you so much," his foster mom said. "We've gotten so attached to you in this past year. We've loved having you living with us. And we want you to be safe. We know you love your parents, but we just feel like you'd be safer with us. But of course we can't entirely decide a thing like that for you, so we wanted to hear your thoughts."

Michael set down his spoon.

His stomach felt achy and strange. It often did, as it had suffered severe damage. In fact, a portion of it had been removed. But this felt different.

"I do kind of feel safer with you," Michael said. "But also . . . they're my parents."

"We know it would be a hard thing for you to have to decide," Mr. Woodbine said. "And we're really not asking you to. Actually, a judge will decide, and he'll probably send you back to your parents because the courts tend to favor the birth parents. It's pretty much going to be decided for us. But we just wanted to be sure you were even okay with our filing to adopt you. With our going to court to fight for it."

Michael's brain felt the way it had when he'd been in the hospital. As though it lived behind a door, one he couldn't breach.

For what felt like a long time, he didn't answer. Because he had no idea what his answer should be.

Then he said, "Why now? I've lived with you for a year. Why is this happening now?"

The adults exchanged a glance.

"Because . . ." Mrs. Woodbine began.

She never finished.

"Your brother has been returned to your birth parents," Mr. Woodbine said. "He hated his foster placement, and he kept asking, and Child Protective Services just recently decided it was okay for him to go home."

"Oh," Michael said.

The word "home" had an odd resonance to his ears. On the one hand, it sounded warm and welcome. Everybody just wants to go home, right? But there was also a tingly fear hiding somewhere in the word.

"I'm not hungry for any more ice cream," Michael said, his eyes cast down to the tabletop. "Can we just go home?"

There was that word again. "Home." He had just used it in reference to the Woodbine household, and, after a year, it sounded like a perfectly normal use of the word.

Where that left Michael's thoughts on the matter, he had no idea. It hurt even to think about it, so he didn't.

At least, as much as such thinking could be avoided.

———

Michael could not have said how much longer it was before the subject came up again. A few months, he might have guessed after the fact, if pressed to estimate. He hadn't been counting the days. Quite the opposite, in fact, if a thing like that can have an opposite. He had been ignoring it as studiously as possible.

He came downstairs from washing his hands to find they were having pizza for dinner, and from his very favorite pizza place. That was unusual, to say the least.

He stood behind his chair, holding its high wooden back with both hands. For a moment it struck him as similar to those movies with the prisoners holding tightly to the bars and peering out. Not that he felt imprisoned in the Woodbine household, but at that moment he would have enjoyed being somewhere else.

There was something coming. He could feel it.

"What's the special occasion?" he asked, even though he was afraid they would tell him.

"We have some news," his foster mom said. "We think it's very good news, and we're hoping you'll think so too."

"What is it?" he asked.

He could feel his face burn, and it was getting harder to breathe.

"Sit down," his foster father said. "Sit down and have some pizza."

Michael sat and watched his foster dad set a slice of pizza on his plate. But he didn't eat it. He only stared at it.

"What is it?" he asked again.

"We're going to be adopting you," his foster mom said.

"The judge decided that?"

"No. We never ended up going in front of a judge. We never ended up needing to. We talked to your birth parents, and we told them how much we love you and how much we want you, and how happy and safe you are here. And we asked them to just think about the idea that maybe you'd be better off here. We have good insurance for your medical needs, and you have all the supervision you need here. We asked them to please just consider that maybe you were happy here and it would be in your best interest if you stayed. They thought about it for a while. And then they agreed that it was probably for the best."

Michael felt his chest and belly tighten, the way it had in the hospital when somebody talked to him about his parents. It didn't hurt as much as it had then. But it hurt.

"But why?" Michael said, trying not to cry.

"For all the reasons we just told you," she said. "They made an unselfish decision because they want what's best for you."

"But why do they want Thomas but they don't want me?"

And with that sentence, Michael lost his battle with the tears.

"Oh, honey," she said, and appeared in the chair next to him, wrapping him up in her arms. "It's not that. It's not like that at all. Thomas was miserable in his foster home, and he doesn't have your special medical needs. They do want you, Michael. They love you. They just want what's best for you, even if it means letting you go."

"But I don't want to be let go."

"Oh, dear," she said. "I was so hoping you'd be happy about this. Not that I don't understand. I do understand. All of this is hard for you, we know. We get that. But we'll make such a good life for you here, Michael. I promise."

"I'm not hungry," he said. "Can I go to my room?"

For a moment she just kept squeezing him. It gave him a claustrophobic feeling, like being held captive. Then she let go and leaned back.

Michael jumped up from the table and ran for the stairs. Just before he did, he noticed that his foster mom was crying as well.

———

It was a few minutes later when his new father came into his room to see him.

Michael had been lying on his back, arms at his sides but out wide like a snow angel's, staring at the ceiling and listening to them argue. The subject was whether Michael should see his birth parents while all this played out. His new father seemed to be for it, his new mother against it.

Michael was not caught up in the outcome, because he didn't want to see those people anyway. In fact, he wasn't caught up in anything. He was only staring at the ceiling.

He could feel the bed sink and shift as his father sat down next to him.

"You probably heard that," he said.

"Kind of."

"I was thinking you might want to see them and talk to them, so you can understand why this is happening the way it is. But your new mom thinks it'll just cause more problems. Like maybe they wouldn't want us to adopt you anymore, but it would be based on purely emotional stuff and not on what's actually best for you. But maybe later, after it's all a done deal . . ."

"It doesn't matter," Michael said. "I don't want to see them anyway."

"Are you sure?"

"Positive."

"You might change your mind later on."

"I won't. I won't ever change my mind. I don't ever want to see them again. They don't want me, so I don't want them."

"They want you, Michael. They just want what's best for you, and they know it isn't them. That's how you know they love you, because they can be unselfish enough to give you up for your own well-being."

That made no sense to Michael, because when you love someone you want them closer, not farther away.

He didn't say so. He didn't say anything.

"Are you doing okay?" his foster father asked. "Is there anything I can do?"

"I hurt *here*," he said, waving one hand over his torso without actually touching it.

"I think what happens is that you get tense when you're upset. You tighten up those muscles, and that causes you pain. Try taking some long, deep breaths with me."

For a minute or two, Michael matched his breath to his new father's.

"Imagine every time you exhale you're letting all the tension flow out of those muscles."

Michael closed his eyes and imagined. And it did flow out. And it did help.

"Is that any better?"

"Yeah, it is, actually."

"You want me to rub some of that cream on you that keeps the scar tissue soft?"

"Yes please."

Michael unbuttoned his shirt while his father went into the bathroom to get the jar of cream.

He lay still on his back while his new dad gently massaged it into the damaged and grafted skin of his belly and chest, and it felt good. Mostly because it was a physical touch from someone who cared about him and wanted him to feel better.

"I was thinking maybe they could write you a letter," his dad said.

"About what?"

"Ah. See? You tighten up. I can feel it under my hand. That's why it hurts more when you're upset. See if you can relax the muscles under my hand again."

"What would they write me a letter about?"

"About why they made the decision they did. You were asking why. I thought maybe I could get you a good answer."

"There are a lot of words I still can't read, you know. I'm only in the second grade."

He should have been in the third grade by then, but he had missed so much school following the accident.

"I could read it to you and explain any words you weren't sure about. And I'm sure they would write it in a way you could understand."

"It wouldn't matter anyway," Michael said, "because whatever they say, I wouldn't believe them."

His father sighed and put the top back on the jar of cream. He wiped his hands on a tissue from the box near the bed. Then he carefully buttoned Michael's shirt.

"Is there anything else I can do to make you feel better?"

"No. I just want to be alone and think."

His father sighed again. Then he kissed Michael on the top of the head and left him alone.

Michael did not think. He only stared at the ceiling. In fact, he would have been hard pressed to remember another time in his life when his brain was so utterly empty and blank.

———

It was something like a week later when Michael came down for breakfast in the morning and saw the envelope propped up on the salt and pepper shakers in the middle of the table.

It had his name written on it in handwriting that he recognized as his mother's. Not the mother who was dishing scrambled eggs onto his plate. His other mother. His first mother. It made his stomach buzz.

His new father was already at the breakfast table, drinking coffee.

"What is that?" Michael said, and took a tentative bite of breakfast.

He thought the eggs needed more salt, but he wasn't willing to touch the envelope to get it.

"It's a letter to you from your birth parents," Mr. Woodbine said. "I told them you were feeling hurt and confused, and that you were afraid they wanted your brother but not you. I told them it might help you if they could explain to you why they decided things the way they did."

Michael shook his head.

"I don't want that," he said.

His mind felt smooth and clear. Cool, almost. He had fixed his mind so that none of this was able to get in and upset him.

"We'll save it for you," Mrs. Woodbine said. "Because there may come a time in your life when you'll want it."

Michael shook his head again. Calm and unruffled, like still water.

"No, I won't. I'll never want that. I don't want them. They don't want me, so I don't want them."

Mr. Woodbine set down his coffee mug and frowned.

"Well, see, that's the problem right there, little buddy. I know you think they don't want you, but I don't think that's what's happening here. So maybe if you read the letter you'd see things differently."

"No," Michael said. "It doesn't matter what they say. I'll never believe them. I'll always know the real why."

He watched his new parents exchange a glance with each other, and he knew this wasn't going away. And he wanted it to go away.

"But I'll take it and save it myself," he said. "For later."

He snatched the envelope off the center of the table, folded it in half, and stuck it in the pocket of his sweatpants.

That seemed to satisfy them.

———

He brought the letter to school with him, where he stood in front of his locker and tore it into pieces the size of confetti. He never opened it. He ripped it up still sealed, envelope and all.

Then he carried the pieces, clutched tightly in his fist, into the boys' room, where he flushed them down the toilet.

They didn't go down properly. They caused a clog, and the toilet overflowed.

And Michael thought, *That figures.*

It was like a sign to him that the envelope and its dreaded contents had been nothing but trouble. Like something that rises up from Hell and still has a little of the evil in it.

He moved out of the stall quickly before any of the toilet water could get on his shoes, and left the whole mess behind him.

MICHAEL,
AGE NINETEEN

Chapter Seven

Madeleine the Fierce

Michael was having "coffee" with Dunning in the student union when he first noticed her.

She was older than a college girl. Maybe thirty, he thought. She had very short dark-blond hair. Surprisingly short, like some kind of punk style. She was wearing a long tan duster coat of a light fabric, like a blazer that just kept flowing down to her ankles. She didn't capture his attention by being exceptionally beautiful, at least not in any obvious or classic way, but his eyes kept being drawn to her. She did have some kind of energy, or style, or way of carrying herself—or all of the above—that struck him as exceptional.

The original reason he noticed her was because she seemed to be staring at his sign on the bulletin board.

Granted, he was sitting in the coffee shop, which put her a good distance away. But something on that board held her attention, and it seemed to be either his notice or one very close to it.

He was briefly grateful that he had left it up, and written his phone number on it, even though he hadn't been getting any more calls.

"You seem far away," Dunning said.

It jolted Michael back into the moment.

"Oh, I'm sorry. I was just watching that woman. I think she's staring at my notice on the board."

"Have you gotten more calls?"

"No. And it seems weird. At first I got three . . . kind of . . . all right on top of one another. And then nothing. Ten people took those little strips of paper with my number on them."

Dunning made a sound in his throat that was something like a grunt. It seemed to indicate that he understood.

That makes one of us, Michael thought.

"People are going to go one way or the other with a thing like that," Dunning said. "They'll jump on it, or they'll talk themselves out of it."

"I guess. I might have enough people already. I know it's only three calls, but then there's you and me. That's five. I was thinking six or seven, but maybe five is enough. What do you think?"

"I think seven might be too many. Five is good. Six is good."

Michael's eyes drifted back to the woman. She was rummaging around in her big, battered leather shoulder bag. She pulled out a cell phone and peered at it, tapping with her right thumb.

Michael's phone rang in his pocket.

"You'll want to get that," Dunning said.

Michael looked away from the woman and to his professor. Dunning had been watching the woman make the phone call as well.

"That might be interview number six," Dunning added. "I should probably be getting home anyway."

He rose and left the table.

Michael answered the phone.

"Hello?"

"Michael?"

"Yes, this is Michael."

"I'm calling about this . . . I don't know what you call it. Ad? Casting notice? It defies description, I guess. I have misgivings."

She paused, so he felt pressured to say something.

"I guess a lot of people do. All ten papers with my number disappeared, but only three out of those ten people called me."

"No, four out of the ten called you. I took one of those papers home. Then I changed my mind and threw it away."

"And now you're calling."

"To state the obvious, yes. I'm calling. But we both knew that."

She had a voice that was strong and sure. Forceful. He felt drawn to it. Drawn to her. Was he drawn to forceful people? Robert Dunning spoke with that same sense of sureness, and Michael would follow him into Hell and back after only a few days of knowing him. Did he envy people like that?

Was that what he aspired to become?

He had no time to think through the idea.

"I need to know if you're for real," she said.

"I'm not sure I follow."

"Not everybody is for real. Not everybody has pure motives for doing what they do. I need to meet you. I need to know where you're coming from."

"If you turn your head," he said, "you'll see me waving to you. I'm in the coffee shop."

She spun around, and their eyes connected, albeit at a distance.

She began to walk in his direction, still talking into the phone.

"What, are you stalking your own sign?"

"No, I was having coffee with my film-workshop professor."

"There's nobody at the table with you."

"He left when I took the call."

She arrived near the edge of his table, stopped, and stared down at him with a look he could only describe as fierce. She had light-colored eyes that looked almost gray. There was something borderline alarming about them.

"Now I'm less sure than ever," she said, ending the call and slipping her phone back into her bag.

"Why? What did I say?"

"Nothing. It's not about what you're saying. I never judge people by what they're saying anyway. People can say whatever they want and I have no way of knowing if it's true. I'm less sure than ever because you're gorgeous. Why would a really handsome guy with a great body make a documentary about people who are uncomfortable with their appearance?"

"You don't know that I have a great body."

"I'm looking at you."

"You're looking at my clothes."

"You're saying there's something under your clothes that explains your interest in body image? Something that would make me believe you're for real?"

"Yes."

"And are *you* one of the subjects in the film?"

"Yes."

"Will people in the film show their bodies on camera?"

"Yes."

"Will *you* show your body on camera?"

"Yes."

"Prove to me that this is true."

"I'm not sure how to—"

Before he could finish the sentence she grabbed hold of his sleeve and tugged him to his feet. Not literally. It was an incitement to stand, and he did.

"Walk with me," she said.

They moved out of the coffee shop and down the hall of the student union, where she opened the door to a single, unisex bathroom and motioned him inside.

"Show me what the world will see when you stand exposed in front of the camera," she said, locking the door behind them.

"I . . ." he began. Then he had absolutely no idea where to go with the sentence.

"You're about to bare yourself on film to everybody who sees your documentary. I'm not saying you have to do it now. Or do anything. I'm not forcing you. I can just not be in the film. But if I'm going to put myself on the line, I don't think it's asking too much. If I'm going to show myself to the world, I want to see what *you* have on the line. I don't want to find out too late it was nothing."

"And not a single one of them will be standing eighteen inches away, in person, staring at me. I've pretty much never taken my shirt off in front of anyone before."

"Oh, come on," she said. "I find that hard to believe."

She was standing closer than absolutely necessary, and her energy was still fierce, but now there was something else mixed in with the fierceness. It felt personal. It felt mildly electric. She felt very much like a woman to him on a purely visceral, nonverbal level, and she seemed to be viewing him as a man. And she was standing so close.

It was making his forehead sweat.

"Well," he said. "My parents have seen all of me. Lots and lots of doctors. Nurses. A few days ago I unbuttoned my shirt for my film-workshop professor. I'd actually never done that before."

"Gym class?"

"I never showered with the other boys. I always kept a T-shirt on."

"And you keep your shirt on when you make love? Or you're a virgin?"

Michael felt his face go hot and flushed.

"That's pretty personal."

"You're right," she said. "I apologize. I tend to be overly direct."

"Yeah, I sensed that."

They stood too close without speaking for several beats.

"Your call," she said.

Then, a minute later, without fully realizing he had decided to, Michael unbuttoned his shirt, slipped it off, and draped it over the sink. He pulled his undershirt off over his head and stood in front of her, the white fabric of it half balled up in, half dangling from, his fist.

It occurred to him, as he waited for her to speak, that she hadn't even told him what it was about her body that made her uncomfortable.

"Okay," she said. "You're for real. I understand why you'd want to make a film about people with body issues. Five months ago I had a double mastectomy. No reconstruction or anything. Just the surgical scars."

His eyes wanted to travel to her chest. He didn't let them.

They looked into each other's eyes for a moment, which Michael found nerve-racking and exhilarating in equal parts.

"Well, if it helps any to know," she said, "I think you're absolutely gorgeous with or without the shirt. I also think I'm too old for you, so I'll just leave this tiny little bathroom before I say or do something I'm likely to regret. You call me when you're putting together the filming, okay? You have my number on your phone."

Then he blinked once or twice and she was gone.

———

When Michael got home, he headed straight for the stairs and his room, but his mother heard him come in and called out to him.

"I made your favorite for dinner," she said.

"Tacos?" he called back. "Or lasagna?"

"Lasagna."

"Excellent. Thanks."

He headed for his room again, but she had more to say.

"Before you go up to your room, honey, you got a box in the mail today from an electronics place. I think it's your new camera."

"My camera," he said, but not so much to her. Not with enough volume for her to hear. He just breathed it out loud to himself.

He grabbed the box off the table by the door, surprised he hadn't noticed it as he came in. Then again, he was still rattled by the sudden meeting with that strangely challenging woman.

It seemed small, the box. He had expected it to be bigger. Then again, electronics got smaller all the time.

He ran upstairs to his room with it, sat cross-legged on the bed, and carefully cut the packing tape with the penknife on his key chain. He pulled the treasure out into the light.

It had a foam-covered microphone that jutted forward on top and a comfortable place to wrap your hand around the body of it. He held it for a moment, swept up in his excitement and admiration.

His phone rang in his pocket.

He pulled it out and picked up the call.

"Hello?"

"It's me," a woman's voice said. "Madeleine."

"I think you have the wrong number."

"This is Michael, right? Madeleine. From the bathroom."

"Oh," he said, drawing the word out long. "*That* Madeleine. You never told me your name."

"Right. I guess I didn't. Sorry. I feel like I owe you an apology for today."

"Any special part of today?"

"Oh, I don't know. Let me think. How about the part where I dragged you into a public restroom, locked the door, and invited you to partially strip for me? You have to understand . . . or at least I hope you'll understand . . . what with the cancer and all, I've just been feeling like I can't take any more shocks right now. Any more disappointments. I knew the minute I saw your sign that I wanted to be part of that project. I knew there was a statement I've been needing to make, but then once I got it in my head that somebody could be using or exploiting people with a thing like that, well . . . I'm just in a place where I can't absorb any more hits. Ever feel that way?"

"Oh yeah," Michael said, his voice quiet.

He still had his hand wrapped around the new camera. He was very aware of the feel of it, and it was a comfort to him.

"And another thing," she said, "if you don't mind me commenting on your body. If I can have permission to do that." She waited, probably in case he wanted not to give it. "I didn't really say much of anything at the time, just that I understand why you wanted to make the film, which might have given the exact opposite impression from what I was feeling. The truth is, I just don't think it's as big a deal as you think it is."

He opened his mouth to respond, but she was still going.

"Oh, don't get me wrong. It's *your* deal, so I don't really get to define how important it is. If it's a big deal to you, then it's a big deal. I'm not trying to minimize your feelings about it, or tell you that you don't feel the way you feel, or even that you *shouldn't* feel the way you feel. I hate it when people do that. I'm just speaking as the universal 'other person.' Obviously you've kept your clothes on all these years because you thought it would be as big a deal to everyone else as it is to you. You made it sound like you've never taken your shirt off in front of a woman. Well, I'm a woman, and you took your shirt off in front of me, and I just don't think it's any big issue."

He waited, in case she had more to say. But he heard only silence on the line.

"It's some pretty extensive scarring," he said.

"So?"

Michael offered no reply to that, because he didn't know what to say.

"Sometimes people have scars," she said. "It's not a deal-breaker for anyone who's not shallow as hell. It just *is*."

Michael glanced down at the precious new camera in his hand and ran the fingers of his other hand along its contours. He had a very clear memory of Robert Dunning standing in front of his class on the first day and saying, "It's not a secret. It's not a scandal. It's not a moral failing on my part. It just *is*."

"When does filming start?" she asked, rescuing him from having to know how to respond.

"I've been trying to figure that out. I have to figure out where I can do the filming. Home won't work. And I just started the class a few days ago, so there's a lot he's going to teach us that he hasn't yet. But still, I think if I can figure out how to get good sound with this camera, I should go ahead and get people on video. I can always edit it and do the credits and stuff closer to the end of the semester. One of the people I'm going to interview, this guy named Rex Aronfeld, is really old. He's so old that he competed in the Olympics when Hitler was in power in Germany. The last thing he said to me was 'Don't slow-walk getting me on film, son. I'm a hundred and three.'"

"Don't slow-walk me either," she said. "But I can go next after Rex. You can use my place if you want."

"For the filming?"

"Right. I live alone, and I have one of those old-fashioned dressing-room screens that people used to go behind to dress or undress. People could take off as much as they planned to take off behind that—while the camera is running, while they're talking to you—and then step out and present themselves."

"That would look great. I love that."

An image of it danced in his brain, and he genuinely loved it.

"Call me if you want to see the place. Call me when you want to start filming. Oh, hell, call me for any damned reason you want, Michael. Just call me."

He opened his mouth to say something. Something on the tentative but affirmative side. But she had already ended the call.

He looked down at the camera again, but his brain and gut were so completely buzzing with energy over her—over the direction things seemed to be going with her—that he couldn't even muster a sense of excitement over the brand-new camera anymore.

Chapter Eight

The Problem with a Fallback Position

Before he even got out of bed the next morning he texted her.

"If that offer still stands . . ." he typed.

The response was instantaneous.

"Ooh. Intriguing."

"I meant the offer to use your place," he typed back, feeling his face redden.

"Oh. That."

What might have been a minute later a little map popped up in the text thread, with a pin on it.

He rose and dressed quickly, brushed his teeth, and headed downstairs.

"I have to leave," he called to his mother, before he was even close enough to the kitchen to see her. "Can I just get breakfast to go? Anything'll do," he added, popping his head into the kitchen. "Toaster pastry. Granola bar. I'm not picky."

"I was just making you bacon and eggs and toast," she said. "But . . . here. Tell you what." She popped two pieces of rye toast out of the toaster as she spoke. "Where are you in such a hurry to get to at this hour of the morning?"

He watched as she carefully laid strips of bacon on one of the pieces of toast.

"It's for my film," he said. "I'm scouting a location."

"Sounds very professional. But what does it mean *really*?"

"Looking for a place to film the interviews."

"You could film here," she said, scooping scrambled eggs onto the bacon and toast with a spatula.

"No, I honestly couldn't."

"Why couldn't you?"

"You'll just have to trust me on this. I couldn't."

She set the second piece of toast on top, making a perfect bacon-and-egg sandwich. She took a big sturdy paper napkin out of a drawer, wrapped it around half of the sandwich, and handed it to him.

"Well, I swear I don't know why not," she said. "But . . . how's this for breakfast to go?"

"You. Are. The. Best."

He kissed her on the temple and ran out the door.

———

When he followed his map app into Madeleine's driveway, he was more than a little surprised. It was nicer than his parents' house. Bigger, too. It was on a huge lot, maybe two acres, surrounded by trees. Two stories, with walls of tall glass windows.

He stopped in front of the house and looked up at it for a time, realizing how much he didn't know about her. When he looked down again, she was standing in the open doorway. She was wearing a robe in a teal color. It looked like some kind of smooth silk.

He stepped out of the car, his heart racing. It was dizzying how fast it pounded.

"I knew you couldn't stay away," she said.

He ignored it. Not because it was unwelcome but because he had no idea how to play on that field.

"I only met you yesterday," he said. "And I thought this was about the film."

"Unless you wanted to see me more than you wanted a place to film interviews."

"I can't film at home. I told you. My mom doesn't work."

"You could've filmed at each person's house."

He stepped up onto the landing, and they stared at each other briefly.

"I thought of that," he said. "But I decided against it. All the different styles of decorating would be a distraction. And the lighting would be different for each interview. Some people's places would be richer and some poorer. I wanted everybody on an even playing field."

"Wow," she said. "I take back everything. You've definitely thought this out. But at least tell me seeing me again is the icing on the cake."

"Of course," he said. "This place is incredible. What do you do for a living?"

"I'm not working. Because of . . . you know."

"Do I know?"

"The cancer."

"Right. Sorry."

She stepped back from the doorway and waved him inside.

Michael was left with the obvious question of how a person could afford such a house without a job. He didn't ask, because it was none of his business.

She seemed to read his thoughts, though.

"This is one of my parents' houses," she said. "They're both in real estate. They have tons of houses. Some of them they flip. Some of them they rent out. They're letting me have this one for . . . you know. A year or so. Here, let me show you the spot I had in mind."

She led him up a flight of carpeted stairs and to what could only have been the main bedroom. He resisted going in, hanging in the doorway instead.

"This whole wall could be a curtain," she said.

She swept across the room to a floor-to-ceiling window and drew the curtain closed across it. It made a fairly flat, featureless off-white backdrop. It was a huge room, so the bed would be nowhere in the frame.

"And this is the dressing screen," she said. "We could put it off-center in front of the curtain."

She pointed to the screen, but did not move it. Michael wondered if she still had physical limitations five months after her surgery. Probably so. It was heavy-looking. Some kind of dark wood, walnut, he thought, ornately carved. Capable of folding like an accordion. It struck him as quite beautiful.

"I think this would be brilliant," he said, still not stepping into the bedroom.

"Then it's all set," she said. "All we need to do now is find you the courage to come in."

He turned his face away and headed toward the stairs.

"I have to get to school," he said as she followed him down. "But I'll call Rex today and arrange the time of the first interview and then run it by you."

He realized as he trotted down the stairs that he was running away. Worse yet, he was running from something he wanted. But he couldn't seem to talk his feet into taking a risk and staying.

He stopped in front of the door, not sure if he should open it himself. She moved around him and held it wide. But for a moment he didn't leave.

"Are you a student at the university?" he asked her, suddenly curious. "I'm trying to figure out how you were . . . you know . . . there."

"I'm taking a class in memoir writing," she said. "I thought it would be nice to get my life down into some kind of coherent story."

"Yeah, good," he said, and immediately felt stupid. "Thanks. For offering this place."

He opened his mouth to say more, but the more was just too mortifying. What if he was mistaken? He felt he could die from the humiliation if he was reading her all wrong.

He closed his mouth again. Then he trotted to his car and drove away.

But his mind was buzzing, and felt almost burning hot with activity.

He stopped at the end of her driveway, picked up his phone. Called her number. Then he put the call on speaker and headed down the road.

"Forget something?" she said when she picked up.

"I'm probably about to make a fool of myself," he said, "because I'm really bad at stuff like this. I think my radar is all out of whack because I never really honed it. So this might be a big mistake, but . . . I feel like you're coming on to me, but I'm so sure I'm wrong that I can't do anything reasonable with the information."

"You think I'm *what*?" she shouted.

"Oh no. Oh crap. I'm so sorry. I'm totally sorry. See, I knew I was wrong. I told you I knew I was wrong. Can you ever—"

"Michael," she said. "I'm yanking your chain. Of course I'm coming on to you. Wow, you *do* have bad radar, because I was being super obvious. But if you don't want me to do it anymore, just say so. I promise you won't have to ask me twice. But yeah. I took my shot. Sue me." A silence. "Do you want me to stop?"

"No," he said.

He meant for the word to be immediately followed by many more words, but they took their time coming.

"It wasn't a complaint," he said after a time. "It's just that . . . you said you were too old for me."

"I figured *you'd* think so," she said. "But *I* don't mind. Do you mind?"

"Not really, no. But you said you'd regret it."

"Yeah, if I'd gone out on a limb and you'd said 'Ew, ick, you're thirty, that's disgusting,' then yeah. I would have regretted putting myself out there. Look. Michael. It wasn't a marriage proposal. I wanted to have a fling. Haven't you ever wanted to have a fling?"

"Some days," he said. "Like, not too many days before I was twelve. But pretty much every day since then."

She laughed, and it was a beautiful sound. He felt it right through to his core, like a perfect note on a wind chime.

"Well, the offer stands," she said.

As tended to be the case with her, he gathered more words and opened his mouth to speak them only to find she had ended the call.

He pulled over onto the shoulder of the road and sat a minute. Not thinking.

Then he swung a U-turn.

———

It dawned on him suddenly that she had opened the huge wall of curtains again in the short time while he was gone. He noticed it long after he should have, as he was lying in bed with her, up against her back, his thumb just barely moving against her bare belly.

It didn't matter, though, because there was nothing outside the wall of window except trees and sky.

It felt radically new—almost alarmingly new—to allow his bare chest and belly to touch someone else's skin. And yet in another way it felt right. More than right, actually. It felt triumphant. Like some wonderful thing he could have done ages ago if only someone would have told him he could. Or if somehow he could have arrived there on his own.

And in daylight. He had always imagined if he took his clothes off with somebody it would be in the dark, but now he couldn't remember what it felt like to think so.

He opened his mouth to try to tell her this, but she spoke first.

"Does anybody ever call you Mike?"

"No. Never. Always Michael. Even when I was little. Like, two. I was still Michael. And my brother's name was Thomas and nobody ever called him Tom. And I honestly have no idea why."

He felt the palm of her hand brush lightly against the fine hairs on his forearm—the arm he had draped over her. It felt like those hairs were standing up at attention in response.

"You could ask them."

"Not really I couldn't. I haven't spoken to them since I was seven."

"But they're alive?"

"As far as I know."

He expected her to ask. She didn't. It reminded him of earlier that morning, when he'd wanted to know how she afforded this beautiful house but had chosen not to ask her. But she had volunteered the information anyway, so he returned the favor.

"After my accident I was put in a foster home, and my parents did time in jail for child endangerment. A year went by, and I guess they were clean, or clean and sober, or whatever, and Thomas had been in a different foster home, and he was unhappy, and he wanted to go home. So Child Protective Services let him go home, and my parents took him back. But they never took me back. My foster parents wanted to adopt me, and my parents just let them. Just gave up their parental rights and let them. They wanted him but they didn't want me. I've never really forgiven them for that, so we haven't spoken since."

"Whoa," Madeleine said. "Poor seven-year-old Michael. That explains so much, though."

"What does it explain?"

"I've been wondering how you got it into your head that you didn't get to have anybody. Lots of people have scars, or some other thing about them that they might worry would be an issue for somebody else, but they still have relationships. They still know they get to have love. I've been wondering why you didn't think you got to have love."

They lay together in silence for a time. Several minutes, from his sense of it. Michael could feel the sun through the gigantic window warming his back.

"I'm not putting all this together," he said.

"You thought it was the reason they didn't want you back."

"I did?"

"I don't know. Didn't you? I mean, they took your brother back but they didn't take you. It must have made you feel like they thought you were damaged goods. It's what I would think if I were seven."

Michael waited for an inner response to her words, but they fell into a very deep, very quiet well. Maybe it was even bottomless.

"I was eight by then."

"It's what I would think if I were eight. But I could be wrong. You were there. You know better than I do."

"I'm not sure either one of those assumptions is true. I guess I was there in a sense. But a lot of that time is just inaccessible to me. I know more from being told about it than from actually remembering."

"Do you remember your accident?"

"I remember a yellow plastic cigarette lighter. And a firefighter watching from up on the bluff."

"That's it?"

"Pretty much."

"Well, maybe it's just as well. Who wants a thing like that in their head? You're skipping classes for me. Where are you supposed to be right now?"

"Math. But I don't even know why. Why am I taking math? I want a career in film."

"Okay, I give up, then. Why are you taking math? Which I realize is a weird question when you just told me you don't know why."

"My parents were hoping I'd go into engineering. Rather than the extremely dependable and lucrative world of film."

"Never hurts to have a fallback position," she said.

"I'm not sure I agree. I'm not a big fan of them. The problem with a fallback position is that you tend to fall back. I'd rather work without a net. Increases your chances of staying on the high wire. I should go to school now. I hate to say it, but I should. I could stay here all day like this, but I don't want to miss film workshop."

"But you'll come back, though. Right?"

"Try to keep me away," he said.

———

He slid into his usual seat, in the front row near Robert Dunning's desk, only about three minutes early. Which for him was essentially late. For a minute or two, the professor just kept reading his magazine.

Then he looked up suddenly, as if shaken from sleep, and looked into Michael's face for a long time.

"I give up," he said. "What's changed?"

"Changed?" Michael asked, though he knew exactly what Dunning meant.

He hadn't expected to be found out so quickly, and he wasn't sure if he was ready to let the whole experience out into the light.

"Something's different. Radically different. But I'm not talking about a new hairstyle or anything like that. I'm talking about something from the inside out. Are you telling me you honestly don't know what I'm talking about?"

Michael glanced over his shoulder to see if anyone was close by. Then he leaned over his desk as far as possible.

"I spent the morning with a girl."

"Spent . . . ? As in . . . ?"

Michael nodded, unable to keep a smile from his face. "But not a girl, really. A woman. She's older. But . . ."

Dunning waited a suitable length of time. Then he said, "But . . . ?"

"No 'buts,'" Michael said. "I just did."

Dunning sat back in his chair.

"Well, good for you, Michael. Seriously, good for you. I wondered when you were going to get it that you're just as free to get involved as anyone."

"She said pretty much the same thing."

"I like her already," Dunning said.

———

When class started, Michael had a devil of a time sitting still.

Halfway through, he slipped his phone out of his pocket and texted her.

"I can't stop thinking about you," he typed. "Is that normal?"

After a brief pause, she responded, "Yes."

After another brief pause she sent him a little smiley-face emoji.

He looked up to see Dunning staring down at him, and he averted his gaze and slipped the phone back in his pocket.

"Sorry," he said.

"One pass," Dunning said. "Because it's a special occasion."

Chapter Nine

If Only I Had Spit on Hitler
When I Had the Chance

"You two seem very comfortable together," Rex Aronfeld said, indicating with a flip of his chin the spot where Madeleine had last stood. "I'm guessing there's a little something there between you two."

He was sitting on a simple wooden stool in front of the wall of curtain. Michael was getting his camera set up on the tripod he had borrowed from Mr. Dunning. Madeleine had been puttering around in the main bedroom with them, but had just slipped downstairs.

"Yes, but the whole thing is kind of new," Michael said. "And what with the age difference and all . . . it's not something I'm sure I want getting around at this point."

"Exactly who would I tell? The only person we both know is her, and she already knows."

"Good point. Now I'm going to turn on the camera," Michael said, and did so. "And we're just going to talk. We can talk for a long time—as long as you want—and I'll take what I need when I'm editing, so feel free to ramble."

"*My* first time was with a woman a lot older than me, too. And I do mean a *lot* older."

"Should I even ask how old you both were?"

"Probably not, but even if you do I know better than to answer. It was a different world back then. I'm not sure how to explain it better than that. I'm just telling you how it was for my first time."

Michael turned the camera off again.

"Why did you say it like that?"

"How did I say it?"

"You said '*My* first' was older, too. How do you know Madeleine was my first?"

"Call it a hunch," Rex said.

Michael waited a minute to be sure they were ready to move on to a more relevant and less embarrassing topic.

Rex was a very small, very thin man. Maybe five foot three, if that. His hair was snow white—what was left of it. His snow-white eyebrows looked almost bushy and dramatic enough to make up for what hair he had lost.

"You ready?" Michael asked.

"When *you* are." Then Rex seemed to remember something suddenly. "Oh. I almost forgot. I brought this along. I meant to show it to you in the car."

He reached down into the canvas bag at his feet and pulled out a framed picture of a young teenager doing gymnastics on a horse. A gym horse, not a live animal.

"May I see that?" Michael asked.

He reached out and took it, and held it in his hands for what felt like a long time.

The boy in the picture was lithe and strong. His arms were bare, and because they were supporting the full weight of his body, every muscle stood out in perfect relief. They looked like a complex set of ropes or cables just underneath his skin. He had a thick shock of reddish-brown hair, cropped short, and piercing light-brown eyes. His face was a mask of concentration.

Michael turned on the camera and took a close-up shot of the framed picture. Then, leaving the camera running, he handed the photo to Rex and asked him to hold it up in front of himself.

Michael zoomed in so both could be easily seen. Then he pulled back out again.

"This has been up on my wall for decades," Rex said. "This picture. Maybe eighty years. Maybe more. So I know it like the back of my hand, but I don't actually see it anymore. Do you know what I mean when I say that? It feels like it's so completely memorized that I can't stand back from it and really see it as though I were seeing it for the first time. It doesn't register anymore. But I have this nurse . . . The county home health service sends a nurse out five days a week to check on me so I can live on my own. She notices this picture, and she starts making a fuss about it. 'Oh my, what a handsome young man,' she says. 'And look at those muscles! Now that's "fitness" with a capital F. Is that your grandson?' I said, 'Honey, that's me.' She was more than a little surprised, to say the least.

"I asked her to take it down and hand it to me. I stared at it for the longest time. I had a strange experience with it, and I think it's what made me want to come here and talk about it for your film. I had this sense of . . . well, grief, I suppose. Like I was grieving for the person in the picture. Or missing him. It was almost like the picture was an old love, or a great friend I hadn't seen in ages. There was this sense of loss.

"Don't get me wrong. I'm happy with my body for one simple reason: It's still going. It got me to a hundred and three. I swear I don't mean it as a complaint. But it's not the same body. Any fool can see that.

"Now I look at this picture every day again. Sometimes I think that's me in the picture and the old man I see in the mirror is a stranger. Other times I look in the mirror and think that's me and the boy in the picture is nearly someone else. Either way, it's strange.

"I don't regret growing older. Hell, consider the alternative, am I right? I loved my body back then because it did everything for me. It got me to the Olympics in '36. Everybody admired me for it. I was so very, very comfortable inside it. So I miss the old days, but I have no real regrets about that. I only have one genuine regret in life, and I told you what it was when I first called you. I wonder if you remember."

Michael remembered. It was hard to forget someone sharing a personal experience they'd had with Adolf Hitler.

"That you shook Hitler's hand at the '36 Olympics in Berlin."

"Yeah, but even more that I didn't spit in his face or at least on his shoes instead. It would have caused an international incident, but I wish I'd done it anyway. It would have been worth any incident."

"But you said you didn't know yet."

"We knew enough. We didn't know millions would be slaughtered. We knew he wasn't allowing Jews to vote or run their businesses, and we knew people were being rounded up and arrested. How much do you need to know before you spit in a man's face? But I was fifteen and he was Adolf Hitler. And I just couldn't do it. Well. Maybe I *could* have. I wasn't physically incapable. But I just couldn't bring myself to do it. I was scared. He had so much power. I felt so small compared to him. Compared to that whole moment."

"I think anyone would have felt that way," Michael said.

"But I still regret it."

"Okay, but you've lived a hundred and three years and you only have one real regret. That's not half bad."

"I suppose you're right," Rex Aronfeld said, "if you want to look at it that way. And it's a good way to look at it, I think. Still, it might only be that one thing, but it's a big thing. It was Hitler. It's just big. But enough about that. Do I take off my clothes? Or keep talking?"

"Up to you," Michael said. "Whatever you're comfortable doing."

For a moment Rex just perched there on his stool. He seemed to be thinking some kind of distant thoughts. It almost gave the impression that he had exited the room but left his body behind. His eyes were the same color of light brown as those of the boy in the photo, but not nearly as clear or intense.

"My wife," Rex said. Then he didn't say more for a time.

"You told me she died when you were seventy."

"Yeah. Fifty-one years we were married. From the time we were nineteen to the time we were seventy."

"What was her name?"

"Elaine. I called her Lainie. Lainie Aronfeld. She was a beauty queen. Literally. I don't just mean in my opinion. She was an actual beauty queen. Miss New Jersey of 1939. You know, with the swimsuit competition and whatnot. It's all frowned upon these days, but it was different back then. The world was different. I'm not saying the world was right then and it's wrong now. I look back and I wince a little. But I can't say it any better than what I already said. It was just a different world. If your wife-to-be won a beauty contest, you were proud. You were considered a lucky man. She was quite a looker, Lainie, with a body to match. When we walked together men's heads turned all the way down the street.

"We grew . . . well, somewhat old together. At the time we thought seventy was old, but now it seems like the prime of my youth. And our faces and bodies changed, of course, but they changed together. I think we accepted that with a fair amount of grace. Couples are doing it all over the world. Have been since the beginning of time. Well, if the guy is a good guy. If he's a rat he goes off after somebody younger."

"But you wouldn't do that," Michael said. "Right?"

"Who knows what a person is or isn't capable of doing, but I can honestly say I never did. There was never anybody else but Lainie, even after she died. Thirty-three years she's been gone. And you know what I miss most about her?"

"I really don't," Michael said.

"I'll let you guess."

Madeleine quietly slid back into the room and touched Michael on the shoulder on her way past. She sat on the edge of the bed to watch.

"I can't guess exactly what it is, but I'm going to go out on a limb and say it's not her body."

"Correct. It's not her body. I miss talking to her. I'd give a hundred thousand dollars for one more conversation with her. Well, no I wouldn't, because I don't have it, but if I had it I'd give it. Not even anything that special of a talk. If I could just sit at the kitchen table with her and have her catch me up on what she's been doing since I last saw her. I'll be honest. It was probably her face and body that got my attention, and vice versa—her with me. You know, back when we were strangers just noticing each other. It might be what I saw that drew me in. But it wasn't what I loved. It definitely wasn't what I loved. And it's not what I remember when I'm looking back over the years."

"That's an important thing to get on film," Michael said. "It's probably enough if you want it to be. But if you have more to say, feel free to go on."

"I watch TV," Rex said.

For a moment he didn't say more, and Michael was unsure of where he was going with the thought.

"The word 'old' means bad. I mean, not in the actual English language it doesn't, but in our comedies on TV. Let's you say you had a blind date and someone asks you how it was. You say 'He was old.' And that means it was terrible, and you don't need to say another word, because the person gets it already. Or they'll say 'That person should be thrown out of Congress because he's too old.' 'Old' means 'bad.' I absorb these hits every day. Sometimes I don't think too much about them at the time. But let me tell you something. It builds up in there. Every time it happens it's like somebody handed you a stone. No big deal. Except after a while you can't even move around because you're so weighted down."

After that he seemed to freeze for a strange length of time. Michael was just beginning to think it might be some kind of medical issue.

He shot Madeleine a sidewise glance, and she shrugged ever so slightly.

Then Rex shook himself as if to wake up. He pulled to his feet with great effort and slowly shuffled behind the ornately carved walnut dressing screen.

Michael could hear the soft fabric-involved sounds of his movements.

"Would you like me to leave the room for this?" Madeleine asked.

"Honey, I don't care," Rex's voice called back. "If I cared, I wouldn't be inviting the boy to film it."

A minute or two later he stepped out, more or less sideways. He had his hands cupped in front of his genitals for privacy. It was the first time Michael had noticed that his hands were huge. Bony, and spotted. And just enormous.

He stopped in front of the stool and stood facing the camera.

His thin skin seemed to hang on his bones, sagging at his chest and abdomen and the insides of his thighs. It fell in fine vertical creases, like a crepe fabric or paper.

"Here I am," he said, accidentally stumbling on the title of the film, which Michael hadn't told him. "What can I say? I accept my body, but I think I might be the only person in the world who does. Or at least I *feel* like I'm the only person in the world who does. And that makes me feel so lonely. It makes me feel like I'm not a part of the world like I used to be. Like I don't fit in anywhere anymore."

For a moment he just stood, staring off into space with that same distant expression.

Then he looked directly into Michael's eyes.

"So what do you think?" He seemed to pull himself together quickly and purposefully, as though he'd suddenly decided enough emotion was enough. "Is that something you can use in your film?"

"I think it's brilliant," Michael said, noticing that he was right on the edge of feeling choked up. It was just a little catch in his throat, but it was there. Undeniable. "I think it's wonderful. I can definitely use it, and right now I'm just feeling really, really happy because you called me."

"Great," Rex Aronfeld said. "Just give me a minute to put on my duds and you can take me home."

———

"You seem far away," she said.

They were lying under a light sheet later that afternoon. Long after Michael had driven Rex home. Michael was propped up on two pillows, his hands clasped behind his head. He had pulled the sheet up to cover his torso, and Madeleine was lying half on her side with the sheet up to her armpits.

For a minute it struck him as strange, since she was always encouraging him to be more open about his body. Then it occurred to him that it was one thing to encourage someone else, and to stand up for their rights. It was quite another to move past your own discomfort.

"I was thinking about that interview," he said.

"It was a good one. It's going to be such a good film if you can get a few more of that quality. Hell of a story that guy has. I just hope it's true."

"It is. You can still look all that stuff up online. All the athletes, all the events. The medalists. He took silver for the USA. But mostly I was thinking about that stuff he was saying about his late wife. I never used to think of my future this way, but I was just picturing having a wife and kids and settling down, and her outliving me and telling somebody that she missed talking to me. And never, not even once, mentioning *this*."

He indicated the length of his torso with a sweep of his hand.

"Of course she wouldn't mention that," Madeleine said. "It wouldn't even cross her mind, unless she was incredibly shallow. And you wouldn't marry and settle down with a woman who was incredibly shallow."

A small cat jumped up onto the bed and eyed Michael cautiously. She—at least she struck Michael as a she—had a surprisingly feminine, delicate face, with faint Siamese-like markings and blue eyes.

"I didn't know you had a cat," he said.

"She usually hides when people are over. She must not have known you were here. Now that she knows she'll scoot again."

The cat continued to stare at Michael for a few more beats. Then she walked right up to him and stepped up onto his belly.

"Lily, no," Madeleine said. "That must hurt. Want me to get her?"

"No, she's okay. She's so light that it hardly hurts. I mean, that was twelve years ago."

"Dude."

"What?"

"Please don't remind me that twelve years ago you were seven. Kind of freaks me out."

"Sorry. It hurt for years, especially when it was cold. The cold weather just made it ache something fierce. I guess it made that scar tissue tighten up. That's why my adoptive parents moved us back to California. For a while we lived in Minnesota. I don't know how it would be now."

He ran a hand down the cat's back, and she blinked sweetly and purred.

"She likes you."

"Too bad I'm going to have to move her in a minute. I said I'd be home for dinner." Then he felt nervous and uncomfortable because he'd just announced he was leaving her company to have family dinner with his parents. "Unless . . . I don't know. You want to come?"

"Oh hell no. One of the best parts of a fling is never having to meet the parents."

"I hear you," he said.

She reached out and lifted the cat off him, and he sat up on the edge of the bed and began to dress.

"You want to go next?" he asked her over his shoulder.

"In what regard?"

"Your interview."

"Oh. That. No, it's okay. I can go last. You're going to do these all in just a couple of weeks, right?"

"That's the plan."

"I'm sure I can hang in that long," she said.

Chapter Ten

The Day We Get to Stop Practicing

"So that's Madeleine," Robert Dunning said.

When he said it, Michael reached out and toggled a switch to turn off the camera.

Dunning was sitting on the wooden stool in Madeleine's main bedroom, facing Michael's new camera. He was wearing jeans and a tweed jacket with elbow patches, with a blazingly white collared shirt underneath. He was leaning forward at an odd angle, as if physically uncomfortable. Or otherwise uncomfortable.

Madeleine had just left, saying she had a headache and would lie down in the guest room.

"Yeah," Michael said. "Why?"

"Just making conversation."

"I was worried there was some kind of judgment coming."

"Why do you think I would judge her? Because she's older? Or because she has such a strong personality?"

"Yes. All of the above."

Michael wanted to turn on the camera, but he didn't want any confidences about Madeleine recorded on video. She might be looking over his shoulder when he edited.

"Are you sensitive about the age difference?" Dunning asked, his head tilted slightly. Curiously.

"Maybe. Maybe a little. I don't know if I care, but I guess I figure everybody else would. I like her personality. She's really strong. And direct. And unafraid. I mean, inside she might be afraid. I don't know. But she presents herself to the world as unafraid. And I think that makes her everything I want to be myself. She's like you that way. I think that's why I like both of you. I want to be just like you two when I grow up."

Dunning smiled a faint smile that Michael could only characterize as sweet. He had never seen a look of sweetness on his professor's face before.

"I do think she's rubbing off on you a little already," Dunning said. "I like who you are since you've been with her, so I like her. As far as the age situation goes, people spend their whole lives together when they have a lot more years separating them. And if you're planning on something short of growing old with her, as is usually the case with first loves, then it doesn't matter at all."

"It's just a fling," Michael said.

He noticed himself directing his eyes down to the carpet as he said it.

"Who defined it that way? Her? Or you? Or was it mutual?"

"It's what she said she wanted. She said she just wanted to have a fling. But now I'm wondering . . . if you're having a fling with someone, are you supposed to not have feelings for them? What if you're not supposed to fall in love but you do anyway?"

He briefly glanced up. Dunning's eyes had grown deeply empathetic. Almost sad. It was another look Michael had never seen on him before. It was also a look he didn't care to see in anyone's eyes in that moment. The last thing he wanted was to be the recipient of anyone's pity.

"No one gets to police your feelings, Michael. A lot of people have casual relationships but still fall in love. It's not against the rules, because there are no rules for feelings. You just have to accept that it's over when it's over."

"I'm going to turn on the camera now," Michael said. Suddenly and forcefully. It was his clear signal that he was moving the conversation in a new direction.

But it seemed the camera was still on—that he had somehow toggled the wrong switch.

He focused it carefully, and chose just the right amount of zoom.

"Thank you for doing this," he said, making eye contact with Dunning again.

"My pleasure," Dunning said. "Though, be prepared. It might cause some minor issues. If I give your film a very good grade—which seems likely based on that unedited interview with Rex Aronfeld you showed me—there might be complaints from another student. Some might think I was biased toward your project because I contributed to it."

"Would that get you in trouble?"

"No. I discussed it with the dean. She trusts me to be impartial."

"I could always make a bad film. That would solve the problem."

"Don't," Dunning said, a tiny smile flickering. "We'll deal with it. Are we filming?"

"We are."

"Okay then. Here goes. My name is Robert Edmund Dunning. I'm fifty-nine years old. I teach film at the college level. Full disclosure, I am Michael's professor, and this documentary is a response to my assignment to create a student film before the end of the semester. I also think Michael's subject matter stemmed from conversations we've had."

"It definitely did," Michael said. "You helped me a lot with what I have to say in a film. But I'm sorry, I didn't mean to interrupt. Go on."

"No worries. You're allowed to talk too. Anyway. On with my story.

"When I was thirteen, I was in the car with my parents and my older sister. We used to go for a drive in the country on Sundays. That was something of a thing back then. I don't see people doing it much these days, but at the time a drive was considered a pleasurable pastime, especially if you could get outside the city and see horses and cows and forests. It was a nice break.

"We were on a four-lane highway—two lanes in each direction, with no divider. I remember I was looking at some horses. A bay and a palomino. Big, nice-looking horses, and they were running together in a pasture, tails up, very free. It was a lovely thing to see.

"And then I heard my father suck in his breath.

"I looked straight ahead again, and there were deer bolting in front of us on the highway. Lots of them. I think seven, though there might have been more I didn't see, or didn't have time to register. My father jammed on the brakes, but he simply didn't have enough space or notice to stop the car. We slammed into this enormous buck. He had a rack of horns like the kind you see on a trophy hunter's wall—the kind that look so big and heavy you can't even imagine how the animal carries all that weight around. It brought the car to a dead stop. Or maybe the brakes had locked. There's just no way to know now.

"There was another car close behind us, but in the left lane. I saw him out of the corner of my eye. He swerved to avoid the deer and plowed right into the back of us.

"It all happened in what felt like just a fraction of a second.

"We didn't know it at the time, but the car my father was driving was one of those problem models. Those poorly designed death traps. The placement of the gas tank was such that it was easily punctured in a rear-end collision. We heard and felt this huge bang, and then the car was enveloped in flames. Just like that. I swear no time elapsed at all.

"Someone pulled me out through the back door, but to this very day I don't know who. Another motorist, I suppose."

"And your parents? Your sister? Did they get out?"

"No," Dunning said. "I was the only survivor."

Michael sat in silence and listened as those words reverberated in the air. Or seemed to, anyway. Maybe it was only inside his own head and gut that they bounced and echoed.

In his head he saw the yellow plastic lighter, and the firefighter looking down from the bluff.

And then that sudden cataclysm. The end of the world.

It took him several seconds to gather himself to ask more.

"Did you have to go into a foster home?"

"No, I was fortunate. Overall, I don't suppose I viewed the whole debacle as particularly lucky, but in that one respect I got a break. My father was an only child, but on my mother's side I had three exceedingly kind, delightfully eccentric aunts, and they all but resorted to fisticuffs over who would have the honor of raising me. I went to live with my aunt Priscilla in Marietta, Ohio. And it was a good upbringing. I'm not suggesting the transition was an easy one, but she made it easier than it might have been. The grief over losing my family was intense, of course, and I suppose there was a degree of survivor's guilt. There was the difficult medical aspect of the whole situation. That's unavoidable. But I don't have to tell you how that goes. And there was the adjustment to the look on people's faces when they saw me. My aunt was hugely helpful with that, I must say. She's the one who taught me the completely shame-free approach. She would say 'Bobby boy, scars are a fact of life. Some people manage to avoid them. Others might incur only the smaller, more subtle varieties. Then there's the vast majority of us who wear their scars on the inside, the truly unlucky souls. They're the ones who come to believe that no one must see their scars. But a scar is not a shameful thing, Bobby. It's just a fact of living, your proof of life, so to speak.' As a result, I grew up defiant. But still, I have to say . . . to this very day, it affects me. That initial wince. That little jump, as if the person has seen a ghost, or a glimpse of their own death. I don't know that a person can ever choose to be entirely unaffected by that. All I can say is that it doesn't grow less troubling, it only grows less new."

"You face it so head-on, though," Michael said. "I just love that about you. I love the way you told the class to go ahead and stare until they'd gotten it out of their system."

"The shame can go both ways, unfortunately. The person meeting me somehow feels like a bad person for noticing, or for flinching, or both. But that's perfectly ridiculous. Anybody would notice. No one is at fault, and yet both parties are somehow left to feel that there's some cause for shame. Well, I myself reject shame outright. Unless I've done something harmful to someone else, which I try not to do, I consider it merely a useless appendage to our lives. And I'm not going to step out from underneath shame without at least offering an escape route to the other party. Now. If you'll excuse me . . ."

Dunning rose and walked behind the dressing screen.

"Ah," he said. "How kind of you to put hangers back here for my clothing."

Less than thirty seconds later he stepped out again, wearing only oversize, baggy white boxer shorts adorned with enormous red hearts.

It was so unexpected from such a sober and serious man. A guffaw of laughter burst out of Michael, driven by the surprise.

"I'm sorry," he said. "I didn't mean to laugh."

"You're supposed to laugh," Dunning said, taking a wide-legged stance in front of the stool. In front of the camera. "My wife bought them for me, specifically for the occasion of this filming. She said they would remind me not to take myself too seriously."

Michael could feel himself grinning widely, and it was such a lovely feeling. Such a relief from the specter of injury and life-changing disaster.

"This is me," Dunning said boldly to the camera. "Get used to it."

He had more burn scars on the left side of his chest and one thigh. But really, after seeing his face and hands, the figure he cut as he stood partially nude before the camera added very little to the story of his scarring.

Michael had gotten used to it.

"I so want to be in that place," Michael said. "I'm trying so hard to get to where you are."

"And you *are* getting there," Dunning said. "You just haven't quite arrived at the destination yet. I'm fifty-nine years old, Michael. Do you remember what I said to you the very first time we spoke?"

"I think I remember everything you've ever said to me. But I'm pretty sure I know the thing you mean. You said, 'Being a person takes practice.'"

"Indeed," Dunning said. "That very thing. And the day we get to stop practicing is the day we die. Now, if you think that's sufficient for what you had in mind, I'm going to put my clothing back on over these silly boxer shorts and go home to my wife."

———

"You want coffee?" Madeleine asked him after Dunning had left.

They were standing in the kitchen, and he was staring out through the huge window at the trees. Had been for some time.

"Actually, I hate coffee," he said, pulling himself back to the moment.

"Since when?"

"Since . . . always?"

"But back when I first met you . . . didn't you say you were having coffee with your professor?"

"Oh. Well. Just as a sort of general term. He was having espresso and I was having orange juice. But who says that? 'My professor and I were having espresso and orange juice.' It just sounds weird."

"I have orange juice," she said, "if you want some."

"Okay. Thanks. How's your headache?"

"A little better. I took a pill."

She poured two tall glasses, handed him one, and then rolled back the sliding glass door and stepped out onto the patio.

"Oh," he said. "We're having it out here?"

"Since you seem so fascinated with something in this direction."

They sat and sipped. And Michael got lost in the trees again.

Lily the cat hopped up onto the deck, making odd little noises in her throat. They were not exactly meows. They were quieter than that, and she seemed to be trying to modulate them, as if speaking.

"There you are," Madeleine said to the cat. "I was looking everywhere for you."

Lily jumped up onto Michael's lap, and they gazed at the trees together.

"You're being awfully quiet," she said after a minute or two. Or maybe it was ten, and he'd lost track of minutes.

"Who? Me or the cat?"

"You."

"Am I being quiet?"

"It was the Dunning guy, wasn't it? He said something negative about us."

"No. He didn't. Not at all. He was very supportive about us. He said he likes who I am since I've been with you, so he likes you. I guess I just started thinking about . . ." He paused for a time, trying to decide if he dared finish the sentence. If he even wanted to. "About, you know, flings. And how they . . . end."

He purposely didn't look at her face.

She reached over and took one of his hands in both of hers. In a move that surprised him, she brought it to her lips and kissed him on the knuckles.

"Everything ends, love," she said.

"I know that. But it doesn't mean I have to be okay about it. I mean, I can accept something and still not like it."

"True."

They sat in silence for another extended time, during which she did not give him his hand back. But that was okay. He didn't particularly want her to let it go.

"We'll make the most of what time we have," she said.

"Sure, I guess. I mean . . . it's not like I have any choice."

"No. It's not one of those things we can control."

Michael pondered that for a time. He would ponder it for days, in fact. Because it seemed like when and whether to end a romance was indeed something the two parties could control.

But he never asked her about it. He just buried his sadness and let the moment for questions pass.

———

"You've been gone so much," his mother said over dinner.

"Well, you know," he said. "I've been working on the film."

"Oh, right. The film. About scars. I'm still not sure—"

But a look from his father stopped her in mid-sentence.

"It's not so much about scars anymore," Michael said, staring at a mouthful of fettuccine wound around his fork but not eating it. "It was going to be. But then it took an unexpected turn. Now it's more about people who just . . . worry about the way they look."

"Everybody worries about the way they look," she said.

"Yeah, I'm gathering that."

"I'm not sure that's true," his father said. "I think there are lots of people who are very happy with their looks."

"But even so," Michael said, "they know it won't last. One guy I interviewed is a hundred and three. He used to be an Olympic gymnast. He loved the way he looked. But now he's . . . you know . . . a hundred and three."

"I guess that sounds interesting," she said. "But it can't take that many hours just getting someone to talk into a camera. You're gone almost all the time now."

"I've made new friends at college, you know."

"Do you have a girlfriend?"

A pall seemed to fall over the table as Michael tried to figure out how to avoid answering.

"You're a very handsome boy," she said. "It's no surprise that you would have a girlfriend. I just think we should meet her."

"Oh no," Michael said, with no forethought whatsoever. "That would be completely humiliating."

"Judy," his father said, "stop treating him like a boy. He's a man now. That custom that a date has to come meet the parents first is for minor teens. Let him live his life."

They ate in silence for an awkward stretch of time.

"I just have one question about this film," his mother said. "You're not thinking of showing your scars on camera, are you?"

Michael set down his fork and felt his appetite abandon him.

"Yes, I absolutely plan on doing just that."

"Why would you do that?"

"Why *wouldn't* I do it, Mom? It's not a secret. It's not a scandal. It's not a moral failing. It just *is*." He realized he was quoting fairly directly from Robert Dunning, but the right words were the right words whether he was their author or not.

He spoke the words with such conviction that she didn't ask any questions for the remainder of the meal, and never brought up the subject again.

Chapter Eleven

The First Deal We Made with the World

"I'm having second thoughts about this," the man said.

It was the man who considered himself too skinny and generally unattractive. But he had admitted that the name he'd given on the phone was false, and Michael still didn't know his real name. He figured the ongoing anonymity and the second thoughts were related.

The man had arrived on time for his interview and willingly followed Michael upstairs to the main bedroom. But now he stood in front of the stool and seemed unwilling to sit.

"Okay," Michael said. "Well. I certainly don't want anyone doing the interview against their will. It's completely up to you."

"It's just . . ." the man began.

Then he didn't speak for a long time. No one did.

He was indeed very thin. His clothes were baggy—maybe purposely so—but the overall shape of him still showed. It was clear how much of the bulk of him was composed of empty pant legs and sleeves. He had deep marks on the skin of his face—maybe from an acne-related condition—and uneven, overlapping teeth. His nose was oddly long and narrow, his eyes small and closely set.

He also looked angry.

"First of all," he said, "I didn't know there would be a woman here."

"Color me gone," Madeleine said.

She jumped up from her perch on the edge of the bed and trotted out of the room. Michael could hear the light brush of her bare feet on the stairs.

"And another thing," the man said. "I figured I'd get here, and take a look at you, and think 'Right. I can see how he'd want to make a film about this.' Instead I show up and you're, like, the best-looking guy in the world. So what's your angle, anyway?"

"I'm not the best-looking guy in the world," Michael said.

"Well, you're at least in the top ten percent. So why would I take my clothes off in front of one of the best-looking guys in the world? Is it so you can feel superior to me?"

Michael sighed deeply.

"You know, it's weird," he said, unbuttoning his shirt. "From the time I was seven until a few weeks ago I never took my shirt off in front of anybody, ever. Not in gym class. Not in front of a girl. Not at the pool or the beach. Well, I didn't go to the pool or the beach. And now it seems like every time I turn around I'm showing someone my chest and stomach."

He let the shirt drop open.

He didn't have to lift or remove an undershirt, because he no longer wore one. He had begun to trust the buttons of his shirt to provide armor enough.

The man's eyes fell onto Michael's scars and stayed there for a long time while no one spoke.

Then the man's gaze came back up to Michael's face again.

"That must be weird," the guy said. "To have people treating you like this almost problematically attractive person because they're not seeing that other thing about you."

"Yeah," Michael said. "It can be weird."

The man sat down on the stool with a sigh.

"You're okay to go forward?" Michael asked. "Can I turn on the camera?"

"Yeah. I'm fine."

Michael turned on the camera and checked the focus and framing before proceeding.

"You want to tell us your name? It's up to you."

"Can I just give my first name?"

"Sure. You can even use the made-up name if you want. I honestly don't care. The names are not what's important here."

"It's Tim. But—you know what? I'm being stupid. I'm a janitor at the college. Most of the people who see this are going to know who I am anyway. It's Tim McDonnell. That's my real name. I'm sorry for getting upset before. I wasn't sure what your angle was for doing this. I wanted to make sure I wasn't going to be a curiosity. You know, like the old-fashioned freak shows. They used to have a thin man in the old-fashioned freak shows."

"I didn't know that," Michael said.

"It was before your time."

"Anyway, I understand. You don't need to apologize."

Michael had purposely left his shirt hanging open, thinking it might make Tim more comfortable. As they spoke, he saw Tim's gaze dart to Michael's torso, then away again.

"It's more than just being skinny," Tim said. "But I think that's the biggest issue to me because it's a power thing. Or I guess I should say a lack-of-power thing. It makes me feel vulnerable, because most men are so much heavier and stronger than me. So there's sort of an added element of threat to that. But the truth is, I'm just not a good-looking guy. I'm not what women are looking for."

Michael started to say that it wasn't an absolute truth, what Tim had said, because not all women were looking for the same thing. Then he decided he should listen to the other person's reality, not mitigate it or minimize it or try to shape it in any way.

"If I'm being completely honest with myself about it," Tim said, "I think it's partly my personality. I think I got bitter and defensive about it at an early age, and now I think that works against me even more than my looks. But however you want to slice it, I've never had a real girlfriend, and I want to have somebody, just like everybody else does. And I don't know what to do about that. What do you do about a thing like that?"

Michael was just about to give an answer no more helpful than an expansive shrug. He was thinking maybe counseling, but he didn't want to be one of those people who tried to solve someone else's pain instead of just listening.

"Never mind," Tim said. "That's really not what we're here to do, is it? This is to talk about a problem, not try to box my way out of it. Besides, let's face it. If there was a way out I probably would have found it a long time ago. It's not like I lack motivation."

Tim sighed deeply. He looked down at the carpet for a moment, then back into the camera.

"When I was younger, I had cystic acne," he said. Quietly, as if sharing a secret. "And I mean I had it bad. All over my face. It was a mess. I'm not sure anybody even noticed how skinny I was back then. I'm not sure they ever looked past my face. And, boy oh boy, I got ragged on for that. And I mean *bad*. Every day at school. It got so miserable that I started getting sick and having to stay home, but it wasn't any special kind of sickness. It wasn't like a cold or the flu. It was more like thinking about going to school made me throw up. They treated me like an animal. Then when I got older it cleared up, but I still had the pockmarks. And then this was around the time the boys around me got into bodybuilding and football and stuff. It was just one bad thing after another. I'd stand in front of the mirror and wish for muscles and clear skin, and I'd try to picture that, and then I'd realize that even if both of those wishes came true I'd still be ugly."

"That's a terrible word," Michael said without thinking.

It was a breach of his promise to himself to stay out of the other person's assessment of their reality. But it just burst out.

"I know what kind of word it is. I heard it every day of my life when I was in school."

"I just think you shouldn't pile on and use it about yourself."

For a time, Tim said nothing. Just squirmed slightly on his stool.

"Here's the thing about that, though," he said. "I had a friend when I was in school. He was the other unpopular kid. The girls would come up to him and pretend to be interested. Pretend to like him. And he thought they really did, which is just so cruel I can hardly even find the words for it. Then they'd go off where he couldn't see and laugh and laugh and laugh. And then I guess I made a decision about the world. You know how we do that when we're young. We sort of make a deal with life to give up something important so we'll be okay. I decided that his situation was even worse than mine because he didn't know he was a joke. I decided the saddest thing in the world—even sadder than being a joke—was to be a joke and not know it. After that I was always careful to be clear about agreeing with the kids who were making my life miserable. I wanted them to know that I knew."

Michael felt something catching in his throat, but he spoke anyway.

"Maybe you don't have to do that now that you're a grown man and not in school."

"Those old original deals are hard to break," he said. "And it's not like I've gotten any prettier since then." He glanced at Michael's chest again. "I think it's brave of you to do this. I think if I were you and I could keep it a secret—the part of my looks I don't like—I'd probably just do it. You know. Keep it to myself."

"You get tired of that after a while," Michael said.

"Yeah. I guess you would. Well, you showed *me*, so . . ." He rose to his feet. "Do I go back behind this screen to get undressed?"

"I figured that would be most comfortable for people."

"I'm leaving my undies on."

"That's fine," Michael said. "This is not a film about anybody's privates."

Tim walked behind the dressing screen with a strange slowness. As though his joints pained him. Or as though something did.

He didn't speak as he undressed. He didn't make a sound back there.

When he stepped out he was wearing white briefs and nothing more. He held both hands in front of his underwear, maybe self-conscious about outlines. He stopped in front of the stool and looked into the camera.

Michael felt almost as though he were looking at the long bones of Tim's arms and legs, because, other than skin, there was not much obscuring them. His chest was narrow, his flesh milky white. Like Michael, he obviously didn't strip down to a bathing suit and spend time in the sun.

"What's this film called?" he asked, seemingly at a loss for what to say.

"It's called *Here I Am.*"

"*Here I Am,*" Tim repeated. "I like that." He stood in silence for a time, and his awkwardness was so obvious that Michael found it contagious. "So, tell me, Michael. What are we doing here? Are we doing any good?"

"With this film, you mean?"

"Right. That. Is it going to change anything?"

"I really don't know, Tim. I don't even know who all will see it. Those who do, maybe it'll make them think a little more. Or maybe they'll just forget what they saw and go to the mall. I don't know. But at least it's *a try* at making a difference. Everybody wants the world to be different, but most people don't do much of anything to try to change it. I mean, it's one thing to try and get nowhere. I can live with that. But I can't be very happy with myself if I don't even try."

The look on Tim's face changed as he spoke. Softened. For the first time since he'd arrived that morning he didn't look bitter, angry, or defensive.

"Yeah," he said. "That's good. I like that. But, you know, it feels weird just standing here like this. All . . . uncovered."

"I hear you."

"Are you going to do this on camera too?"

"Oh, absolutely."

"Good. That's good. Can I put on my clothes now?"

"Of course. We can be done if you want. It was a good interview. Thank you."

"I'm glad we did it," Tim said. "I don't usually talk about this whole situation much. Maybe I should. It felt good to talk about it out loud for a change. It felt like a good thing to do."

Then he bolted for the safety of his clothes.

———

"You should ask your mother to show you her belly," the woman said.

He knew her name was Tanya, though she hadn't formally stated it for the camera. She was fortysomething, with red hair that could not have occurred naturally. She hadn't so much as glanced at the dressing screen. Before she said an official word on camera she simply slipped off her light coat and let it fall onto the rug. Underneath she was wearing only a fairly modest two-piece bathing suit. She seemed to have no intention of sitting.

"Wait, I should do *what?*" Michael asked.

He had heard her. But he hadn't quite managed to absorb the suggestion.

"Ask her to show you her belly. The reason I say it is because everybody loves their mother. If they saw *this* in a movie or a magazine ad or a TV commercial . . ."

She indicated her belly with both hands.

It was as she had described it on the phone, her belly. Stretch marks, excess skin, and puckering. Normal for a woman with five children, three of whom were triplets, but nothing a person would likely see on TV.

"They'd say 'Ick. That's not the way a woman's supposed to look.' Well, maybe *you* wouldn't. You seem willing to look underneath all this garbage. But most people would. But nobody criticizes their mother for a thing like that. Her stretched-out belly is the reason you're here. Right? Everybody's mother gave birth. Nobody wants anybody looking down on her for the results of it."

She paused, and looked right into Michael's eyes. As if waiting for a reaction from him. Some kind of answer.

"My mother never gave birth," he said.

She laughed. But when he didn't, her face changed. Her expression grew more questioning.

"Is that a joke?"

"I'm adopted."

Her face changed again. This time it collapsed into embarrassment and shame.

"Oh, no. Oh, I'm sorry. I'm so stupid. Why didn't I think of that?"

"You're not stupid," he said.

"But here we are, trying to be the sensitive ones. You know. With more respect for other people's different experiences. And here I forget to consider that not everybody's mother gave birth to them."

"It's really not a big deal."

"Feels like one to me," she said. "Are you already filming this?"

"Yeah. I have been all along."

"Oh. Well. That's okay, I guess. I was stupid in front of everybody who sees this. But maybe they'll learn from my mistake. Don't assume. You're not in contact with your birth mother?"

Which struck Michael as potentially stepping out of one mistake and into another.

"No. I haven't seen her since I was seven."

"Oh. Wow. Then she didn't give you up at birth. There must be a story behind that."

"Maybe we can—" he began.

But he didn't need to finish the whole sentence before she got the idea.

"Right. Sorry. I'll confine my discussion to myself from here on out. I'm okay with this," she said, indicating her belly again. "I accept it. I love my children and it's a small price to pay. What I can't accept is the standard that's shoved in my face. The rail-thin, flat, absolutely zero-fat belly. Real women don't look like that. Maybe when they're fourteen. But by the time you get to my age—even without the addition of childbirth—you either spend most of your life energy trying to have it, or you have cosmetic procedures trying to have it, or you don't have it, but you live under this cloud that says you're supposed to. That says what you are is not attractive. Not right. It bothers me a lot, and I don't know how to change it. So I'm doing this. Your little film. But I don't know if it'll change anything."

"I don't know either," Michael said.

She turned her head and glanced over her shoulder, as if to look out the window. But the curtains were closed. She turned back and drilled her gaze into Michael's eyes again.

"Why do they do it to us?" she asked him. "Do they *want* us to feel like crap about ourselves? And what do they gain by that? What kind of motive is it?"

"Probably money," he said. "The ads make us feel bad about something and then offer a product to change it. They're selling something."

"And movies and TV? What are they selling?"

"The movie or the show, I guess. People like idealized life better than real life. But it's not like I'm any expert on this."

"You make a lot of sense, though," she said.

And with that sentence, she seemed to deflate. For the first time since arriving, she sat down on the stool with a deep sigh.

"What about you?" she said, breaking her earlier promise. "What's your connection to all this?"

Michael sighed.

"I'm getting so tired of taking my shirt off in front of people," he said. "Maybe you could just trust that I do have a connection? It'll all come clear in the finished film."

"Ah," she said. "It's a secret."

"Well, it won't be for long," Michael said.

Chapter Twelve

What If We Won't Always Have Paris?

"Who's next?" Madeleine asked him when Tanya had gone.

She was lying on the bed in the main bedroom, looking tired.

"Interview-wise, you mean? That's everybody. Except you and me."

"I don't want to do mine now," she said. "My head hurts."

"I'll go home and leave you alone."

"No," she said. "Don't. Stay with me."

She had never said anything like that to him before, and he found it quite surprising. All the way down to his gut he felt the surprise of it.

He opened his mouth to answer, but she was still talking.

"Spend the night. You never do. I'll make us a nice dinner. I'll feel fresher in the morning and I can do my interview then. It's Sunday tomorrow. We can sleep in and then have brunch."

"But you don't want to cook dinner with a headache."

"Okay, then you'll go out and get us a nice takeout dinner. Is that too weird? Not the dinner part, but the having to tell your parents you're spending the night?"

"Potentially," he said. "But watch me do it anyway."

He dug his phone out of his jacket pocket, where it hung on a chair. He carried it downstairs, hovered by the front door, and called his father's cell phone.

His father picked up on the second ring.

"Michael," he said. "Everything okay?"

"Sure, why wouldn't it be okay?"

"You usually don't call. You usually just come home."

"Yeah. About that . . ." He ran his fingers along the wood molding of the glass inset on the door, but he wasn't sure why. Something related to nerves. "I need to ask you a big favor."

"Try me," his father said.

"I need you to tell Mom I'm not coming home tonight, and then stand there and take all the flak that comes back from her, because I won't be there to take it. I'll be here."

He waited, but probably not very long. Probably it just seemed long.

"I think I can manage that," his father said.

"Really?"

Michael found himself surprised. He had not expected this call to be easy.

"I was a young man myself once, you know. I realize it's hard to imagine now."

"I owe you one."

"You do. No, you know what? I take that back. You don't. Have a good time, be safe, and we're even."

And with that, his father ended the call.

He carried the phone back upstairs and slipped it into his jacket pocket again.

Madeleine was still lying on the bed, now with her eyes closed.

He sat gently on the edge of the bed with her.

"You okay?"

"Yeah. Pretty much. I took a painkiller. It'll kick in anytime now."

He didn't know if she meant an over-the-counter painkiller or something stronger. And he didn't ask.

———

She woke him in the morning with breakfast in bed. Waffles with fresh strawberries and whipped cream. Two of them together on one plate.

"You must be feeling better," he said as he sat up and tried to prop pillows behind his back.

"A little. If I was feeling all better I'd have made waffles from scratch. These are only toaster waffles."

"In my whole life I don't think I ever had a homemade waffle except maybe in a restaurant. Which I guess is technically not a home."

"We'll have to fix that," she said. "One of these days."

She sat on the edge of the bed and cut a bite-size piece with the edge of the only fork she'd brought. Apparently it was a sharing sort of thing.

She was wearing his shirt, which was long on her, like a short dress. She looked good in it, and it showed off her amazing legs. But it meant he had nothing to wear on the top half of himself, and had to eat breakfast more or less exposed.

She fed him the bite of waffle.

"Still good," he said. "Toaster or not."

"I'm ready to do my interview when you are," she said. "As soon as we eat I'm ready to get this over with. Oh, I don't mean that the way it sounds. It's not a bad thing. Well, I sort of mean it the way it sounds, because I think I'm nervous about it now that I know you so well. But, anyway, we'll eat. And then we'll get it done."

———

She sat on the stool in front of the camera, with the wall of curtain as a backdrop.

He nodded to her when he had the camera running.

Rather than relying on words to begin the interview, she unbuttoned his shirt and slid it off her shoulders, allowing it to arrange itself in a sort of soft fabric puddle around her hips and lower arms.

"I've never really done this in front of you," she said, her voice small. "Not so open like this."

And it was true, though only in a subtle sense. She'd had a series of gestures like turning slightly away in the light, or moving an arm over herself. It wasn't that she had kept her chest covered, but more that she had kept it from being examined in too direct a way.

"And that's my shirt," he said, "so I never really sat here bare-chested in front of you, except just now at breakfast."

He tried to keep his eyes tuned to her face, but they dipped down, as if powered and directed by a mind of their own. The scars were long, and covered her chest from one side to the other, not quite touching in the middle. They still looked angry and maybe somewhat painful. He wasn't sure. Whether or not they pained her, he could feel a sickening sensation of pain on her behalf. It trickled down through his belly like something liquid and cold, and continued along the insides of his thighs.

He could see the marks where the stitches had been.

"It's not really what you were expecting," she said, "is it?"

"I'm not sure what I was expecting."

"I can tell you what *I* was expecting. It seems naive now, though. My mother asked more questions of the oncologists than I did. I guess I didn't want to know. I pictured my chest looking like a boy's chest, or like a younger girl who hasn't developed yet. But in addition to the obvious scars, the absence of nipples kind of blows that theory out of the water. It doesn't look like no breasts were ever there, which I guess is more what I was picturing. It looks like there were breasts there and a surgeon came along and removed them by cutting—which shouldn't surprise me, since that's exactly what happened. And I expected the whole thing to be . . . you know. More . . . even. Like, I looked in the mirror and thought, 'Jeez. You could at least have been neater about the whole thing.' Right?"

She stopped talking for a few seconds, and he had no idea what to say to even begin to fill the void.

Before he could find anything she continued.

"My mother wanted me to have reconstructive surgery. And I mean, she was adamant about that. She pushed and pushed. And: Look, Mom. I know you'll probably see this at some point, and I'm not insulting you. I know you only want what's best for me. But seriously. Sign up for two more surgeries just so I can look more like I used to look, and for how long? A year? Why would I do that, and who would I be doing it for? I'm trying to fit in as much life as I can here . . ."

She paused, giving Michael a second to interject his confusion.

"Wait," he said. "Back up."

"Okay."

"For a year? Reconstructive surgery only lasts a year?"

She laughed slightly, which struck him as a thing out of place. Laughter was the furthest thing from his mind. It usually was. It particularly was in that moment.

"No, silly. The surgery lasts as long as I do. It's me who's only going to last for about a year."

A long silence fell. Long and stunned, as if he'd just been mildly electrocuted. During it, she pulled his shirt back up onto her shoulders and buttoned it, as though retreating into a shell.

His face felt tingly and cold.

"But you knew that," she said, as if nudging him to agree. And the sooner the better.

"I did *not* know that," he said, hearing his own words more than he felt himself speak them.

"I told you. More than once."

"I think I would have remembered if you had."

"You said Rex told you not to slow-walk his interview because he's a hundred and three, and I said, 'Don't slow-walk mine either.'"

"I thought you were just referring to yourself as the impatient sort."

"And when you said you'd do all the interviews in a couple of weeks I said I was pretty sure I could last that long. Or words to that effect.

And we had that talk about flings being over, and I said it was out of our control, and we'd just make the most of whatever time we had . . ."

"Doesn't everybody say stuff like that?"

"And I said my parents were letting me use this house for about a year."

"I figured that's when you thought you'd be ready to work again."

"And that I was trying to get my life story written down into a memoir . . ."

"Right. I guess you did say that," he said, suddenly feeling entirely stupid.

"Look, I know I didn't, like . . . spell it out. I didn't tell you exactly what the doctors gave me as a prognosis. Not exact numbers of the range of months or anything." Her voice seemed to be taking on panic as the speech rolled along. "But I swear I thought you were following me."

He opened his mouth to admit how much he had not been following her, but was hit by a wave of nausea.

"I need to use the bathroom," he said.

He raced for it and closed himself in, locking the door behind him. Then he knelt bare-chested in front of the toilet, feeling exposed and cold.

Nothing happened. The feeling seemed to ease.

In time he heard a light rap on the door.

"Honey? You okay?"

"I think so. Yeah. I thought I was going to throw up, but now I'm pretty sure the feeling passed."

A silence.

"I'm so sorry," she said through the door. "I guess I was being too subtle. Which is not something I normally have to worry about."

"Or I'm just really stupid."

"Stop that. You're not stupid."

"I thought when they do a mastectomy, then . . . you know . . . you don't have to die from cancer anymore."

"That's always the hope," she said. "But not everything turns out the way we hope it will."

"No kidding," he said.

He pulled himself up from his knees and lowered the lid of the toilet. Then he sat on it, wrapping his arms around his bare torso and shivering. It was not cold in the house in any real sense.

"But you knew one way or another this was going to end," she said. "I know you knew that. We talked about it more than once, and pretty directly."

"Yeah," he said. "I knew *this* would end. I didn't know *you* would. I didn't know that after it was over you wouldn't exist anywhere on the planet at all. I thought we'd go our own ways with this sort of bittersweet energy, and years from now I'd run into you at the mall or the library, and we'd get together and have coffee and do one of those 'We'll always have Paris' talks."

"You hate coffee," she said.

For a moment, no one spoke.

Then Michael barked out a short laugh. Probably more a release of stress than anything else.

"Good point," he said. "Yeah."

Then, when a fair amount of time had passed and she had offered nothing more, he said, "Is it that you refused to have any more surgeries?" He went ahead and asked it because he felt he needed to, though he was unclear as to whether it was in fact his business or not.

"Oh hell no. If they thought they could get at this new tumor, I'd let them. If they could turn a surgery into more time for me I'd be the first on board. But I'm afraid it's just not one of those tumors. It's in my brain, and not in one of the better spots. It's just inoperable. Come on out. Let's finish the interview. If I can even think of anything more that needs saying."

He rose, unlocked the door, and stepped out.

She had retaken her position on the stool in front of the camera.

"Were you taping that whole time?" she asked.

"I never turned off the camera. But there was nobody in front of it."

"You think the audio picked up that whole conversation?"

"I'm not sure."

"If it did, will you keep it in?"

"Maybe," he said. "Probably, yeah. I mean, it's the damn truth. Which is kind of what I was hoping this film could be about."

———

"Men are weird about women's breasts," she said when they had gotten themselves together to continue the interview. "Granted, not all men. You haven't been weird about it. And I really appreciate that. I needed that. You have no idea how much that helped me."

"You haven't been weird about my situation, either."

"That's different, though," she said. "You have a chest and a stomach. They definitely look like they've been through a huge trauma, but they exist. I'm not comparing the two. I mean, I am and I'm not. I'm not saying my pain is more valid than yours. I'm almost saying the opposite. I'm saying it's a bigger deal that you're able to be so matter-of-fact and accepting with me, because breasts are a body part that people tend to associate with being a woman, and mine are literally gone. Like, they do not exist anymore."

"Here's the thing, though," he said. "I don't think the point is how bad any of this stuff is, or for what reason. I think the point is that none of it matters. At all. Our own stuff might matter to us, and that's valid, but when you love someone, none of that matters. Like when Rex was talking about his late wife. Thirty-some years later he just wants to sit down at the kitchen table with her and hear what she's been doing since he last saw her. A hundred thousand dollars' worth, he wants that. All that body and appearance stuff is nothing. It never was anything. It was never the part about his loving her that was real."

"Nice," she said. "That's so right. That's so on point. I think you figured out what you have to say with your film."

"Yeah. Maybe so."

"I'm sorry I wasn't clear about—"

"No," he said, cutting her off. "The word 'sorry' will not appear in this film. Or, at least, not unchallenged it won't. It's not about being sorry about how you look or how you feel about how you look, or how you think you mishandled a tough emotional situation. It's about being unapologetic."

"I used to think I was good at that."

"And I used to think I wasn't," he said.

Chapter Thirteen

Part of the Foundation of the House He Built

"Are you sure you want to do this *now?*" she asked him.

She was sitting behind the camera wearing a light bathrobe. She had given him back his shirt to wear on video.

"I've never been surer of anything in my life," he said.

"But you're still upset."

"And you figure tomorrow I won't be?"

"I figure in a few days you can put the thing in perspective."

"I don't want to wait until I find a way to bury all this again, or even kind of halfway distance myself from it. I want everything that just hit me to end up on film. So go ahead and turn on the camera. I'm doing this thing."

He saw a little red light come on beside the lens. He hadn't even known there was a little red light on the camera. Everything was so different from this side.

He opened his mouth, but his breath seemed to leave his body. It just flew off and abandoned him.

He took several seconds to compose himself. Maybe he would edit those seconds out later. Maybe not.

"I'm Michael," he said when he could. "I've been behind the camera all this time, and you've just been hearing my voice. But now . . . here I am.

"Wow. I'm a lot more nervous than I thought I was going to be.

"My story. Yeah. It was easier when it was everybody else's story. But anyway, this is mine."

He worked for a moment to catch his breath. He hoped it wouldn't show.

"When I was seven I had a serious accident with professional-grade fireworks. Serious enough that my chances of making it through that first night were pretty slim. I don't really remember the accident, though. I can only tell you what other people have told me about it. All I remember was a yellow plastic lighter my brother was holding, and I remember a firefighter looking down on us from a bluff. But I don't even know why I'm so sure he was a firefighter. It was half dark, and I don't know that I could make a positive identification of a uniform in that light. Especially at that age. But I'm just positive that's what he was, and I don't know why.

"Most people who have a run-in with fireworks take the damage to their faces and hands. In fact, when I was in the hospital there was this older boy in the next bed who was having surgery on his hands because of fireworks, and I think he'd lost some fingers. But for some reason I took it in the stomach and chest. Somehow I was on top of that damn thing when it went off, and nobody can tell me why. Maybe I leaned over it at exactly the wrong time? Tripped and fell on it? I can't imagine I would have put my body on top of a thing like that on purpose.

"Not only do I not remember the accident, but I've lost quite a bit of time leading up to it. At least a year. The doctors said it might come back, but it never did."

He glanced at the red light again, and again felt that strange sensation of his breath leaving him, or somehow moving beyond his reach. Madeleine's face was just above and behind it, but he didn't dare look. He wasn't sure he could hold it together if he looked.

"I was in the hospital for about six weeks, and when I was discharged, I didn't get to go home. I was sent to a foster home with the very good people I now call my parents. The reason I didn't get to go home is that my birth parents were charged with child endangerment, because it turns out they were leaving us unattended to go back and forth to the car to take bumps of cocaine. Also they had a lot of pot in their systems, and their blood-alcohol level was about two and a half times the legal limit. Well, my mother's was. My father's was just under two times.

"And then after about a year my brother got to go home, but my foster parents wanted to adopt me, and my birth parents let them. And I've got to be honest here. That hurt more than the accident, and the accident hurt more than I can even describe. They took my brother back, but they let me go. It actually never consciously occurred to me until Madeleine said something about it, but I think I must have figured they didn't want me because I was so physically damaged. So scarred. Of course I'm older now, and I very much doubt that's what happened. I honestly don't know what happened. I can't even imagine the reasons that would cause a parent to give away an eight-year-old child. But of course when you're that age you just sort of . . . internalize things. Whatever you perceive about the world, right or wrong, it just gets in there and becomes your reality, and it's hard to get it out again, because it's like part of the foundation of the house you're building as you grow up."

He stopped. Swallowed hard. Pushed himself harder.

"Looking back on all of it, I suppose it explains why I kept the scarring a secret. I guess I thought if people knew, they'd reject me. But objectively that's obviously not true. Or at least, as Madeleine says, not for anybody who's not incredibly shallow. But you get used to holding a thing like that close to your chest—and no, I didn't just do that on purpose. I'm in no mood for making puns.

"As to what changed all of a sudden . . . I met my film-workshop professor, Mr. Dunning. Who you know too now. You kind of met him, in a sense. He was my first exposure to someone who just took a whole different attitude about a thing like that. On the first day of class he said, 'It's not a secret, it's not a scandal, it's not a moral failing. It just *is*.' And I guess until that moment I didn't realize how tired I was of keeping secrets, and how I never deserved to have to live that way. Especially when you have to sacrifice so many things when you always keep all your clothes on all the time. I never went swimming. I never showered with the boys after gym class. I was a virgin."

He glanced nervously at Madeleine, sitting behind the camera.

"I guess I never said that straight out."

"I had a pretty good idea," she said.

"Oh no. Does that mean . . . ?"

"No. No. It was always good. You were just . . . you know. Vulnerable and scared. It was kind of sweet. Probably not a fun feeling for you, though."

"Well, I don't want to do the hiding thing anymore. So I'm not going to. That's it. I'm done."

He rose and took a step toward the dressing screen.

"Wait," Madeleine said. "Is it okay if I ask something?"

He stopped. Turned toward the camera again.

"Yeah. Of course."

"You're such a handsome guy. Weren't girls just throwing themselves at you all the time? Every day?"

Michael stood awkwardly and asked his brain to go deeper. He tried to turn inside himself to find an answer to her question. But there was no answer in there. He honestly didn't know.

"I'm so lost trying to answer that," he said. "I mean . . . girls came up and talked to me. I think . . . I think if you *want* a girl to be attracted to you, you develop some kind of radar for whether she's flirting or not. I never developed that. I wanted them to stay away, so I had no idea what they were thinking. I just held everybody at arm's length, and I was so shut down. I honestly don't know how to answer the question any better than that."

He stood awkwardly for another moment. In case she said more. Then he walked behind the screen.

His heart hammered at an alarming rate, and his face felt bloodless and cold. Now and then a soft border of white appeared at the edges of his vision as he undressed, as if he might be about to pass out.

He hung his shirt and jeans over the pegs on the back of the screen. He dropped his underwear onto the floor.

Covering himself with his cupped hands, he stepped back out into the camera's view, and turned to face its very live and active lens.

He stopped, stared into it, and realized he was perilously close to tears and that he was holding them back with the sheer force of his will. It felt like more pressure than this fragile moment could support.

"Here I am," he said. "Get used to it. I sort of didn't entirely mean that last sentence. Well, I meant it, but I wasn't very comfortable saying it. But I put it out there so I can grow into it."

He fell silent, and watched the red light on the camera. It felt like some kind of x-ray, looking too deeply into him. Showing more than he had ever meant to show.

And still the tears threatened.

"The scars on my thighs are the places where they harvested skin to graft onto my stomach and chest. But that's not the heart of what I'm standing here wanting to say. I feel like I'm about to cry and maybe in a minute there won't be much I can do about that. And I think it might come off wrong, like sadness or even weakness. The truth is, I tend to get tears in my eyes when I'm angry, which is just so inconvenient I can hardly stand it. Just as I'm trying to project strength, that happens. I *am* sad. I won't say I'm not. I'm sad about what I just found out about Madeleine's cancer. But I'm also furious. At cancer. And I'm mad that I spent all those years not able to do what I'm doing right this minute. And also I think there are some tears of relief because I'm just so, so relieved that I'm finally doing it now."

And with that, they let go. He could feel the wetness of them on his cheeks.

He almost raised a hand to brush them away, then realized his hands needed to stay exactly where they were. And in a minute his nose was going to run.

He tried to wipe a tear on his shoulder, but it didn't work. Eyes don't reach shoulders when your arms are down.

He struggled with that ridiculous helplessness for what felt like a long moment, but probably wasn't. Then he moved carefully sideways toward the screen.

"Madeleine, turn off the camera," he said. He reached the safety of the area behind the screen and sighed. And cried. "Just turn it off, okay?"

He dressed quickly and stepped out.

She was still sitting behind the camera, looking lost in thought. The red light was off.

"You can't edit that part out," she said.

"Why can't I?"

"Because it's too good. It's the perfect ending to your film. I turn off the camera. The screen goes black. Roll credits over the black screen. That's it."

"Hmm," he said. "I kind of see what you mean. It was a pretty vulnerable moment, though."

"Isn't that the whole point?"

———

"I finished the filming," Michael said. "I have all the interviews on tape."

He was having espresso and orange juice in the student union with Mr. Dunning.

"Including your own?"

"Yeah, everything. And maybe I shouldn't say this myself, but I think it's good."

"Or maybe it's just good, and you see that, and you shouldn't have to feel bad about thinking so or saying so."

"Right. Got it." He stared out the window. Sipped at his juice. "I just don't exactly know how to tackle editing it all together."

"You're in luck," Dunning said, "because that's next up in class."

"Good. I need that. Even though . . . I mean, I need to know how to stitch it all together smoothly into one cohesive whole, but I'm actually not planning to edit much out. Some things happened that I definitely didn't expect, but I don't think I'll take them out."

"What kinds of things happened?"

"Like . . . I found out Madeleine still has cancer. And the prognosis is not good."

"Oh, no. I'm so sorry, Michael. For both of you. You literally learned that while the camera was rolling?"

"Yeah. Literally."

"Wow. Did you ask her how she feels about leaving that in?"

"She's all for it. She wants everything in."

"Then leave it in."

"Here's another thing, though," Michael said. He glanced out the window again, despite there being nothing much to see out there. "This is why I asked if you had time to talk. I wanted your opinion on this. Your advice. Remember that conversation we had about Madeleine right before your interview? When I told you I was worried I was falling in love with her and I wasn't supposed to? I thought I'd turned off the camera for that. But I hadn't. I was still getting used to the camera, and I made some kind of mistake. And it turns out I have that whole thing on video. And I'm not sure if I should edit it out or not."

"Why would you edit it out? Because you're admitting that you care for her?"

"I guess. I don't know. It just seems like a personal moment."

"It's entirely up to you."

"I guess the film is supposed to be personal," Michael said. "I mean . . . isn't it?"

"Also up to you."

"But I want your advice."

"My advice is to be true to yourself. Make it the film you honestly think it should be, and try to make sure it says what you set out to say."

"Right," Michael said. "Then I guess I'll need to leave it in."

———

"I want you to look at this," Michael said.

He was at Madeleine's house, in her office, because she had a much better computer for video editing. Michael's poor little laptop didn't have much RAM and wasn't up to the task.

"Okay."

She came up behind where he sat at the computer. He felt her hands rest on his shoulders. It was a warm and comfortable feeling, but he couldn't shake the idea that it would disappear. That she would disappear.

"What am I looking at?" she asked.

"It's a part of my interview with Robert Dunning. It was sort of . . . before the interview. Before I thought we were officially starting. Like an aside. I never exactly meant to tape it, but I wasn't familiar enough with the camera to turn it off right, especially when I was only half paying attention. I figured I'd just cut it later. But now I'm not sure. I want you to watch it and tell me if you think it should stay in or not."

"Were you two talking about me?"

"Kind of. Yeah."

"Then he did say something bad about me."

"No. Not at all. It's nothing like what you're thinking. Just watch."

Michael pressed "play" on the clip.

He was not on camera, of course. Only Dunning was. And that eased some, but not all, of Michael's discomfort.

She watched and listened from behind him as they discussed the age difference, the strength of her personality. The fact that she was the one who had deemed their involvement a fling.

As she watched, she set her chin down on the top of his head.

They listened together as Michael discussed his fear that he was falling in love with her when that was somehow against some invisible rule. His face tingled and felt hot as he heard himself saying it.

When the interview had moved on, he reached out and stopped the play.

"I didn't come off badly in that," she said.

"I never said you did."

"Why would you cut it? Because you admitted that you care about me?"

"After you said it was just a fling."

"It *has* to be a fling," she said. "I'm not in *anything* for the long haul."

"So . . . use it?"

"Of course use it."

She turned and moved away. To leave the room, Michael thought, though he didn't turn his head to see.

A couple of seconds later she came back, leaned over, and kissed the top of his head.

"I love you, too," she said.

Then she was gone.

MICHAEL,
AGE NINETEEN
AND A HALF

Chapter Fourteen

When You Can Do That, You Will Have Arrived

Michael sat in the dark, in Mr. Dunning's film workshop, watching himself on video. Watching his video image try to wipe his eyes without moving his hands away from their position guarding his private areas. Watching himself retreat behind the dressing screen. The portion of the room in the frame—the stool in front of the wall of curtains—was empty and blank, but he could hear his voice asking Madeleine to turn off the camera.

The screen went black.

The first credit was a dedication to the memory of Rex Aronfeld, who had died three months short of his 104th birthday, before the film project was due.

For a moment it filled Michael with a nearly overwhelming sadness. The kind that threatens to drown a person. Then he pictured Rex sitting at a kitchen table with Lainie Aronfeld, finally hearing what she'd been doing since he last saw her, and that seemed to pull him away from the edge of oblivion. Somewhat.

The other credits were simple. First and sometimes last names of participants, then every possible filmmaking role needed for a simple documentary short like this one. They rolled by one at a time, all followed by the name "Michael Woodbine."

When the last credit had faded away, leaving the screen empty, Mr. Dunning flipped on the lights.

Michael blinked and winced at their brightness.

He waited for some reaction from the class, but heard only a stunned and stunning silence. There was not even so much as a rustle of movement.

He felt much the way he had felt behind the dressing screen as he'd begun to strip away his clothes. His heart pounded. His face felt cold, as if every drop of blood had drained out of it. The world appeared threateningly white at the edges of his vision.

Still no one moved or spoke.

"I showed you this film," Dunning said loudly, making Michael jump, "for what should be an obvious reason. We can screen some of the others in future classes if you'd like, but I needed you to see this one now because—as I'm sure you all couldn't fail to notice—I participated in this one. I did not participate in any of the others. Hopefully you understand why, but if not, here's your chance to say so. Then again, no one *asked* me to participate in any of the others.

"I gave this film a very strong grade. An A-plus, which is the highest grade I give, and it was the only A-plus I gave out this semester. I gave Mr. Woodbine's work an A-plus not because I participated in the film but because I honestly felt it deserved it. If any of you don't, or if you question that grading decision in any way, I invite you to speak up now."

He moved to the center of the classroom floor, directly in front of his desk, and looked up and around, scanning the faces for a long time. Long enough to make Michael feel truly desperate. Still no one spoke or glanced around. No one scratched an itch, or checked their phone, or looked for something in their backpack.

"I guess we're agreed, then," Dunning said. "Let's take it a little further. What do you think about the film you just watched?"

A long, long silence reigned. The room spun slightly around Michael's field of vision. It was a dangerous feeling. As though it might suddenly career out of control.

"Good," a young man in the back said.

"I was hoping for a bit more detail," Dunning said, "but okay. What was good about it? Anybody?"

"It had something to say," another young man's voice said.

"It did. Of course. It had quite a lot to say. And therein lies the A-plus. The technical aspects of the film, if I were grading only on that, were about a B-plus. Better than average, definitely good enough, but not exceptional. But it had something to say, and did an exceptional job saying it. And, as I told you on the first day of class all those months ago, that is the ultimate goal. Nothing is more important."

Michael felt a whispered gasp of breath come into his body. Surely he had been breathing before, but obviously not much. They liked the film. Still, he couldn't shake the idea that every student sitting in the room with him had watched him physically and emotionally bare himself. He had let them in, and now there would be no way to force them out again.

"Can we go a little deeper?" Dunning asked the class.

A young woman in the second row raised her hand.

"Just jump in," Dunning said. "You don't need my permission to speak."

"It made me feel," she said.

"Okay, good. But *what* did it make you feel?"

"It made me feel different about . . . people. Oh, but . . . I actually didn't even mean that the way it sounded. I guess that sounded like I meant it made me feel different about *other* people, like people who seem different from me. But that's not what I meant at all. I'm not sure how to say it. It made me feel different about *me*. About how I feel about being a person. Does that make sense?"

"It does," Dunning said. "Different in a good way or a bad way?"

"Both," she said. "Like on the one hand it's okay to be a person, but on the other hand it's scary and hard."

"Both true," Dunning said. "And thank you. Now we're getting down closer to the bone of the thing. You can have something to say about an infinite number of topics, but if you want to move anybody, or change anybody, you'd better have something to say about the human condition. About—as Ms. Deluca just described—how it feels to be a person. You won't be able to say anything entirely new about the human condition because, as the man says, there's nothing new under the sun. But you can shine a light on humanity in a way that makes the viewer see it differently. That makes them *feel* it differently. If you can make your viewer feel more human, while at the same time making them feel that being human is not the bad news, you will have arrived. And you will have made a good film."

He waited, but still no one stirred.

"Any last thoughts?"

"I feel like it should be in . . . I don't know. Film festivals or something," a different girl said. "Or like when I'm streaming stuff online on Netflix or Hulu or something, this should be one of my choices. Because there's a ton of stuff out there that's not nearly this good."

"I think submitting it to film festivals is a fine idea," Dunning said. "And Mr. Woodbine and I will discuss that more after class. Anyone else?"

A thin, shy-sounding female voice rose up from the last row of the classroom.

"Is Madeleine . . . you know . . . still . . ." Long pause, which felt unnerving even though Michael knew what was coming. Everyone did. "Okay?"

Michael realized he was being asked a direct question. It made his throat feel like it was tightening. Squeezing closed.

He looked over his shoulder, but couldn't see who had spoken. But he did see faces looking back at him. Lots of faces. And the expressions on those faces were not what he had expected. No one looked like they pitied him. They looked almost envious, as though looking up to him in some undefinable way.

"I'm not sure if 'okay' is the right word for it," he said in the general direction of the back of the classroom. "She's having a hard time. But if you mean is she still alive, yes. She is. She's still here. Thank you for asking."

It wasn't until he spoke that last sentence that he realized the true weight of her question, and its reflection on his own situation. She had asked because she cared enough to ask. And she cared because he had made her care.

And he had made her care with his film.

———

"Walk with me," Dunning said, and they left the empty classroom together.

He handed Michael several sheets of paper as they stepped out into the light of the sunny afternoon.

"Here's a list of film festivals that accept documentary shorts. Thirteen are in California, but that number goes down a bit if you subtract the ones that are special category."

"Special category?" Michael asked blankly, blinking into the bright daylight.

He felt mildly surprised that the world was still there, intact and waiting for him, unchanged, after being so lost in a dark screening.

"Asian American or Jewish films. That sort of thing. There's a big one in LA that's just for shorts. Then you can also venture outside California if you like. They're all over the country. Thing is, if they accept your film you'll want to attend the screening, and that amounts to a lot of traveling."

They began walking side by side through the quad. Michael was looking down at the sheets, flipping pages, overwhelmed by the sheer number of listings. And yet, in another way, he was not taking in anything he saw on the papers.

"Sticking to California makes sense in another way," Dunning said. "If you can get your film accepted in one or more of them here in the state, then it becomes fodder for the big-city California newspapers. 'Local College Boy Makes Good.' That sort of thing. And that can bring more attention to the film, which can only do you good."

"Wait," Michael said, and stopped walking.

Dunning stopped too, and examined Michael's face quizzically in the silence. But Michael couldn't seem to pull his thoughts together.

"Okay. I'm waiting."

"I don't know how to submit to film festivals."

"Keep flipping pages," Dunning said. "That's in there too."

"But how do I pick which one?"

"You don't submit it to one. You submit it to as many as you can. Some are free, but most have a fee. Not huge, but it'll start to add up. But you need the sheer numbers, because it's very competitive. The smallest of these festivals might have a ten-in-a-hundred acceptance rate. The bigger ones are more like one in a hundred. You need to buy a lot of tickets to win that lottery."

Dunning began to move off, but Michael stopped him.

"Wait," he said again.

Another silence fell. Dunning seemed surprisingly patient, under the circumstances.

"Yes?" he asked after a time.

"You didn't tell us we'd be submitting to film festivals."

"We?"

"Yeah. The class. We. At the beginning of the semester, you didn't tell us. I thought I was just making this for a grade. And for practice. You didn't say we'd be submitting to film festivals."

"Michael," Dunning said. And then, for a few beats, he said nothing more.

Michael got the impression that he was missing something very basic, and that Dunning was waiting for him to fill it in on his own.

"What?"

"Do you have any idea how long I've been teaching this class at this college? I've had this list from the beginning. I update it every year. And this is the first time I have ever suggested to any student that their work was submission quality."

"It's that good?" Michael asked, his head swimming slightly. Again.

"It has that much to say. Now, go home and get this rather daunting process started. You have a lot of work to do."

———

When he got to Madeleine's house, he found her in bed in the main bedroom, the curtains drawn against the afternoon light. The more time went on, the more she had become unable to tolerate light.

"Hey," he said, and sat down on the edge of the bed.

"Hey yourself, sweetie."

"How're you feeling?"

"Eh."

He kissed her on the temple, and she smiled.

He settled beside her, on top of the covers. She set her head on his shoulder and he stroked her hair, which had grown longer. It was more like an average short haircut and less like a radical one. It felt fine and silky under his fingers.

"How did the screening go?" she asked him.

Her voice sounded small, and a little weak. As if it were gradually leaving. Growing an inch or two farther away every day.

"It was weird. But good."

"Weird how and good how?"

"Good because people liked it. I mean, liked it so much that they had a hard time even finding words for what they felt when they saw it. Weird because it felt like I let everybody in the world into this very private place. Well. Not everybody in the world. There are just maybe three dozen people in the class. But still. It's like, once you open the door, it's open. Anybody can come in. So you've pretty much invited the whole world. And that definitely feels weird. And then I found out that my professor wants me to submit it to a bunch of film festivals. And he's never suggested that to any of his other students."

"That's good," she said.

"Is it?"

"Isn't it?"

"I'm having trouble deciding."

They lay together in silence for a long time. Maybe five minutes. Maybe she was literally giving him time to decide. But his thoughts on the subject were as muddled as they had ever been. They felt almost out of his reach. As though he couldn't sort or analyze them because he couldn't corral them.

"I understand it's a little scary," she said when it was clear he didn't plan to restart the conversation.

"I'll say."

"But it's your very first film. Your freshman-year-of-college film. *So what* if it doesn't get accepted? You'll have so many others."

"That's what you think I'm afraid of? That it won't get accepted?"

A pause.

Then she said, "Oh. Okay. I get it. You're afraid it *will*. But you made it to be seen. That's what it's for, right? To be seen."

"It was just so weird," he said. "Sitting there in the dark. Watching people watch it. It was just such a helpless feeling. Like the door to my house was propped open and just anybody could come into my private space. But I guess I keep saying that, don't I? I was practically having a panic attack. A mild one anyway. My heart was going a mile a minute. I thought I was going to pass out."

"Good," she said.

She was clearly not kidding. Neither was she being mean. He wasn't sure what she was doing or being.

"How is that good?"

"It's good because it's being alive. And I don't mean being alive as in not dead. Really alive. Most of the world is sitting on the couch watching TV and trying to get to bed every night without anything challenging happening. You're taking risks and you're out on the edge of the cliff, and you're freaking alive, and you're scared because everything is real and you can feel it all. Take it from someone who doesn't get to have enough of the alive thing. Run with that feeling. Have a real life and take the risks. Live like living *means* something. Like you're lucky to have the chance."

They lay together for a long time. Michael was vaguely aware of daylight fading on the other side of the drawn drapes.

"Okay," he said after a time. "I think I need to borrow your computer again."

Chapter Fifteen

It's All about Exposure, in Just So Many Ways

Michael sat alone at a small two-person table in the student union, staring out the window without directly focusing on anything.

He was unclear whether or not Mr. Dunning would join him. Leaving the classroom a few minutes earlier, Michael had mentioned that he would come here for a juice. Dunning had said something noncommittal. "Right," or "Okay."

Michael just figured he would wait and see.

He slipped his phone out of his pocket and texted Madeleine.

"Hey" was all he typed.

Then he died a little inside waiting to see if she would answer.

It was like this every time. Except it kept getting harder.

The light *boop* of her text coming in on an already open thread made him jump, even though it was quiet. But then relief rose up around him as though he were sinking into it, drowning in an ocean of relief.

"Hey," it said.

In the time between texts, it broke through to him that he was slumping. Allowing his shoulders to curl forward. "Protecting his soft underbelly," a doctor had told his mother, in the process of trying to convince her that his posture problem likely had no physical root.

Michael had improved his posture a lot since then. But now Madeleine was in a fight to the death with her disease, and he was slumping again. So clearly his old injuries were not the only soft underbelly he was trying to protect.

He forced himself to sit up straighter.

Boop. "You there?"

"Yeah, sorry," he typed.

Boop. "You at school?"

"Yeah."

Then he had no idea what to type.

A minute passed. At least, he thought it was a minute. Could have been ten seconds or five minutes. It wasn't like there was much he could use to gauge its passing.

Boop. "I know why you do these hey texts."

"Sorry."

Boop. "Don't be."

"I'll come by soon."

Boop. "You'd better."

He closed the thread and looked up to see Dunning standing over the empty chair, holding his small espresso cup on a saucer.

"Am I interrupting?"

"Not at all. I was just checking in on Madeleine."

Dunning sat.

"How's she doing?"

"Eh," Michael said, borrowing her response.

"How's she holding up emotionally?"

"Surprisingly well. I have no idea how she does it."

"And you?"

"What about me?"

"How are *you* holding up?"

"It's not about *me*," Michael said, unable to mask his surprise. "She's the one people need to ask about."

"Right," Dunning said. "That's very true. Which is why I was concerned that nobody was asking about you."

But Michael had no idea how to express his thoughts on the subject. He wasn't even sure where they lived. So he said nothing.

Dunning sipped his espresso in silence for a few moments. He seemed to be both waiting—in case Michael wanted to say more on the subject—and instinctively knowing the answer to that question. Or maybe Michael was reading too much into the pause. But probably not. They seemed to function well together without a lot of talking.

"How's the submission process going?" Dunning asked after a time.

"I've done seven," Michael said, correcting his posture again. "Mostly the ones I could drive to. You know. On the off chance I need to drive to them. LA, Palm Springs, San Francisco. Sebastopol. Seattle. Of course, Santa Barbara is the close one. And I guess I'm forgetting one. I'd have to look at my notes."

"That's a good start," Dunning said.

"It's more than a start. It ran me out of money for submission fees."

"Oh. Well, yes. That can happen."

They sipped in silence for what felt like a long time.

"I have a friend," Dunning said. "Old friend. I've probably known him more than thirty years. He's still working in the industry. Well, actually he's in television now, but he still knows everybody on every side of the business. I was thinking maybe I'd show your film to him. He has connections. Might open some doors that don't require an entry fee to unlock the way the 'over the transom' submissions do."

Michael only froze. Almost literally, from the feel of it. There was a shocking coldness to his reaction. He did not immediately answer.

"But of course I would never do that without your permission," Dunning added.

For a split second, Michael could see and feel himself poised at the edge of that cliff Madeleine had described. Except this time it was not an "I might sprain an ankle" exposure looming below him. This was a fall to a nearly certain death.

But as the split second faded and he felt himself back in the moment, he remembered the next thing she had said.

"Take it from someone who doesn't get to have enough of the alive thing. Take the risks."

She hadn't actually said "Be alive for me. Have the life I can't have. Take the risks on my behalf." But he had inferred it all the same.

Then Michael was filled with an easier, more comforting thought. Sure, it was nice to have a friend in the business. But still, most of those connections led nowhere. Everybody was trying to get ahead in that business.

What were the chances, really?

"Sure," Michael said. "Thank you. That would be great."

———

It was about eight days later, and Michael was running in the park. He was sprinting along the jogging and bike path around the lake. It was a small man-made lake, thick with lily pads and with a fountain of water jetting out of the middle.

The worse things had gotten with Madeleine's health, the longer and faster he had tended to run.

His phone rang in his pocket.

He pulled it out and looked at its screen without slowing. It was a 310 area code, so Southern California. LA. Probably a junk call. He almost slid the phone back into his pocket, but for no special reason—or at least for no reason he could identify—he clicked onto the call.

"Hello?" he managed to gasp out, though he was quite breathless.

"Michael Woodbine?" a male stranger's voice asked. An older man, from the sound of it.

Michael stopped suddenly on the dirt path and was nearly mowed down by a bicycle from behind.

"Yes, this is Michael," he said.

"You okay? You sound like you can't breathe."

"I was running."

"You want me to let you finish up with that and you can call me back?"

But by then Michael was curious as to who this person was and what he wanted.

"No, that's okay," he said, and started to walk at a leisurely pace.

"My name is Jonah Levy. I'm a friend of Bob Dunning. I hope you don't mind. He gave me your number."

"I don't mind. Are you his friend who works in the industry? The one who's going to look at my film?"

"I looked at your film the minute he sent it to me," Jonah said. "In fact, I've been talking it up to a friend of mine who licenses properties at Netflix."

Michael stopped again.

He was right across from the fountain in the middle of the lake. It roared and splashed, and blood roared in his ears. It amounted to a lot of noise.

"Netflix?"

"Right."

"*The* Netflix?"

"The one and only."

"Wait."

"For what exactly?"

"Netflix takes documentary shorts?"

"They absolutely do. You might not see them on their home page all that often, but if you go out and search in their categories, you'll see. Anyway. Here's the thing. I told him about your short, and he's definitely interested. It's a subject they like a lot. I haven't shown it to him yet. I'm wondering if you could get free for a couple or three days and come down to LA. I'd like to work with you on polishing it up."

"I'm . . . not sure," Michael said, thinking immediately about Madeleine. About how much support he was providing for her lately. Maybe there was someone else who could look in on her while he was gone. "I could . . . you know . . . see if I can get away."

"You're worried about leaving Madeleine."

It hit Michael like a physical shock, leaving his ears ringing. He felt as though this man had looked right through him and seen things he was never meant to see.

"How did you know that?"

"I watched the film."

"Oh. Right. Of course."

"Only if you can manage it," Jonah said. "Don't get me wrong. It's already good. It's just kind of plain. Visually plain. I like the way you spliced in pictures from these people's pasts. I'd actually like to see more of that. More of a break from just talking heads. Well. Talking whole bodies, I guess, in this case. I want to show you how to make these smooth, professional-looking transitions. And how to punch up the credits. I think it would elevate it from a very good student film to just a very good film. Period. No need to qualify the phrase. But I'll be honest and say there's a pretty good chance he'd take it as is. But a lot of people will see it, so I'm thinking why not put your best foot forward with it? You know?"

Michael walked again, aimlessly. He was vaguely aware that he couldn't feel his feet touching the ground. He felt slightly dizzy. Maybe from bringing his heart rate down so fast. Maybe not.

"You really think my film could stream on Netflix?"

"I really do. I think it's got a great shot. But just so you know, they'd want it exclusively. And we're not talking about a lot of money. Maybe just a flat few hundred dollars."

"I wasn't even thinking about money. Just . . ."

"Right," Jonah said. "It's all about exposure."

Michael laughed. It came out sounding a little more bitter than he had intended.

"Yeah. As somebody who stood buck naked in front of the camera for this, I definitely agree that it's all about exposure. I haven't even shown it to my mother yet. And people are going to be streaming it on Netflix?"

"I hope you're not getting cold feet. Because if you're serious about looking for a future in this business, I'd hate to see you let a chance like this go by."

"I'm not getting cold feet," Michael said. "Well, that's a lie. I am. But I'm not going to let it stop me. I'll warm them up and keep going. When would you need me down there?"

"When you can. Just call me back when you figure out how soon you can get away."

———

Michael let himself into Madeleine's house with his key. He vaulted up the stairs two at a time and into the main bedroom.

Madeleine was not alone. There was a woman her age, or maybe a few years older, sitting by the side of her bed. Petting the cat with her free hand. She looked a little like Madeleine, except she had a massive volume of wavy brown hair.

"Michael," Madeleine said, her voice thin. "This is my sister, Patricia."

Michael stepped closer to shake the woman's hand, but she didn't extend hers. Just looked him up and down.

"You're Michael?" She sounded surprised. Doubtful, even.

"I . . . am," he said, but it sounded hesitant. As if he weren't sure either.

"I was picturing you differently somehow."

"Older," he said.

She twisted her face as if to dismiss his comment.

"Maybe not so handsome."

"Older and not so handsome. Got it." He turned his attention onto Madeleine. "I just got the most amazing phone call. What would you say if I told you our film might end up streaming on Netflix?"

"Netflix?" both women said at the same time.

"*The* Netflix?" Madeleine asked. "I didn't even know they streamed documentary shorts."

"That's exactly what I said!" Michael shouted. He hadn't meant it to come out so loud, but he was filled with a nervousness and excitement he had not yet vented.

"I'm going to leave you two alone to talk about this big news," Patricia said.

"Wait," Madeleine said. "Before you go. While I have you both in the same room. It's about the cat. I know we said you'd take Lily, Patricia. You know. After I'm gone. But you have those two big dogs. And so. Many. Kids."

Michael was curious how many, but he wasn't sure it was his business to ask.

"And she really, really likes Michael," Madeleine continued. "Anyway, I was thinking . . . not to hurt your feelings, Patricia . . ."

"You think it hurts my feelings not to have to be screaming 'Stop chasing the cat!' at two dogs and five kids from dawn till dark?"

"I'll take Lily," Michael said.

"Are you sure it's okay?"

She didn't say straight out *Are you sure your parents would allow it?* But he knew that was what she meant. And he knew why she didn't say it.

"Positive," he said.

If he had to, he would get his own place. One way or another, he was taking the cat. Still, just talking about it left a figurative bad taste in his mouth. The idea that the cat was about to need a new person made the whole thing feel suddenly, painfully real.

"Then it's settled," Patricia said. "I'm going to go make us some tea."

―――

"You seemed so surprised when you saw my sister here," she said while Patricia was downstairs. "I told you she was coming."

"You did?"

"Pretty sure."

"Really sure?"

"I'm not really sure of anything these days. But I swear I thought I told you. So tell me about this Netflix thing. It's incredible. How did it happen?"

Michael sat down on the bed with her. Slipped his shoes off and propped his feet up on the duvet.

"It was Mr. Dunning. He has a friend who has a friend. It's not definite. But he's seen the film and told his friend at Netflix about it, and he honestly likes my chances. Only problem is, he wants me to go down there for two or three days so we can work on it a little. Punch up the production values."

"That's not a problem," Madeleine said. "Go."

"I worry about leaving you."

"My sister is here."

He slid an arm around her shoulder, and she set her head down on his chest.

"Yeah," he said. "That's amazing. Just when we needed it."

"It's not amazing," she said. "Never talk about things of that nature like they're out of the ordinary. The universe pushes us around. All the time. In a good way, I mean. It knows which way it wants us to go, so when we turn in the right direction it puts a wind at our backs."

Michael sat in silence for a time, letting that idea run around inside him. He'd never stopped to consider what he believed in that respect. He wondered if she saw through the thin veil of life more clearly as she reached the end of it. He felt happy that she believed in something bigger than this.

"I still worry about leaving you," he said. "I'm afraid . . . I just don't want to miss . . . anything."

"We need to start calling things exactly what they are," she said.

He could feel her jaw move against his chest as she spoke. It was comforting somehow.

"We do?"

"I think so. You're afraid I'm going to die while you're away."

"Um . . . yeah. That's pretty direct, but yes."

"Well, I don't think I am. I can't sign a written guarantee for you, but it doesn't feel that close, so go do this important thing. I never got a chance to finish my memoir, and I'm counting on this film to immortalize me. So go get it done."

"When you put it like that," he said, "the way seems pretty clear."

Chapter Sixteen

Borrowed Swim Trunks and a
Special Kind of Freedom

When Michael looked up from his host's computer—which he hadn't done for hours—he was struck again by the sweeping view of the city of Los Angeles through Jonah's huge home-office windows. The Levys' house was high in the hills over the city, nestled in a dense lot of tall trees.

"It makes such a difference," he said to Jonah, nodding toward the monitor.

He didn't say what "it" was exactly. He trusted his host to know.

"It so does," Jonah said. "Sometimes the viewer might not even be able to put their finger on the differences. Especially the transitions. Transitions are a little bit like subliminal advertising. They affect you, but you don't even know it in most cases."

He was a man in his mid-seventies, unusually tall, with a full head of silver hair and a quick smile. His husband, Dennis, had been in to bring cookies and iced tea since lunch.

Michael stared out at the astounding view for a minute or longer without speaking.

"I want to ask a question," he said. "But I'm not sure how to find the door into it."

"Okay."

Another brief pause.

"This stuff we did today . . . is this stuff that Mr. Dunning doesn't know how to do?"

"At this level of filmmaking," Jonah said, "there's nothing Bob doesn't know how to do. And it's not that he didn't want to take the time to help you, if that's your concern. He thinks very highly of you. If you mull it over, I think you'll see why we agreed that I should be the one to work with you on it."

While Michael was waiting for something obvious to pop into his brain, he was vaguely aware of the film paused on the massive monitor in front of him. It was frozen on the closing credits, with his name hanging there, larger than life.

"I guess I'm not a good muller," he said.

"He already *appeared* in your film. That's enough to potentially raise eyebrows among the other students or their parents. But that's a little different. Speaking on camera. Adding content. This is actually sitting down with you at the computer and helping you make your production values look professional. He's not doing that for any of his other students, so how can he do it for you?"

"Right," Michael said. "What a stupid question I just asked. How did I not think of that?"

"It's hard to see the world through anybody's eyes but your own. Let's run this one more time and make absolutely sure we think it's ready to submit."

With a couple of clicks, he started Michael's film playing from the beginning.

It felt strange watching it now. Partly it was strange because it was overly familiar—nearly memorized. Now and then a piece of dialogue would break through and register with him, but usually not the ones he would have expected.

Partly the strangeness came from the fact that it was now so smooth and so professionally made that it didn't seem like it could be his film at all. In that sense, the overly familiar had taken on a nearly unfamiliar feel.

"This is such a beautiful moment," Jonah said.

It was the interview with Madeleine. The moment when she corrected his misunderstanding of her many hints regarding her life expectancy.

"I hope you know what I mean when I say 'beautiful,'" Jonah added. "Of course it's painful and sad, but in a beautiful way. Please tell me it's not scripted."

While he spoke, on-screen Michael was running to the bathroom, thinking he was about to throw up, and Madeleine was following him to the bathroom door. The scene played out in quiet overheard dialogue against a backdrop of empty set.

"Nothing in the film was scripted," Michael said.

"So this is really you finding out while the camera is going."

"Believe me," Michael said. "I'm not that good an actor."

They fell silent through the rest of the film.

When the credits rolled, for at least the seventh time, Jonah said, "I'm happy with it."

"I think it's great," Michael said.

"Then we made short work of that. Finished it in one day."

Michael looked out the window again and was surprised to see that dusk had begun to fall.

"You ready for me to send it to him?" Jonah asked. "And look, before I do . . . I know we've been at this all day and we both think it's perfect. But just to warn you, if they license it, they have a right to make certain edits, and they might."

"Edits?"

"I don't mean they'll cut scenes or censor your interviews, most likely. I mean like logos, new opening and closing credits, even though ours are so beautiful. Maybe other details. It's one of the ironies of this business. You make it perfect so they'll take it, and then they change it to their version of perfection."

"I guess so long as the words and the messages stay the same."

"I wouldn't worry about that. It's what they're buying. It's the part they know they want. I'm going to upload this to a private page of my website, and when it's loaded I'll send him a link. And look. You might want to show this to your mother. Because she won't want to be the last person in the world to see it."

"But even if he takes it, I have some time. Right?"

"Usually. Yeah. I mean, at very least we have to send them a high-quality digital copy and deal with chain-of-title stuff, which should be easy in this case. And we need to provide release documents. You got a release from the man who passed away, right? Please say yes."

"I got a release from everybody. Mr. Dunning covered that in class."

"Good. Then it should be straightforward. Sometimes there are delays, but it can also happen fast. If I were you I'd show it to your mother."

"It's just weird," Michael said. "Thinking of sitting in the dark with her while she watches me standing there with my hands in front of my privates, crying. It's embarrassing."

"If you want I'll send you the same link I send Eric at Netflix and she can see it while you're gone. You're at least staying one night, right? It's such a long drive, and it's almost dark, and never underestimate what eyestrain does to you after a day like this. We have a separate little guesthouse."

"I guess I'll take you up on that. Thanks."

He said it partly because he was hungry and didn't want to leave before dinner, but mostly because there was a feeling in this new world, and he was enjoying being a part of that feeling. Something about the home of an entertainment professional, and the way Michael was being welcomed, treated as a person who fit here. And then there was the city stretched out below the yard.

"Done," Jonah said. "I sent him the link. I sent you the link. I sent Bob the link, just so he can see what a great job we did. Now we just wait."

"For how long?"

"Wouldn't life be nice if questions like that could be answered? Go get your bag out of the car. Dennis is making fajitas for dinner. If you want you can take a swim while we're waiting."

———

Michael stood at the edge of the pool, fully dressed. It was illuminated from below, and sent lightly swaying reflections through the water onto him and his host, who stood at his side. Beyond its surface, the ground dropped away precipitously, leaving the impression that the pool was almost floating above the city without support.

Lights were coming on in the dusky neighborhoods below, and shining in tall office buildings downtown. The lighted streets seemed to stretch on forever.

"I haven't been swimming since I was seven," Michael said.

"That's a big nice thing about what you just did on film," Jonah said. "I've seen your interview. Dennis has seen it. A lot more people are about to see it, and that's a good start toward defusing going shirtless in just about any situation. It's like you've already broken the ice, and you can be a little more comfortable because the others know what they'll see and have already acclimated. And the pool is heated to a glorious temperature if I do say so myself. I can lend you a clean pair of swim trunks."

"You know what? I was just about to say no. But I'm not sure why. Force of habit maybe, because I just realized I can say yes. And it feels like a kind of freedom."

"It *is* a kind of freedom," Jonah said. "One of the best kinds there is. The freedom to be exactly as you are with no secrets and no apologies. Too bad more people haven't tried it out."

———

"I was afraid I wouldn't remember how to swim," Michael said. "But it came right back to me."

He was treading water in the deep end, talking to Jonah, who was sitting in a poolside lounge chair staring intently at his phone.

"Your cells remember something so basic," Jonah said without looking up. "It's in your DNA."

Michael turned his head and looked out over the view of LA. It was fully dark now, and the lights glistened. It was almost like looking at a sky full of stars, in the sense that he had to marvel at the sheer vastness of the numbers. Points of light all the way to infinity.

The pool water was heated to somewhere in the eighties and felt heavenly against his skin.

"The water is great," he said. "And I'm floating here totally enjoying it, and at the same time there's this kind of deep sense of sadness because I didn't put on swim trunks and get into a pool sooner."

"You're only . . . what? Twenty?"

"Nineteen. I'll be twenty in a little over two months."

"You have no idea how many people take their insecurities to their grave. You didn't do badly."

Michael opened his mouth to answer, but a sharp bell tone sounded on Jonah's phone.

Jonah held it closer to his face and squinted at the incoming text.

"Oh," he said, and Michael could hear his disappointment. "Bob says hi and that we did a great job."

"Oh," Michael said. A sort of echo of disappointment.

He pushed off from the side and swam several laps. The backstroke, which was the bravest stroke under the circumstances. Not that anyone was watching. Jonah was staring at his phone and Dennis was in the kitchen working on dinner.

"He admires you," Jonah said.

But Michael had to stop, bring his head fully up out of the water, and ask his host to repeat the sentence.

"Who? Mr. Dunning?"

"Right. Bob. He admires you."

Michael swam to the edge of the pool and held its concrete rim.

"How could he?"

"Why wouldn't he?"

"Because he's . . . so . . . he's like . . . *everything*. How could *he* admire *me*?"

"Men like Bob and me have had more life experience. And it took us a while. But I think he sees you breaking ground and doing it young. You shouldn't compare yourself to him, or me, or anybody for that matter. But especially not anybody much older. You know what Bob always says."

"'Being a person takes practice.'"

"Ah. You do know." He looked up from his phone and straight into Michael's face. "I hope somebody is looking in on Madeleine while you're gone."

"Her sister is in town."

"Good." He stared at his phone for another minute. "Is she your first love?"

Michael pulled himself up and out of the pool and sat dripping in a lounge chair a few feet from Jonah. There was outdoor lighting. Plenty of it. To sit there in nothing but swim trunks was definitely the new Michael. He was aware of it. But he was not distressed.

"She's my first everything," he said. "I never let a girl anywhere near me before this."

The evening breeze felt cool on his skin, and he thought he could feel drops of pool water evaporating one at a time. He felt strangely aware of his body, but in a comfortable way.

"I'm sure it was easier for both of you," Jonah said. "Each knowing in advance that the other had misgivings, and why. I just hope you know it doesn't always have to be that way. You don't have to go through life looking for someone else who's scarred. Look at Bob and Ellen."

"I don't know Mr. Dunning's wife."

"No, I guess you wouldn't. Since you only see him on campus."

"I have to admit I wondered, though. But it felt like an inappropriate question."

"Lovely young woman. Well, not young, I guess. Mid-fifties. When you're my age that seems young. She just always loved him for exactly who he is."

"Good," Michael said. "I'm glad to know that exists."

"Oh, it definitely exists. You just have to hold out for it."

His phone let out that bell tone again, and it made Michael jump.

"It's just Dennis," Jonah said. "He wants us to come in for dinner."

———

Dennis handed him a stack of towels and washcloths and a bottle of drinking water at the guesthouse door.

All the exterior lights had been turned off, but a lamp glowed inside, and the lights of the city below added a surprising illumination to the scene.

"I sure appreciate all the hospitality," Michael said. "Dinner was great. I'm sorry if I ate too much, but I was just so hungry."

"Nonsense. I made it to be eaten. Jonah and I were so happy to have you here. I just loved your film. I would have told you over dinner, but you and Jonah seemed so lost in conversation." He scrubbed a hand over his gray beard as he spoke. "I loved it at a level I'm not even sure I knew I had. It hit me in a very deep place."

"That's a nice thing to hear."

"Maybe this is more than you wanted to know, but when I was a kid I was overweight and I had braces on my teeth. And I mean those super-radical braces that rubber-band to a strap behind your head. And I had my father's nose, which was not a good thing to have. I'm ashamed to admit I got it fixed when I was seventeen. At my parents' encouragement."

"Not sure why you'd be ashamed of that."

"Because now, at this time in my life, you couldn't pay me enough to go under the knife for purely cosmetic reasons. But back then my confidence was at an all-time low. I guess I just needed it. Then I got into my twenties and felt a lot better about myself. But now Jonah and I are in our seventies, and there's an adjustment to that—as the late Rex Aronfeld so eloquently pointed out. We're lucky because we get to adjust together. But it's just so hard for older people who are still looking for someone. Or looking for someone again. Anyway, sorry if that was too much information. I just wasn't sure if you knew how deeply this topic resonates and for how many people."

"I didn't," Michael said. "When I first came up with the idea I honestly didn't. But it's really opened my eyes."

"Well, I know you're exhausted, and I'll stop bending your ear and let you get some sleep." Dennis walked several steps back toward the house, then stopped and turned back in the dim glow. "I just want you to know I'm remembering Madeleine in my nontraditional prayers."

"Thank you," Michael said.

He could hear in his own voice that he could almost have cried in that moment. If he hadn't held it back. He wasn't sure if Dennis could hear it too.

Then the older man turned away and was gone.

Michael let himself inside the little guest cottage and plugged his phone into its charger.

He called Madeleine. An actual voice call. Which he usually didn't. But it was her sister who picked up her phone.

"Oh, it's you," he said.

He couldn't remember her name.

"She's asleep. I thought it would be best to just let her sleep."

"Yeah. Yeah, of course. Just tell her I'm coming home tomorrow, okay?"

"Will do."

Michael clicked off the call and felt himself overwhelmed by a virtual fire hose of sadness. He sat without moving, thinking as little as possible, for what might have been five or ten minutes.

A knock on the door startled him into a standing position.

"Sorry to bother you, Michael," Jonah's voice said through the door. "But I have news."

Michael ran to the door and threw it wide.

He knew just by Jonah's face that the news was good.

"I hope you showed it to your mother," he said. "Because it'll be streaming in possibly less than thirty days. Barring unforeseen holdups. Exclusive licensing. Seven hundred fifty dollars flat. Like I said, not a lot of money."

"But I'll take it!" Michael said.

The sudden news had propelled him out of his sadness and into a nearly dangerous-feeling elation. It made him feel almost ill to change mood so suddenly, like a diver who gets the bends from surfacing too fast.

"We'll talk more over breakfast," Jonah said. "I'll let you pretend you can get some sleep."

He walked back to the house, and Michael stood leaning in the doorway for a long time, watching him go. Then watching the space where he had been. Eventually he stepped back inside and closed the door.

He called Madeleine's phone a second time.

"Michael," her sister said. "Again."

"Sorry, but I have big news. And I didn't have it a minute ago. When she wakes up, tell her I said she should consider herself immortalized."

"I have no idea what that means, but okay."

"She'll know."

He clicked off the call and emailed the link to the newly revised film to his parents.

Then he texted his mother.

"Hey. I just emailed you a link to my film. Watch it now, because it's going to be streaming on Netflix in maybe thirty days. Didn't want you to feel like the last to know."

Then he turned off his phone and tried to get some sleep.

As Jonah had predicted, the best he could do was pretend.

———

When he arrived home at a little after eleven the following morning, both his parents were waiting for him at the door. He found himself walking directly into his mother's waiting arms.

She held him tightly for what felt like a long time before speaking.

"I am so, so proud of you," she said into his ear.

Then she let go and bustled away as if she were simply too busy to hang out and chat.

He looked up at his father, who nodded back at him.

"She wasn't freaked out by it?" he asked his dad.

"She was a little freaked out by it. But she really is proud of you. We both are."

MICHAEL,
AGE TWENTY

Chapter Seventeen

All Kinds of News in the Wrong Order

Michael caught up with Mr. Dunning just after the older man locked up his classroom at the end of the day. And he only just barely caught him. Michael had to run to pull level with Dunning as he walked to his car.

"Hey," Michael said, a little breathlessly.

"Hey yourself."

"I need to ask you a question. Do you have any idea why I would get voicemail messages from three big newspapers in one day? Like, in a span of five hours?"

Dunning stopped walking. He stared down at the sidewalk for a moment as if lost in thought.

"Did you send out a press release?" he asked after a time.

"No. If I had, it wouldn't be a question."

"Sounds like *somebody* did. Why not just ask the journalists who called you?"

"I've only managed to reach one so far. I called them all back, but I had to leave voicemails for two of them. The one I actually talked to, he swore he didn't know. He said he just had a note on his desk telling him to call me and set up an interview."

"Somebody must have sent out press releases," Dunning said.

"Would Netflix do that?"

"Not in a way that would have the papers calling *you*, I wouldn't think."

"Maybe one of the film festivals?"

He had received acceptances from three in the past two and a half months.

"I doubt any of them want to help you do publicity for your film, in light of that fact that you had to tell them it was exclusively licensed and they probably couldn't screen it."

"Where does that leave the question?"

Dunning began to walk again, and Michael fell into step with him.

"My best guess would be the college," Dunning said. "They're understandably proud of you. All colleges like to see good things coming out of their education, and of course they want everyone to know about it. Goes directly to private funding and such. I enjoy teaching here, but let's face it—this place is not Harvard. They want all the accolades they can get. You can ask Mrs. Framingham in the dean's office. She would be in charge of that kind of publicity outreach."

"Wait," Michael said. While they waited, Michael realized he used that word a lot when confused or caught off guard. "Wouldn't they tell me if they were going to send out press releases about my film?"

"One would think," Dunning said.

They walked silently to the parking lot. Michael wasn't sure why he wasn't just letting Dunning go, but he wasn't. His mind was spinning, and it seemed to be preventing him from making a new plan.

Dunning stopped in front of his car, a silver Volvo SUV.

"This is me," he said, bouncing the smart key on his palm.

"I'll let you go."

"Before we do . . . I'm curious. You said big newspapers. How big are we talking?"

"The *LA Times*, the *San Francisco Chronicle*, and the *Santa Barbara Independent*."

"Oh, my," Dunning said. "I would call those big, yes."

———

Michael stepped into Mrs. Framingham's outer office. She had a secretary or assistant who looked up and smiled. But the smile seemed rehearsed and insincere.

"And you are . . . ?"

"Michael Woodbine."

"And this is your appointment time?"

"I don't have an appointment."

"Really? I thought we made an appointment for you."

"Not that I know of," Michael said.

The door to the inner office flew open, and a person he could only assume to be Mrs. Framingham stood in the open doorway. She looked about fifty, with an efficient short haircut and a bright-red skirt suit.

"Mr. Woodbine," she said, leading Michael to believe that the walls were thin. "I've been expecting you. Come right in."

Michael's head swam slightly as he stepped into her office. He sat on a modern-looking chair with a thinly padded leather seat, and immediately lost the thread of how to sit comfortably and what to do with his hands.

"How could you be expecting me?" he asked. "*I* didn't even know I was about to come see you."

"You got a call asking you to come in, right? I wanted to talk to you about your film. We're so proud of your success with it, what with the project coming straight from one of our classes as it did. We wanted to tell you we plan to send out press releases."

Michael sat for a second or two, feeling that swimmy sensation in his head again.

"Nobody called me and told me to come in," he said. "And I think you already sent out press releases."

"That seems odd."

She had been fiddling with a silver pen as she spoke, and she used it to press a button on her desk phone, which apparently enabled an intercom.

"Maggie," she said in the general direction of the phone. "You made an appointment for Mr. Woodbine, didn't you?"

"I was just looking that up in my schedule," Maggie said, her voice tinny over the phone speaker. "Turns out I was going to, but you asked me to postpone because of your uncle's memorial."

"You didn't send out the press releases yet, though, right?"

"I did. I'm sorry if that was wrong. You didn't ask me to postpone that. Just the in-person appointment."

"Oh, dear. Well. Thanks." She clicked the intercom line closed with her pen and looked up into Michael's face, her own face embarrassed. "Well, I'm awfully sorry," she said. "This is a busy, busy place and we do our best to keep things happening, but sometimes in all the confusion they all happen at once or in the wrong order. So tell me. You had already said you thought we sent out press releases. Have you gotten responses? Is that how you knew?"

"The *LA Times*, the *San Francisco Chronicle*, and the *Santa Barbara Independent.*"

Mrs. Framingham's face lit up. Positively illuminated.

"Splendid! That's fabulous. Mention the college a lot. Please. Oh, I know that sounds self-serving, and I'm not asking you to do it in an artificial-sounding way. Just . . ."

"None of it would have happened if I hadn't taken Mr. Dunning's film class," he said to fill in the pause. "So it shouldn't be hard."

"Perfect. Exactly like that. And just so you know, we're arranging a screening of your film, with you there for a Q-and-A and discussion afterward. Lots of local publicity."

Michael opened his mouth to object, but she kept going.

"Oh, I know. I know. Exclusively licensed. But we're going through the proper channels to get permission for one screening. We think they might say yes, since we're just a local college, but if they say no it won't change our plans much. People can read the publicity about the event and watch the film at home before coming. One way or another we can make a great event out of a discussion of the film. It's very thought-provoking. I thought we'd invite Robert Dunning to sit on the stage with you and join the discussion. We thought of asking all the people you interviewed, but the older man passed away and we know Madeleine is very sick. It didn't feel right to have some but not all of the people, so just the two of you should be fine. As soon as we pencil in a date we'll let you know. And good luck with the newspaper interviews."

"Um . . ." Michael said. "Thanks."

He honestly couldn't think of one other thing to say.

———

"Absolutely not," Dunning said.

Michael was more than a little stunned by his reaction.

He had found the professor at his desk, in his classroom, just before first period the following morning.

Michael stood with his hands in his jeans pockets, unsure how to respond. The first words out of his mouth were the most honest and vulnerable reaction possible.

"Just me? All alone on that stage?"

"You'll do fine," Dunning said. "You know what you wanted to say with the film, and you can speak to that better than anyone."

"But *why?*"

"Because it's not my film. It's yours. To sit next to you and answer questions about the film suggests I take some credit for it. I don't. You're not a child, and I don't want to appear to be hand-holding you through the process. *You* made this film. You and you alone. I will sit in the audience and applaud your accomplishment, and you will sit under the spotlight and take the credit, and we will not confuse anyone into thinking you couldn't have done it without me or anyone else. You may still be a college student, but you're a professional filmmaker now."

"I'm not a professional filmmaker."

Dunning's eyes came sharply up to his and engaged. It almost sent Michael back a step.

"Excuse me. Beg to differ. You just licensed your film to a major online streaming service. You're a pro. Step into the role. I'll support you in the background, but in public you stand alone, because no one deserves the credit but you. Now if you'll excuse me, it's time for my first class to begin."

———

Michael opened the door to Madeleine's house with his key. As he stepped in, he nearly ran smack into a woman stepping out. He backed up quickly.

It was not the home health nurse.

She was a woman in about her mid-sixties, with perfectly styled hair. She looked as though she had just stepped out of a beauty salon and driven here with the car windows closed. She wore a surprising amount of makeup.

"Oh," she said.

Then they stood considering each other for a moment. He wanted to ask who she was, but he didn't want to seem rude. She appeared to feel quite confident in her right to be there. He was considering the idea that she might be Madeleine's mother.

"I'm Michael," he said.

"Oh, I know who you are."

Her voice, her tone, pierced him. It put him in mind of the term "bloodcurdling." He thought he knew now, for the first time, how something could curdle his blood.

He wasn't speaking, so she added another curt sentence in that same dreadful tone.

"I saw your movie."

"You're not a fan?"

He tried to keep it light. It didn't work.

"The whole world did not need to see that."

"I very much doubt the whole world will watch it," he said.

"Lots of people are watching it. Nobody needed to see that."

Michael stood curdled another moment, then decided he was done being intimidated. Especially about the message in his film. It had become the one thing in life he knew he believed.

"She had a reason to feel she needed to show it," he said. "Everyone who appeared in the film had something important to say. And since it's her body . . ."

"Yes, I know it was her decision," she said, her tone softened somewhat. "But I'm her mother, and I've watched her make awful decisions for thirty-one years."

Michael honestly doubted that Madeleine had made awful decisions as an infant, or that he would have agreed with her mother's disapproval of every one of her decisions since. But he had no more interest in talking to this woman.

"She's an adult," he said, and pushed by her toward the stairs.

"Yes, I'm glad one of you is old enough to drink," she said to his retreating back.

He ignored the dig.

He found Madeleine in bed. Of course. He had not expected to find her anywhere else.

He sat down on the edge of the bed and gave his vision a minute to adjust to the dimness. Her eyes had become more recessed, as if she were retreating into herself. It scared him, because he felt as though she had been leaving in some very real way.

"Come lie down with me," she said, her voice so small it bordered on nonexistent. "I missed you."

He kicked off his shoes and lay beside her, and she moved closer and eased an arm across his chest. She lifted her head cautiously and set it down on his shoulder.

For a moment they enjoyed the warmth of each other before speaking.

"You met my mother?" she asked after a time.

"I did."

"Sorry about that."

Michael laughed, but carefully. The last thing he wanted to do was bounce her head around.

"She wants to call in hospice," Madeleine said quietly.

Michael felt her words like little ice crystals dancing in his torso.

"Is that what you want?"

"I told her you're taking good care of me. But hospice takes care of you with those excellent next-level pain meds. So I told her she could call them on Monday."

"Okay," he said. But still the ice crystals danced. "I have news," he added, happy to change the subject. "A guy from the *LA Times* is coming to interview me tomorrow about the film. And two more big papers are interested in scheduling interviews. They're going to hold a big event at the college with a discussion of the film."

"That's great," Madeleine said.

Her voice did not betray much enthusiasm, but he didn't take it personally. He knew she honestly did think it was great. She simply had no energy to get excited about anything anymore, or at least to reflect it in her voice.

"I was hoping he could come here," he said.

"Of course. You practically live here."

"But will your mom be here, though?"

"No, she and my dad are leaving tomorrow to check on two houses they have up in Big Sur. They won't be back till Monday."

"Okay, good. He was hoping to be able to talk to you. The reporter. Just briefly. I told him I'd ask you. But I also told him that, even if you say yes, right up to the last minute it's going to hinge on how you feel."

"No pictures, though," she said. "This is not the way I want people to remember me."

"No. No pictures. I told him if he brought a camera he should leave it in the car. He can get a picture of me on his way out if he wants. Outside. He couldn't very well take a picture of you anyway because there's no light in here. And I'm sure not letting him set off a flash in your face. But I thought it was good, though, that he's coming. We're immortalizing you."

"We are."

They lay in silence for a time. She rolled away onto her side and tugged his arm so he would roll with her, ending up with his chest up against her back. Pressed close.

"You need a girlfriend," she said in that barely there voice.

And with that, the dormant ice crystals danced again.

"I have a girlfriend."

"Not really you don't. You have a terminal patient."

"Who's still my girlfriend. Can we talk about something else?"

"First I want you to make me a promise. At least when I'm gone, I want you to start again with somebody else. Somebody your own age. And I want you to promise you won't go purposely looking for a girl who has some huge reason to feel insecure about her looks, like that's the only way she'd want to be with you. Just find a nice girl who you can love, and trust her not to be shallow."

"I'd still like to talk about something else. Or nothing."

"Sure. As soon as you promise."

"Okay. Fine. I promise."

He wasn't sure he meant it. He just wanted to change the subject. But he knew it was his job to step into meaning it as soon as possible.

It was a final promise, as far as he knew.

They lay together in silence for fifteen or twenty minutes. Michael's stomach was cramped with hunger, but he didn't want to let her go.

In time he could hear by her breathing that she was asleep, so he gently drew away and walked downstairs to make himself a sandwich.

Her mother was still there.

She sat at the kitchen table, hunched over a cup of coffee. He could tell what she was drinking from the aroma. She was leaning her forehead into one hand in a way that obscured her eyes.

"There's coffee," she said.

"Thanks, but I don't drink it. I'm just going to make myself a sandwich."

"Who's keeping the fridge full of food?"

"That would be me," he said.

"And are you also the one refilling her prescriptions and keeping the place so clean?"

"Yeah," he said. "Still me."

"Well then. I guess despite my personal feelings about your age and your movie, I suppose she's lucky to have you."

The whole time Michael made and ate his food, she said no more. Neither one of them did.

Chapter Eighteen

He Really Only Kept His Shirt on So No One Would See His Wings

The reporter arrived at a little after ten the following morning. Michael had been watching for him, and stepped out to meet his car.

He was not at all what Michael had been expecting. He'd expected a man significantly older than himself. Someone he'd be tempted to call "sir." Instead the reporter looked to be just a handful of years older than Michael, with a wild head of brown hair and a cheerful face.

"Zach Brownstein," he said, and shook Michael's hand. "You sure you want the camera to stay in the car?"

"If you wouldn't mind."

Zach shrugged, and they walked toward the front door together.

"I gotta tell you," he said, "when I first called you, I hadn't seen your documentary. I just had this note on my desk to call you and set something up, like I said. I'm kind of the new kid on the block at the paper, if you know what I mean. Not exactly in the middle of the decision-making process. But after we talked, I watched it. And I really loved what you did with it. *Really* loved it. It moved me."

"Thank you. That's great to hear."

They stepped up onto the porch together. Michael could tell Zach had something to say, and that it would come from a deep place and feel personal. It was a sensation to which Michael was growing accustomed.

"My mom is a big woman," Zach said.

For a moment it seemed he would say no more. And yet Michael expected Zach to find more within himself, and say it. Michael didn't speak, or try to move them into the house. He just left the space open.

"All my life I've had to watch the way she's treated," Zach said after a time, "and it's just sickening what people do to her. Total strangers who stare and feel free to comment. Like anything about her is any of their business. Watching her try to get medical care. Once she went to the doctor for a rash on her arm and all he would do was give her a brochure about bariatric surgery. He never treated her. He just gave her unwanted advice and then sent her away. The whole time I was watching your film I felt like you were speaking up for her. Like you were striking a blow in her defense."

"I hope I was," Michael said.

"I'm sorry if that was too much information."

"No, it's fine. I get where you're coming from."

Michael opened the door, and they stepped inside.

"So, do I get to talk to Madeleine? Her part in the film was so touching."

"She said yes, but we just have to be so watchful for signs that we're tiring her out. And if that happens I want us out of the room immediately. She's fragile. Sometimes she'll be having a conversation with you and everything seems fine, and then all of a sudden she'll slur her words, or say a sentence that's just meaningless. That just adds up to nothing. Or you'll say something perfectly short and simple and she can't understand it. She has good moments and bad moments. We can try, but I'm going to be very quick to shut it down if I feel like it's stressing her in any way."

They moved together toward the staircase.

Zach stopped on the bottom step.

"You're very protective of her," he said.

"Yeah, of course I am. And I make no apologies for that. Somebody needs to look after her, because she's too sick to do it herself."

"Hey," Zach said. "Buddy." His voice sounded soft. He very briefly laid a hand on Michael's upper arm. "It wasn't a criticism."

———

Michael pulled a straight-backed wooden chair up to Madeleine's bed, and Zach sat in it. He had brought a miniature tape recorder, which he switched on and set on the bedside table.

Michael stood in the doorway, feeling somehow that Madeleine had a right to her privacy in that moment. It was one thing to monitor her strength, her energy, her needs, and her pain. But her words, her thoughts, her answers to a reporter's questions . . . he did not want to hover over those.

He heard Zach ask her, "What did you want to get across to the public when you agreed to appear in the documentary?"

He did not hear her answer, because her voice was very small.

He heard Zach say, "Michael takes good care of you, doesn't he?"

He leaned in, figuratively. Tried to set his ears on some kind of higher volume, which of course could only be accomplished in his imagination. He did not move closer.

"I'm going to talk to Michael and let you get some rest," Zach said. "You look like you could use some rest."

He clicked off the recorder, rose, and joined Michael in the doorway.

"Thanks for keeping that short," Michael said. "We'll sit out on the patio."

He led the reporter down the stairs and through the sliding glass door off the kitchen.

The day had become ominous with clouds that threatened rain. Michael hadn't bothered to look at a weather forecast, but he could feel the charge of it in the air, and in the warm wind. And the sky was positively black.

"We can go inside if it rains," Michael said.

"Or just get wet," Zach said.

———

A good twenty-five minutes and one brief photoshoot later, when Michael had covered the most basic, most logistic information about his journey through the project, Zach looked up into Michael's face.

"Now, on a more personal note . . ." he said.

Michael was suddenly aware of the red light on the mini recorder, like an eavesdropping presence. He was aware of the warm but threatening wind blowing his hair across his forehead and into his eyes.

"What did making this documentary change about you? How are you a different person now than you were before you got the idea to do it?"

"Oh," Michael said. "That's a very good question."

"Thank you."

"I guess . . ." Then he paused there in the wind for a time, waiting to access more thoughts. "I guess more than anything, I honestly had no idea how many people were feeling stressed about how they look. Like . . . when I first put up a notice on the college bulletin board, looking for participants, I left it kind of vague. I don't remember the exact wording, but it was something about people who felt worried and uncomfortable about their bodies. I didn't think everybody who responded would have extensive scarring like me, but I kind of expected it to go in that general direction. I thought the people who stepped up would have some huge, obvious thing that would make me think 'Wow, yeah, I can see how that could be troubling.' I had no idea this was something that's an issue for just about everybody, at one level or another. So I guess the biggest change is that I used to think my problem with body image set me apart, like that one lonely guy on the dark side of the moon. I thought it isolated me, and made me different from everybody else. And now it feels like a thing that makes me even more human and binds me to everybody else. Like I'm in a big club instead of standing outside alone, staring in the window at the people I always figured were doing fine. Does that make sense?"

"Perfect sense," Zach said. "And I really think it's all I need."

And just in that moment, as if on cue, the rain let go all at once.

———

Michael joined Madeleine in bed.

He lay down on top of the covers, close against her back, and threw one arm over her waist.

"Is it raining?" she asked.

"Yeah. Hard."

"I thought I was dreaming."

"Not about that you weren't."

"Don't go," she said.

And, just on those two words, her voice rang out stronger than he'd heard it in months. Just in that moment she was herself again. For a brief instance she was his lover, Madeleine. A woman he'd thought he might never see again.

"I'm not going," he said. "I just got here."

"No, I mean don't go at all," she said, and her voice was miles away again. "Don't even go to the bathroom if you can manage it. Stay here with me. Stay close, okay?"

"Yeah. Of course. I'm right here."

They lay together in silence for what must have been an hour or more. Michael was wearing a watch, but didn't want to disturb her by moving his arm, so he only lay still and listened to sheets of rain drumming on the roof.

Then she spoke, surprising him.

"Remember when I pinned you in a bathroom in the student union and got you to take off your shirt?"

"That would be hard to forget."

Another few minutes of silence, save for the rain, passed.

"Did that really happen?" she asked.

"Yeah. It really happened."

"Oh." More rain-punctuated silence. "Is it okay that it happened?"

"Of course it's okay."

"Kind of rude."

"But look at all the good things that came of it."

"Did we make a movie together?"

"We did."

"Are people watching it?"

"Oh yeah. Thousands of people."

"Good. I thought I just dreamed that."

"No. That was very, very real."

After that she seemed to have no more to say.

Michael was hungry, and could have used a quick trip to the bathroom. But he had promised her he would stay close.

In time, he fell asleep.

When he woke, he had no idea what time it was or how long he had been asleep. But as to Madeleine, lying in the bed with him, he knew. He could feel the difference in her physical presence against him. The different feel of her. She was no longer yielding, or warm.

He waited for the sensation of her breath against his chest, even though he already knew it would never come.

It never came.

She was no longer there.

———

The memorial was held in Santa Cruz, because her parents were in charge of planning it, and that was where they lived.

Michael left his parents' house at four in the morning to be sure he would be there on time, even if there were holdups on the highway.

He stopped in the nearly nonexistent town of Chualar and filled his tank with gas. And while he was inside paying for it, he picked up a copy of the *LA Times*.

The article was there, in the Arts and Leisure section. As he separated out the sections, he saw his own face smiling back at himself from just below the fold.

He ran his finger down the text, skipping over the parts in which his own words were quoted. Later he would read them, just to see what words had and had not made the cut, but he knew what he'd said. He still did not know what she had said.

He skipped over the description of her condition when Zach interviewed her, and zeroed in on her answers.

"What did you want to get across to the public when you agreed to appear in the documentary?"

"I guess something about what it means to be a woman. And what it means to be beautiful. Because it's not always what we make it out to be. Either one. I think we mostly have a basic confusion about both things."

"Michael takes good care of you, doesn't he?"

"He's an angel. An actual, literal angel. Well, no, not literally literal. He's a human guy. But to me, he flew right down from Heaven with his great big puffy wings. How lucky was I to get him?"

Michael threw the paper down on the passenger seat and drove again. And he didn't stop driving once after that, even though he never did stop crying.

Chapter Nineteen

Blood Brothers

When the lights in the college auditorium came up, they glared into Michael's eyes, and he lost sight of his emotional anchors in the front row. Mr. Dunning was there with his wife, and Michael's parents were there. And he could no longer see them.

And he needed them.

He sat alone in a very uncomfortable chair on the stage. He could feel his right hand locked in a death grip on the microphone he'd been given.

He knew he would be asked to speak in a matter of seconds, but his heart hammered so hard he could hear it like a throbbing in his ears, and it felt impossible to breathe. And his throat was trying to close up on him.

A spotlight landed on the audience, and Michael could see people lining up behind a microphone on a stand in the center aisle. The man in the front of the line tapped the head of the mic lightly, to be sure it was on. It was a big noise, and it made Michael jump.

"Hey," the man said. It sounded like some kind of soft, familiar greeting.

"Hey," Michael said into his own microphone.

The man was beefy and solidly built. About forty, with short, ginger-red hair and a freckled face. Michael could see the man's face surprisingly well in the spotlight. He seemed to be reaching out to Michael in some indefinable way. He seemed about to deliver a message that felt important to him.

"So, I saw your film," the man said. "Some neighbors told me to see it, and I think you'll understand why in a minute. They said, 'Hey, didn't you go through something like this?'"

Michael began to relax slightly. Because this was a scene that had become quite familiar to him. Someone had had a similar injury or experience, and felt moved to share it.

The feeling didn't last.

"You said in the film there's a lot you don't remember from that night. You said you only remember a yellow plastic lighter and a firefighter looking down at you and your brother from the bluff. And you said you had no idea what you were doing on top of the rocket when it went off. If you tripped and fell on it, or what. And I just thought I should come fill in some of those blanks for you."

In the silence before he answered, Michael could feel his face suddenly tingly and hot. His first thought was that this man was somehow not of sound mind, which seemed like a weird way for his big, important Q and A to start.

"How can you do that?" Michael said into the mic. It came out much louder than he had expected.

"Because I was there," the man said. "You threw yourself down on top of the rocket, purposely, because you were trying to hide it. You were trying to cover up what you and your brother had done. You didn't know your brother had lit the fuse, because you weren't looking when he did that. You were looking up at me."

Michael swallowed hard, wondering if his voice was about to fail him.

"You're the firefighter," he said.

He said it quietly, almost to himself, but the microphone made it big.

So much blood roared through his ears that it didn't even sound like his voice saying the words. Even through the roar of blood, though, Michael could hear a murmur of sound from the audience—a collective reaction to the unexpected nature of the moment.

It hit him, as he sat absorbing the news, that he had spent his life not feeling as though the firefighter actually existed. Not quite believing he lived somewhere out in the world, remembering that night. The firefighter had always felt more like something Michael had dreamed. A figure in a story, purely from seven-year-old Michael's point of view.

"I *was*," the man said. "I left the department not too long after that night. It was a pretty traumatic experience for me too. Not as much as it was for you. Don't get me wrong—I'm sure you had a much worse night than I did. But by the time I got down there you were losing so much blood from that explosion right against your torso, and you weren't breathing, and I was trying to do CPR, but it's hard to do chest compressions on a little kid who doesn't exactly have a chest anymore. And I had so much of your blood all over me."

"I'm so sorry," Michael said, sounding almost winded. And feeling almost winded. "I never once thought about how that night might have been for anybody who wasn't me or my family."

"And you shouldn't have had to. We were the grown-ups. We were the professionals. You were just a little kid, and you had enough on your plate. But after that I decided to teach the fourth grade, and I think that was a good choice for me. I've been a lot happier and more relaxed since then. I followed your progress as much as I could after that night to see how you made out, but all I knew was that you'd survived. I wasn't blood family, and nobody was going to tell me any more than that. But I've got to tell you, speaking of blood family, when you have to wash that much of someone's blood off your hands and out of your clothes, you feel connected. It's a hard bond to let go of."

He stopped talking, and no one else started. No one stepped up to try to replace the man at the microphone, and Michael had no idea what to say.

The silence felt stunning, awkward and long, though it might only have been a handful of seconds. Michael pushed himself hard to break it.

"You probably saved my life."

"Maybe," the man said. "I don't know. But then another part of me thinks, if only I hadn't followed you, probably you would have set off the rocket successfully. It was my being there on the bluff that made you throw yourself on it, and I think about that a lot. It used to keep me up at night. More than I care to admit, really. But anyway, I didn't come here to get credit for saving you, and I didn't come here to ease my own guilt over possibly causing the accident. I just wanted to say hi and see in person how you look now that you're all grown up, because last time I saw you it didn't seem likely you'd ever get there."

Michael set down the microphone and stood. He walked to the stairs of the stage, down into the audience, and up the center aisle. He stopped in front of the man at the microphone, and they looked into each other's faces at very close range.

Then Michael reached out—tentatively, just in case it wasn't a welcome gesture—and wrapped his arms around the former firefighter, who embraced him in return.

"Thank you," he said quietly into the man's ear.

"Anytime."

"That night, or . . . actually all this time since, I was thinking of you as some big enforcer type. This authority figure who sort of only existed to get us in trouble. And actually you were trying to keep us from getting ourselves killed."

"And I almost missed."

Michael pulled back.

He knew he had to retake the stage, but he felt shocked and displaced, and wasn't sure how to do normal things like move his limbs. In time he did walk back to his seat on the stage, though he seemed to be watching the motions from outside himself. He couldn't quite feel his feet touch the floor.

He sat down and picked up his mic again, but did not immediately speak.

"Anyway," the man said. "I just wanted to tell you that. And also . . . good film, by the way. I liked the way you took the worst thing that ever happened to you and turned it into the best stuff you could give to everybody else. That's such a great thing to be able to do. I admire that. I'm Jerry Fitzgerald, by the way. And I'm listed, if you ever want to call and chat."

And then, just like that, he was gone. Faded into a part of the aisle not spotlighted, an area bathed in shadow.

A woman stepped up to the mic. She was his mother's age, or a little younger. Her dark hair was short, and she smiled at Michael in a natural way that broke through his shock and helped ease him.

"I haven't had any specific experience that makes me relate to your film," she said, "but I loved it, and I wanted to tell you that. And I wanted to tell you why. I loved it because it was so honest. It was all centered around telling the truth about a subject we're encouraged to lie about. And I just feel like . . . I feel like every time somebody sets a tone of emotional honesty like that, it breaks down the wall of lies just a little bit. The more you do it, the more we all get to do it. So I wanted to thank you for that."

She peeled away from the mic and faded into the shadows.

"Thank *you*," Michael said. "That's such a nice compliment. I could really feel that. All the way in."

A much younger woman stood at the mic now. College-age, and slender, with waist-length straight blond hair.

"I kind of *do* have something that ties me to the film," she said. "But it's embarrassing, and I keep going back and forth about whether I'm going to say it in front of all these people. But then I figured, if you can do it, then I should probably do it too. I never . . . really . . . developed. Above the waist, I mean. I have no . . . bust. Well, hardly any. I'm just super flat-chested. And I really heard—and kind of felt—what Madeleine was saying about how men sort of see breasts as being what makes you a woman."

Her name was a dagger in Michael's chest, but he had to hold it together. And the young woman had more to say.

"Every time you open a magazine or watch a commercial, you see what men find important. And I don't have it. And I don't know if it's worse to have them and then have to lose them or to never know what it would even feel like to have them in the first place."

She seemed to pause, as if Michael would weigh in. Michael weighed in.

"I think part of the point of the film," he said, "is getting past comparing one person's experience to another. It's not about who has it worse. Our problems are our problems, and I think sometimes they get compared to other people's problems in a way that makes us feel like we don't have a right to feel the way we feel about them."

"Oh," she said. "I never thought about it that way. But anyway, since I saw your movie I've been grateful for what I do have. You know. In that department. So that's good, I guess. Anyway, I just wanted to tell you that."

"Thank you," he said.

But she was already gone.

A young man stood at the mic. He was a few years older than Michael, by the look of him, with a wild head of curly blond hair that fell over his face and collar. He stood with his hands stuffed deeply into his jeans pockets, and smiled at Michael in a way that felt oddly familiar.

"I noticed it kind of threw you before when somebody jumped up out of your past." Those were the first words out of the young man's mouth.

"I guess it was just unexpected," Michael said.

"Yeah. Well. I'm doing this anyway. I saw your film for the same reason he did, except it wasn't neighbors that told me to watch it. It was this guy from work and his wife. He said, 'You should see this.' It was because of that part when you were describing being in the hospital after the run-in with the fireworks. I think they thought I'd find it kind of similar to something I went through. I don't think they could possibly have known it was actually me you were talking about."

"Wait," Michael said. "When was I talking about you?"

"You said there was this older boy in the next bed who was having surgery on his hands because of fireworks, and you thought he'd lost some of his fingers."

He pulled his hands out of his pockets and held them up in the light for Michael to see. They were deeply scarred, and he was missing four fingers—three on his right hand and one on his left.

"Jeffrey," Michael said, feeling bowled over and knocked off his inner foundation again.

"Wow," Jeffrey said. "You remembered my name after all these years. That's so nice. Do you remember what I told you in the hospital? I gave you some advice."

"Yeah, I do. You told me not to look until I was out of the hospital and feeling safer and more used to things. And it was good advice. I waited till I'd been in my foster home for a couple of weeks and was feeling more settled there. And then I told my new mom I wanted to see, and I looked in a mirror while she was changing the bandages. And, wow, let me tell you, I'm glad I didn't do it any sooner. It was just a lot to take in all at once."

"It *was* a lot," Jeffrey said. "I mean, at least I got to go home to the same family. But anyway, I'm glad I could help."

"You helped me just by being there," Michael said. "You were the only person there who was anything like me. Everybody else was a nurse or a social worker or a doctor or a cop. And you were a kid who'd tried to mess with fireworks, just like me, and I just can't tell you how comforting that was."

"Then I guess our message is 'Don't play with fireworks.'"

"Amen."

"The other guy got a hug," Jeffrey said.

And with that, Jeffrey left the mic and walked up onto the stage. Michael stood and opened his arms, and then they were filled with Jeffrey.

It was a more enthusiastic hug than the one he'd shared with the firefighter. It was something like an embrace from a long-lost brother. And Michael had lost a brother. And he had lost Madeleine only thirty-five days earlier. And it was getting harder to hold it together.

"Thanks so much for coming here tonight," he said near Jeffrey's ear. "It means a lot."

"We made it, Michael. We survived."

"*Yeah* we did."

He clapped Michael on the back and returned to the audience.

And though it would have been easy to curl up into a limp, exhausted ball and sleep for weeks, Michael pushed down all the feelings that weren't helping him in that moment.

Then he sat in his chair on the stage and held still for another hour of comments and questions.

———

After the president of the college made his wrap-up remarks, Michael was just standing to leave the stage when he noticed the young woman.

The audience was milling toward the doors, and she was the only one who had come down to the stage. She stood almost leaning on it now, looking up at him, her hands over the edge of its boards.

She was not spotlighted, but he could see her fairly well. She had curly dark-brown hair that fell just past her shoulders and very white teeth. He could tell because she was smiling at him. A little nervously. A little shyly.

She was pretty.

It was unusual for him to observe that a woman was pretty. It was a new and unfamiliar experience. Before he'd met Madeleine he had not allowed himself to consciously go there with anyone. And after he'd met Madeleine there had been Madeleine.

He was too tired to give her anything. Even words or attention. He felt almost literally wrung out, as though he might fall right over at the slightest push. His brain screamed for unchallenging silence. He felt as though he were a car that had been running its headlights for hours with the engine off. There was nothing left.

He took a deep, bracing breath and moved forward to talk to her anyway.

He crouched on his haunches at the edge of the stage and looked down into her face.

"You look tired," she said.

"You could say that."

"I won't keep you. I just wanted to meet you. I just wanted to tell you that I've seen your film four times, and I'll probably see it again. And I just think you're wonderful. Really handsome and kind. I'm not a crazy stalker or anything. I just wanted to tell you that. I know you have a girlfriend."

He teetered a moment, feeling the reference to his loss slash through him.

She must have seen his reaction, because she backpedaled into apology.

"Oh, no. I'm sorry. Did you break up with Madeleine?"

He cut his eyes down to the stage to keep her out. Then shook his head very slightly. It was such a subtle movement that he wasn't positive it had actually happened out in the world, and not just in his head.

"Oh, no," she said. "Now I'm *really* sorry. Oh, I'm so sorry I even brought it up. I'm so sorry for your loss. That's terrible. Nobody asked about her tonight. I was surprised."

"They didn't dare," Michael said, still avoiding her gaze. "Too much time has gone by. Too much chance that the news is bad."

"Well, anyway, please don't take this the wrong way, but I'm writing down my phone number for you. Just in case you ever want to talk. And if not, that's okay too. But just let me do this. I'm a good listener."

A few seconds later a slip of paper appeared between his eyes and the stage.

He took it.

On it was written the name "Caroline," in careful script, and a phone number.

He looked up, but she was gone.

———

"I owe you an apology," his mother said from the front passenger seat on the drive home.

"For what?" he asked, wishing no one would talk.

"For acting like you shouldn't make that film because it was so personal. And that's why it makes me uneasy, because it's so personal, but I listened to all those people tonight, and I realized that's actually the point. That's why it's obviously good for people. Because it was so personal. And it was so clear tonight that it was a good thing you did."

"Thank you," Michael said. "That means a lot."

"I'm sorry if it seemed like I encouraged you to hide your scars. I was just trying to protect you."

"I know you were."

"I know it's been hard for you since your friend died."

"She wasn't his friend, Judy," his father said from behind the wheel. "She was more than his friend."

"Sorry. Your girlfriend. I haven't known what to do to help."

"There's nothing you can do, Mom," Michael said. "I just need time."

"Understood. I'll leave you be."

They pulled into the driveway, and Michael went straight to his room. Or tried to. But his mother spoke out to him as he moved through the house from the front door.

"We should have that nice man to dinner."

"What nice man?"

"The firefighter."

"He's not a firefighter anymore. He's a fourth-grade teacher."

"The former firefighter. We should have him to dinner. Don't you think?"

"Yeah. I think that would be nice. I'm just too tired to think about anything else tonight."

He slipped into his room and closed the door.

He opened his laptop and sat with it on the bed, and hit the bookmarked link for his film on Netflix.

Lily the cat jumped up onto the bed with him, making those little modulated sounds in her throat. He pulled her close to his chest, advanced the film to a time mark he knew by heart, and pressed "play."

"You'll get used to it here," he told the cat as he stroked her fur. "We'll take care of you."

As he spoke, his eyes remained on the screen, where Madeleine let his shirt fall into a puddle on her hips and lap.

"I've never really done this in front of you," Screen Madeleine said. "Not so open like this."

He watched as she talked about what she had expected of the surgery, and how she had argued with her mother about reconstruction.

He stopped it before the part where he questioned the words "a year." Before she had a chance to answer.

Then he backed up and played it again. And again. And again. And again.

———

When he undressed for bed, he took the slip of paper with Caroline's phone number out of his pocket. Until he checked his pockets before throwing his clothes in the hamper, he had forgotten it was there.

He stared at it for a moment too long, as if trying to make sense of it. It looked almost unfamiliar to him, though at one level he remembered what it was. He was just too mentally exhausted to grasp much.

He threw it in the bathroom trash, brushed his teeth quickly, and put himself to bed.

Then he got up, rescued the slip of paper, and tucked it into the drawer of his bedside table.

Not because he actually wanted to. Only because he had promised.

Chapter Twenty

What Other People Think He'll Want, Given Time

It was a little over three weeks later when Michael came home from classes at the end of the day and found the letter sitting on his bed.

It was a real old-fashioned letter. The kind you almost never saw these days. A handwritten address in cursive on a pink stationery-size envelope, with a postage stamp and a return address in the upper left-hand corner. The return address had no name above it, though. Just a street address in Duarte, California.

He sat with it on the edge of the bed, and Lily the cat walked back and forth on his lap, purring, as he tore it open.

"Our Dear Michael," it began.

For a moment, he fell into confused thoughts and did not read more. *Our Dear Michael?*

What two or more people in the world would call him that? For a moment he thought it was from his parents, but they didn't live in Duarte. They lived under the same roof with him. And not once since he had come to live with them as a child had they written out their thoughts for him rather than speaking to him directly.

With a growing sense of dread, he read on.

"Your father and I saw your film a few weeks ago, and ever since then we've been talking about whether we should try to reach out to you."

He stopped reading again, and felt his chest and belly fill with rage. He did nothing outwardly to express his anger, but the cat jumped down off his lap immediately and slithered under the bed.

He knew now who the letter was from. What he couldn't possibly imagine was how his birth mother had found the nerve to refer to them as "Your father and I." In what world did you get to give away an eight-year-old child and then years later refer to yourself as his parents? In what universe had they been parents to him since that awful day when he was seven?

He looked back down at the text and briefly thought about throwing the letter away unread. But he did read it, mostly because he wanted the feeling of rage now, and it felt satisfying to stoke it.

"We almost came to that lecture you gave at your college, but we were afraid it might seem like ambushing you. We know from watching the film that your feelings about us are not good. We heard you say that you thought we rejected you because of your scarring, and of course it just ripped our hearts out to hear that."

Gosh, Michael thought. *Sorry if this was hard for* you.

"Of course it was nothing of the sort. We sent you a letter at the time, trying to explain why we did what we did. Did you not get it, or not understand it, or . . . ?"

Michael closed his eyes and pressed his memory into action. Did he remember a letter from his birth parents? He did not.

"Anyway, looking back, I guess what we told you in that long-ago letter was just the part of the thing a boy your age could understand. There's probably more to it—all our failings and none of your own. It's just so heartbreaking to think you might be holding on to wrong ideas about it after all these years, and we wonder if you might be open to meeting with us, now that you're an adult. I promise you we'd be completely honest in every respect about why that whole disaster played out the way it did.

"I'll put our phone number below, or you can just write back.

"With love and more apologies than I could possibly fit into a letter,

"Your mom and dad,

"Olivia and Miles Costa"

Below that she had written a phone number.

Michael threw the letter on the floor and stomped on it. The soles of his shoes marked it with dirt and tread imprints.

"You are *not* my mom and dad!" he shouted at the letter.

He left it on his bedroom rug and found his real mom in the kitchen. She was mixing a meat loaf with her hands. She looked up at him, and her face changed when she took in his expression.

"Did you know who that letter was from when you left it on my bed?"

"Honey, I don't read your mail," she said. "Who was it from?"

"Those people."

"I'm sorry, baby. You're going to have to narrow it down more than that."

"The people who gave birth to me and then threw me away."

"Oh." Her hands stopped moving in the gooey egg-and-ground-beef mixture. "*Those* people. I don't think it's fair to say they threw you away. Your father and I are a lot better than a trash can."

"Of course you are. I didn't mean it like that. They said they sent me a letter. You know. Way back at the time. But I have no memory of a letter. Do you?"

"Oh, yes," she said. She had begun wiping her hands on a paper towel, even though the meat loaf was clearly not properly mixed. "There was definitely a letter."

"What happened to it?"

"Well, I don't know, dear. At first you wouldn't go near it at all. You just kept saying you didn't want it. You said they didn't want you so you didn't want them. But then you turned on a dime and took it. For later, you said. I have no idea what happened to it after that."

But as she spoke, Michael knew. The knowing came in the form of a visual memory. In a stall in the boys' room at school, watching the tiny pieces of torn paper swirling in the bowl as he tried to flush them. Coming up with the water level instead of going down as intended.

"Never mind," he said. "It's gone."

"What did they say this time?"

"They want to meet me and explain in person."

"Are you going to do it?"

"Absolutely not," Michael said.

He turned, stomped back to his room, and slammed the door. He grabbed the letter off his rug and threw it in the bathroom trash. Then he flopped on the bed, hoping the cat would come and talk to him. But his mood was apparently still causing her to keep her distance.

In time he heard a light, tentative knock on the door.

"What?" he shouted.

"May I come in?"

"I guess," he said, his voice softer.

She came in and sat on the edge of his bed and brushed the hair off his forehead with her fingers.

"I know how you feel about them, Michael," she said. "But just hear me out. The way you talked about them in your film was just so hard to hear, because it showed us you still have so much anger and so much hurt that you're having to deal with. Maybe it's time to find out why they really let you be adopted. You know. Put some of those old child-size ideas to rest."

He opened his mouth to argue, but she put a finger to his lips to shush him.

"Don't answer now," she said. "We all know what your answer is now. Just think about it. Not for a few minutes. For a few weeks, or a few months. Sit with the feelings and see if they change. If you decide to do it, you'll be doing it for yourself, not for them."

She took her finger back, leaned in, and kissed him on the forehead. Then she let herself out.

———

The following day while he was at school she cleaned his room.

When he got home, he noticed she had emptied the bathroom trash. But the letter from his birth parents hadn't gone out with the rest of the bathroom garbage.

It was lying—looking quite stomped-on and disrespected—in the middle of his bed.

He put it in the drawer of his bedside table, alongside Caroline's phone number. It had become his equivalent of filing things under the heading of "I don't want that, but other people think I might someday."

———

"I used to talk to Madeleine about things like this," Michael said, "and she always gave me such good advice."

"And it must be very hard that you can't talk to her now," Dunning said.

They were sitting at their usual table in the coffee shop in the student union. Drinking their usual drinks.

"You have no idea," Michael said.

"I've lost people."

It hit Michael, as a sinking feeling in his gut, what a colossal mistake he had just made.

"Oh crap. Of course you have. I'm so sorry. You lost your whole family. And here I am talking like I'm the only one who knows loss. And there you are being all calm about reminding me, instead of slapping me halfway across the room like you had every right to do."

"Partly I took it as a figure of speech. Partly I know how isolating it is to be in the middle of losing someone. It's hard to imagine that other people know how you feel. I'm no substitute for her, of course, but I don't mind your talking to me about things like this, if it helps."

"What do you think I should do? You think I should hear their side of the story?"

Dunning sipped his espresso, which was clearly still too hot.

"I think I want to be careful not to overpower your own thoughts on the matter, or drive them off track. But if you're asking what *I* would do . . ."

Then he left a space for Michael to fill.

"I am. That's exactly what I'm asking. What would you do if you were me?"

"I would hear them out. Maybe not today. Maybe not next week. But I think I would."

"Because . . . ?"

"Because you have some old notions of what happened, and they're not a very happy part of your life. And I honestly don't think they're serving you, so go ahead and debunk them. I guarantee you it's more complicated than eight-year-old Michael perceived it to be. And also because, in this life, it seems to follow almost without exception that our regrets are made up of the things we didn't do. Almost any mistake can be lived with, because you gave it a shot. But we regret the chances we let go by."

If only I had spit on Hitler when I had the chance, Michael thought. He knew it was a paraphrasing of the original statement, but still he heard the sentence in Rex Aronfeld's voice.

"You know who I'd really like to talk to?" Michael said. "My brother. I'm kind of mad at him too. But I have a feeling he blames himself for the accident. And he does bear some blame, at least from what he told the police, but not all of it. Anyway, he was just a kid too. It's my parents who were supposed to be in charge of things. I'd just like to hear his side of the story. You know. How it felt to get to go home when I didn't."

"Fine. Start by talking to your brother."

"I have no idea where he is."

"But they undoubtedly do. And you said they gave you their phone number. So call them up and say you may or may not be ready to talk to them at some future date, but in the meantime you want to talk to . . . what did you say his name was?"

"Thomas."

"Right. Tell them you want to talk to Thomas."

"Thanks," Michael said. "I have this weird idea in the back of my brain that Madeleine would have said pretty much the same thing."

———

Michael did not call them. He tried to force himself to do it. Twice. But both times he got caught up in—and overwhelmed by—imaginings of the different ways the conversation could run out of his control.

Instead he sent them a note in the mail.

It was written on the bottom of their letter. He told himself he did that to save the trouble of finding a suitable piece of paper, but in the back of his mind he was aware that he enjoyed the mental image of them seeing how thoroughly he had stomped on their letter.

All he said was "Maybe someday. I would like to talk to Thomas, though."

So many weeks went by after mailing it that he dropped the whole idea in his mind and came to believe it would never happen. After all, that was his birth parents in a nutshell. What you expected them to do simply never materialized.

———

It was three months to the day after losing Madeleine when Michael got a text message from an unknown number.

"It's me," the text said. "Patricia."

He texted back, "I think you have the wrong number."

He watched the bubble of the other person typing for a minute or so.

"No, Michael, it's me. Madeleine's sister. You know it's been three months, right?"

"I'm painfully aware," he typed back.

"I promised her I'd get in touch with you in three months and see if you were dating again. She wanted you to be dating again."

"I'm painfully aware of that as well."

"Is that a no?"

"That's a no."

"Well, okay. But don't be surprised if you hear from me again in exactly another three months. I swear it's not in my nature to bug you, but she wanted this, and I promised."

"Yeah," Michael typed. "I know all about those promises."

She never replied. Or, in any case, she was saving her reply for exactly three months.

MICHAEL, AGE TWENTY AND A HALF

Chapter Twenty-One

When Too Much Is Not Too Much

It was a quiet two and a half months later when Michael got home from running to find an older, disheveled car idling in front of the house.

As he pulled level with it the driver leaned over, powered down the passenger window, and addressed Michael directly.

"Dude," the guy said. "Get in."

Michael backed up several steps and said nothing.

"Seriously. Dude. Get in. I don't have all day."

Michael backed up another step or two.

The guy was a handful of years older than Michael, with shoulder-length, thick, shaggy hair and a T-shirt with a frayed hole in one sleeve. He wore dark sunglasses and a backward baseball cap.

"I don't know who you are or what you want," Michael said, "but I have my phone in my hand and I've already hit the nine and the first one."

The man sighed deeply and pulled off his cap and sunglasses.

"Mike, you jerk. It's me."

But Michael still did not know who he was.

"Me who?"

"Me Tom."

"I don't know any guys named Tom."

"Tom your brother, idiot."

Michael stepped closer to the car for a better look. He didn't look much like the Thomas he'd known as a boy. Not enough so that Michael could have picked him out of a lineup. But if he tried hard he could almost see Thomas in there somewhere.

It struck Michael that Thomas had an advantage in recognizing him, as he had undoubtedly seen Michael's film.

He opened the passenger door of the car and got in.

They sat still a moment, staring at each other.

"Your personality hasn't changed at all," Michael said, "has it?"

"I was just thinking the exact same thing about you."

"You don't go by Thomas anymore?"

"No, why would I? Who *does* that? I mean, other than Mom and Dad. Makes you sound like you're walking around with a stick up your butt. I mean, you don't still go by Michael, right?"

"Yeah, I do."

"Yeah. I should've seen that one coming."

"Did you ever ask them why they were so into full names with no nicknames? I never got to ask."

"Maybe," Thomas said. "I don't know. 'Dignity and some kind of sense of self-worth, blah blah blah, yada yada.' You want to go get a cup of coffee or something?"

"Yeah, or something," Michael said.

———

As it turned out, Thomas's idea of "or something" consisted of a couple of frozen bananas with a nut-studded chocolate coating, purchased from a street vendor near the park.

Michael paid for both.

They walked as they talked, and Thomas had no issues about speaking with his mouth full.

"Here's the main thing I have to say to you," Thomas said.

Michael braced for some form of apology and said nothing in the waiting.

"You dodged a bullet."

Michael thought his brother might have been talking about the simple act of surviving, but he wasn't sure. And Thomas was still talking.

"You think I was lucky 'cause I got to go home. Ha! Some luck. I got pulled out of there twice more by Child Protective Services. I spent more time in foster homes than I did with them. And the rest of the time the county should've come and taken me away, but they just didn't know what our parents were up to."

"What were they doing?"

"Always the same stuff. Lots of drinks, lots of drugs. You're the lucky one. You landed in a home that actually made sense and held still, and you've gotten to be there all this time with people who take care of you."

"I don't know. My adoptive mom is one of those helicopter parents. I think she takes *too* good care of me."

"Oh boo-hoo," Thomas said. "That must be awful, to have someone take *too* good care of you. I'm just going to play tiny violins for you everywhere you go. Get a real set of problems before you start complaining, you know?"

They walked without talking for a time. Past the lily pads on the lake and the noisy fountain. Past kids on bicycles who rang the bells on their handlebars before passing.

Michael found he wasn't taking his brother's harsh words too seriously, because that was just Thomas. He had never spoken to Michael any other way. It was familiar. It was a known quantity, which carried an odd, conflicted sense of comfort.

"Why did you wait all these months without a word," Michael said, "and then just suddenly show up with no warning?"

He expected an emotionally revealing answer. Something about his brother's dread over facing the events of their past.

"I drive Uber," Thomas said. "And I almost never get up here. I had to drive somebody to, like, ten miles from here. I figured I'd take a shot. See if you were home."

"Oh."

They walked in silence again for a minute or two. Or three. It struck Michael as sad that he could go so many years without seeing his brother and still they would have nothing to say to each other.

"You could've just called."

"You said you wanted to see me."

"I thought I just said I wanted to talk to you."

"That's not the way I heard it, but it wouldn't be the first time our parents got something wrong."

Michael wanted to open the dreaded package of Thomas's involvement in that night, but he wasn't sure of the best way in. Or even if there *was* any good way to enter.

Thomas seemed to read his thoughts in the silence.

"Look, of course I'm sorry for what happened to you," he said. "I never meant for you to get hurt so bad you nearly died. Obviously I didn't. I didn't figure you were gonna throw yourself on the thing. You know? I mean, you were a dork of a little kid, but everybody knows better than to do crap like that."

"But you did something purposely, right? You told the police it was your fault."

"No, the *police* told *me* it was my fault. I told them I tricked you into stealing the rocket so we could go way down the beach and set it off. I didn't trick you into getting near it once it was lit. But they were all like, 'The first thing led to the second thing and blah blah, yada yada.' And I almost ended up in reform school for it. Meanwhile you got to go to a normal house with normal people. And I never quite got over that. I mean, Mom and Dad admitted they couldn't take care of you and you should be with someone who could. So what was I? Chopped liver? I didn't need taking care of? I didn't deserve a better place?"

"Whoa," Michael said.

It was all he could manage on the outside. But on the inside, he clearly saw something he had never understood before. Never even imagined before.

"Whoa what?"

"I'm not sure if I could even put it into words. But you wanted to go home. Right? They told me you wanted to go home."

"I was in a terrible foster home, so yeah. I wanted them to take me back. If I'd known they were never gonna get their act together maybe I would've just asked for a better foster home instead. Or . . . I don't know. Maybe I always would have wanted to go home because it was home and they were my parents. But now that I'm looking back, I feel like I could've done better. Maybe if it wasn't for all the bouncing around I wouldn't have had so many of the problems I've had in my life. Maybe I wouldn't have had to do time."

"What did you do time for? If it's okay to ask."

"Drugs."

"Seriously? After everything you watched our parents go through?"

"I don't know what to tell you, Mikey. You swear to yourself you're never going to be like them and then you turn around and look back and there you are. No idea how it even happened. Anyway, you should talk to them. They're not terrible people. They're kind of screwups, but they mean well. I know you think they didn't care about you, but Mom cried for weeks when you got adopted. She wanted to keep you. Dad pretty much put his foot down and said 'We can't do it. We just can't.' But they argued about it a lot. It wasn't just a thing they did without thinking, like they didn't even care."

"That's good to know, I guess."

Thomas's phone let out a sharp tone. He pulled it out of his pocket and stared at it, shielding its screen from the sunlight.

"That's it," he said. "I gotta go. I gotta pick up this guy again and take him back to LA. I'll drop you back, though. But we gotta hurry."

"Just go," Michael said. "It's okay. It's not far. I can walk."

———

When he got home, he found his mother in the kitchen, fixing dinner. Frying something at the stove.

"That was a long run," she said.

"I ran into somebody I used to know."

He walked up behind her and wrapped his arms around her waist, pulling her into a tight bear hug. He leaned around and kissed her on the cheek.

"Oh, my," she said, setting down her spatula and resting her hands on his arms. "What did I do to deserve that?"

"Took good care of me."

"I thought you were of the opinion that I hover too much. That I take *too* good care of you."

"Yeah, I guess I might have thought that on occasion," Michael said. "But it turns out that's not the worst thing that can happen to a guy."

———

"You seem so quiet and far away," she said over dinner. "Is anything wrong?"

"No, not really," he said. "I was just thinking."

She did not ask him *what* he was just thinking, which was progress for her. He decided to reward her restraint by volunteering the information.

"I was thinking maybe I really *should* sit down with my parents and hear what they have to say."

Both his mom and his dad set their forks down abruptly.

"I didn't mean my parents," Michael added quickly. "*You're* my parents. Obviously *you're* my parents. My birth parents, I meant to say."

"That's quite an about-face," his father said. "What brought on this change of heart, if it's okay to ask?"

"Actually . . . I had a conversation with Thomas."

"Oh," his mother said.

"It was a real eye-opener of a thing, talking to him."

"In what way, honey?"

"Well. You know how all those years I was upset because I felt like they wanted him but they didn't want me? Well, it turns out Thomas has been upset all this time because they recognized that I needed better care than they could give me, but they took him back and just sort of . . . didn't take care of him. So he's thinking 'What, he needs a good home with supervision and I don't?' And it makes sense from that point of view. It's like two totally different sides to the thing, but they both make sense. Apparently they never got clean for very long and he got taken away and put in foster homes a couple more times, and he's had a hard life because of it. Now I'm thinking I definitely got the better end of the deal."

His father picked up his fork again and resumed eating. His mother continued to lean on the heel of her hand and stare into Michael's face with fascination. And maybe a hint of trepidation.

"That's nice that you had a good talk with him."

"Oh, it wasn't a good talk," Michael said. Not surprisingly, that seemed to surprise her. "Not at all. He's a real jerk. He kind of always was, but somehow I thought he'd outgrow it. But he hasn't changed at all. I always pictured him racked with guilt about the accident, and I was all ready to let him off the hook. Turns out he let himself off the hook years ago. Or maybe he never thought he was on it. But still, it helped me, because the whole situation just looked so different to me after I talked to him. My whole past just looked different. It got me thinking that maybe I should talk to my birth parents and see how *that* changes the past. Only problem is, I don't have their number anymore. I sent them back that letter without writing it down. But I know they live in Duarte, and I thought it might be listed."

His father's fork stopped in midair on its way to his mouth. As though the family dinner were a video and someone had hit "pause."

He watched his parents exchange a glance with one another that was hard to read. It was followed by a tiny mutual nod.

"We have their number," his father said.

"Oh," Michael said. Then he had to take a few seconds to register how he felt about that. "I hope you're not going to tell me you've kept in touch with them all this time."

"No," his father said. "Absolutely not. Nothing like that. We hadn't spoken to them since the adoption. And then all of a sudden they got in touch with us a few months ago, right after they saw your film. They wanted us to arrange a meeting with you. We flat-out refused. We didn't want to get in the middle of a thing like that, and we didn't want to influence your thinking on the matter. We told them you were a grown man and if they wanted to speak to you they'd have to go directly to you."

"But you still have their number."

"We do."

"Okay then. I guess this is really happening."

It was the first time it had felt to Michael like a thing that would really happen. It set up a buzzing upset in his stomach that would prove slow to fade. He knew if he followed through on the idea fairly quickly it would be in an effort to make that awful feeling go away.

———

In spite of the buzzing upset, it took him three days to get up the nerve to call. When he did, his heart pounded as it rang, and he was flooded with relief when the call went to voicemail.

"If you're willing to make the drive up here," he said on the recorded message, "I'll sit down and hear you out. One dinner, in a public place. If I can't handle what I'm hearing I reserve the right to get up and walk away. If you can accept those conditions, call me back."

He realized after he'd hung up that he hadn't said who he was. But he didn't think it mattered much. He figured they'd know.

Chapter Twenty-Two

You Don't Know How Anyone Hurts

When he stepped into the restaurant, they were already there. He saw them immediately, and he knew them as soon as he saw them.

In some ways they had changed.

Of course they were older. Everyone is thirteen years older after a thirteen-year gap. But it hadn't changed their appearance all that much.

What had changed was Michael's sense of their size and power. They looked smaller in stature than he remembered. They did not look invincible and strong. They looked vulnerable, lost, and more than a little bit scared.

They jumped to their feet when they saw him approach the table.

"Michael," his birth mother said.

"Mrs. Costa," he said. "Mr. Costa."

He sat.

He had planned and rehearsed the greeting to make it ever so clear that he did not see them as his real parents. Still, it came out more formal and colder than he could have imagined.

"Look at you!" Livie said. "So handsome!"

She reached out a hand to touch the hair falling onto his forehead. Probably to brush it aside. He flinched away involuntarily, and her hand missed. And she never touched him.

"Can we just—" he began. But he could find no ending to that sentence. "I hardly know you."

Her face fell. Crumbled, in fact. It reminded him of those videos of demolition crews bringing down a building. The way the structure implodes on itself.

"How can you say that, Michael? I grew you in my womb."

"Yeah, well, that was a long time ago, wasn't it?"

"We raised you for seven years."

"Did you? Did you really? Or were Thomas and I just sort of hanging around the house and, as luck would have it, nothing terrible happened to us until the night it did?" As the statement wrapped up, Michael realized he was on his feet, though he honestly didn't remember standing. It felt as though his anger had an energy, a buoyancy, that had brought him upright. "I don't think this is working out for me," he said. "I think I'm just going to go."

"Please, Michael," she said. "We drove for hours. Please hear us out."

The energy drained away, and he sank back into his chair, missing the safety of his anger.

"Look, I don't mean to be cruel," he said. "Honestly. I don't. I didn't come here to try to lash out at you. But I'm just on edge, and this is hard for me. Can we just . . . you had something you wanted to say to me, so please just go ahead and say it."

But at that moment a waiter appeared at their table to take drink orders.

"The wife and I will have this local merlot," Miles said. "This one is too young to drink."

"I'll have an iced tea," Michael said.

When the waiter had picked up the wine lists and left, Michael couldn't help taking the conversation in a new direction.

"You're drinking?"

"Just wine," Livie said.

"I thought you quit drinking."

"We didn't have a problem with *wine*," Miles said. "Mostly drugs, and sometimes the hard liquor we tended toward when we were using them. This is not even hard liquor."

"Liquor is liquor," Michael said. "It's all the same."

"It's not all the same. Allow me to educate you, son. Wine only has about twelve percent alcohol. Hard liquor has forty percent."

"Let me educate *you*," Michael said. "A shot of hard alcohol is about one or one and a half ounces. A glass of wine is about five ounces. Do the math."

"I thought you wanted to hear what we had to say."

"Fine," Michael said. "Talk."

It actually was an important part of the picture to him, whether they had ever genuinely gotten sober. It felt relevant. But it was not as though anybody could change anybody else's thinking about a thing like that.

For a moment a powerful silence fell around the table. Almost fell *onto* the table, from the feel of it. Michael thought it had a thumping quality to the way it landed, but he knew that was only his imagination.

"You deserved to be with people who could take care of you," Livie said.

"But you had two sons. Thomas didn't deserve that?"

"Hoo boy," Miles said. "Somebody's been talking to Thomas."

"It's a good thing for you I *did* talk to Thomas. The only reason I'm here is because he told me she cried for weeks after I was adopted. He didn't tell me anything nearly so comforting about you. He said you insisted you couldn't keep me. But Thomas you could keep."

"Thomas is very different from you," Livie said.

"He's an ass," Miles interjected. The statement was followed by a grunt of pain that suggested he had been kicked under the table.

"He's your son," Livie said.

"The two are not mutually exclusive."

"Just hush for a minute, Miles. For once in your life just be quiet. I'm trying to talk to Michael." She turned her full attention on him.

"From the time you were born, you weren't like Thomas. He was tough. He took care of himself. You were more sensitive than he was. You needed more. You hurt at a much deeper level."

"You have no idea how other people hurt," Michael said. "None of us do. You only know what they tell you about it, or what they let you see."

The waiter arrived with their bottle of wine and Michael's iced tea. "Are we ready to order?" he asked.

Miles said "Yes" and Livie said "No" at almost exactly the same time.

"We could use a minute," she said.

When he'd left, she turned her full attention onto Michael again, and it nearly burned.

"I told you we'd be completely honest and tell you some of the parts of the thing we wouldn't have told an eight-year-old. So here goes. We got clean in jail—of course, what choice did we have?—and we stayed clean for what we hoped would be long enough to get you kids back. But we honestly didn't expect it would last. We'd already done time for child endangerment. What if something else had happened to you? What if we'd turned our backs for a split second and some other terrible thing had happened? It wouldn't have been our first offense. We could have gone to prison for years."

"And . . . ?" Michael began, hoping she'd follow him there.

"And what?"

"And something terrible would have happened to me."

"Oh. Of course, honey, of course. That goes without saying. It wasn't all about us. We were terrified that something would happen to you because suddenly it seemed like it would. Before, we always figured nothing would happen to you kids because it never had. All of a sudden you seemed so vulnerable. Like it would be so easy for you to be killed."

The waiter appeared near their table, took a quick scan of their faces, and peeled away again.

"Pretty much flesh and blood like everybody else," Michael said.

"I'm talking about the things a person's subconscious tells them."

"You're forgetting the obvious other option," Michael said. "You could have actually stopped drinking and using and been parents to us. But you didn't do that, did you? You gave me away!"

The last sentence came out too loudly, and nearby diners fell silent and craned their necks to look.

A woman of about sixty leaned over from the table behind him and tapped him on the shoulder.

"I know this is none of my business," she said, "and I promise to butt out if you ask me to. But a lot of times parents give up a baby for very unselfish reasons."

It was a stunningly inappropriate thing for a stranger to say, and he had to work to absorb and then push through the strangeness of the moment.

Michael felt his gaze harden. His face felt set hard. When he spoke, his voice came out hard.

"I was eight," he told her.

"Oh," the woman said.

She turned back to her dinner companions without further comment, and Michael did his best to shake off the odd distraction.

"You're forgetting a very important element," Miles said. "You had medical needs. You needed surgeries. You'd already had three surgeries and you needed at least four more."

"I know all about the surgeries," Michael said. "I was there. I think they were more trouble for me than they would have been for you."

"You're missing the point, honey," Livie said. "We had no insurance."

For a moment Michael only held still and let that sink in.

"You had two kids and no insurance? How did I get the first three surgeries? How was I in the hospital for weeks?"

"We had Medi-Cal," she said. "The whole time you boys were little we were low-income enough to qualify for Medi-Cal. But then in that year when you were in the foster home, your father got a better job, and it paid more. And it took us up just over the limit. We lost our Medi-Cal, but we couldn't possibly have afforded to pay for all your medical stuff out of pocket. And the job didn't come with insurance. You needed a lot. What could we have done? We couldn't just take you back and not follow up on your care. You needed it."

"And what about Thomas? What if he'd gotten sick or had an accident?"

"Well, we got lucky," Miles said, "and he didn't."

The waiter reappeared and this time dared to approach them.

The Costas both ordered prime rib. Michael, who had completely lost his appetite, ordered fettuccine Alfredo, because it was his mother's favorite. He figured he could pick at it and bring the rest home to her.

Meanwhile Michael could feel himself losing the last of the clean, powerful anger that had shielded him through the early parts of the meeting. Not because the Costas had convinced him that they were good people who had done the right thing, but because he had accepted, on a deep level, that they weren't and they hadn't. They had been a mess when he was growing up, they were still a mess, and it had nothing to do with him.

He remembered Thomas saying, "They're kind of screwups, but they mean well."

The deficiency was theirs.

"Okay," he said when the waiter had left. "I know you want me to say I forgive you. Fine. Here goes. I forgive you. Except I don't honestly mean that. I mean it like an intention, but it doesn't match with how I'm feeling. Maybe years from now it will, but I don't expect to see you again, so I'm putting it out there now, and I'll try to step up to it. You did your best, and it was not great, but it was what you could manage. But just so you know, to the extent that I'm forgiving you, I'm forgiving you more for myself than for you. I don't want to carry all this stuff around anymore. I've been doing it for too long and I'm tired. Does that help you at all?"

"It feels like a start," Livie said.

"No. It's not a start. It's the whole thing. It's everything I have for you, and to me it feels like a lot. It's more than I ever thought I could manage. This is not the beginning of a relationship for us. I'm hearing you out, I'm forgiving you. It's a onetime deal. After this I plan to get on with my life."

Then he just sat. Still and silent. Waiting. A nagging feeling at the back of his brain questioned whether what he'd said was too harsh, even under the circumstances.

"I guess it's still better than what we had before," Miles said.

———

"What are you going to do next?" Livie asked him while he picked at his food.

"In what respect?"

"You're going to make another movie, right?"

"Well, yeah."

"What about?"

"I have absolutely no idea."

He picked a little more. Livie stuffed her mouth with prime rib and spoke while still chewing.

"When Miles and I watched it, we were shocked."

"Because people took their clothes off in it?"

"Oh no, not that. We're all for that. Seeing your chest and stomach, I mean. We heard about it, and we tried to picture it. And we knew you almost died. But to actually see the damage it did to you, and how bad it still was all these years later. It just made the whole thing very real. You're not touching your food. Are you not hungry?"

"I lost my appetite a long time ago," he said. "Pretty much as I came through the door."

Michael flagged down the waiter as he passed the table and asked for his food to be wrapped to go.

"I'm not sure what to make of what you just told me," he said to Livie. "Are you saying I look totally awful compared to what you imagined, or are you saying the whole time I was fighting for my life it never felt very real to you?"

"So sensitive," Miles said. "It was a perfectly reasonable comment she made."

"It really wasn't," Michael said.

"You're too sensitive."

"Or maybe you're not sensitive enough," Michael said, heady with the freedom of being able to say what he felt. "Whenever I hear anybody tell anybody else they're too sensitive, all I hear is 'I want to feel free to say offensive things to you and it really inconveniences me when you mind.'"

"We can't win with you."

"Leave him alone, Miles," Livie said. "I'm sorry if that came out wrong, Michael. I didn't mean you look terrible. I mean . . . Well, it *is* shocking. Very hard to look at. But I didn't mean to insult you."

Michael sat in silence and felt each of her observations like punches raining down on him in a boxing ring. He wordlessly acknowledged that it simply *was* that way with them. That it always *would* be that way with them.

"But to be honest," she said, "it kind of *didn't* feel real. I mean, I'm sorry, but that's just the truth. We never saw any of it with our own eyes. It felt different to see it. I don't know how to explain it any better than that. But it was a good film. We were so proud of you."

He wanted to tell her that it wasn't right to be proud, because pride suggested some connection to the achievement. He didn't tell her that. He was exhausted, and completely beyond thinking anything he said would change them. He just wanted to get his to-go bag for his mom and head home.

When the waiter arrived with the bag, he rose.

"I'm just going to take off," he said.

"So soon?" Miles asked.

"I feel like we're just small-talking now. I heard what you had to say. Now I just want to go home."

He stood quietly for a moment, hoping they would say something. "Goodbye," or words to that effect. Something that would clear him emotionally to go.

After a few more awkward beats Miles said, "You're leaving us with the check?"

Michael felt his mouth fall open.

"You thought *I* was buying *you* dinner?"

"Well. You're a big-time moviemaker now."

"I'm a college student."

"You sold a film to Netflix."

"For seven hundred and fifty dollars. Months ago."

"Oh. I thought they paid a lot better than that."

"It's a documentary short. It's a miracle they even license them."

Miles offered no response. He seemed moored to his position.

Michael sighed. He pulled his wallet out of his back pocket and fished out a twenty and a ten and dropped them on the table.

"This should cover mine," he said.

"Wait, honey," Livie said. "Please don't go away mad. Isn't there anything else I can do for you?"

Pick up the check, he thought. *This was all your idea.*

But all he said was "Just give me Thomas's number and we're good."

"I don't have anything to write with."

"Here. Just put it in my phone."

She entered the number with one thumb and handed the phone back to him.

"I'm sorry this didn't go well," she said.

"It went a lot better than I thought it would."

Michael almost said *See you,* but he wouldn't see them. He was tempted to say *Have a nice life,* but it sounded too dismissive and cold.

"Anyway, thanks for telling me what really happened," he said.

Then he walked to his car and headed home.

———

He called Thomas from a stoplight and set the call to speaker.

As he waited for the light to turn—and for his brother to pick up the call—a hard rain let go, beading up on his windshield and giving the world a pebbly, muted appearance. The sound of it drumming on the roof of his car reminded him of the afternoon Madeleine died. It was a sensation something like being stabbed.

The light turned, and he drove, the phone sitting faceup on his thigh.

"Hello?" Thomas's voice said.

"It's Michael."

Michael switched on the windshield wipers against the downpour.

"Michael who?"

"Your brother."

"Oh. How'd you get this number?"

"Don't worry. I won't call you again after tonight. I just wanted to tell you this one thing. It wasn't about you, the way it went down all those years ago. It had nothing to do with you. They didn't judge one of us more worthy of care than the other. They were just scared of me. Of all the surgeries I needed, and how they would pay for it, and going to jail for decades if anything else ever happened to me. They thought nothing would ever happen to you because nothing ever did, and that I would keep blowing up and nearly dying because I had already. Because they were using this sort of reptile part of their brain instead of their logic. We both felt like they cared about the other more, but actually they cared about themselves more than anybody. It was never a reflection on us. They're just screwups. You said so yourself. They would have kept me and ignored me too if they hadn't been afraid they wouldn't get away with it. It was never about our value in any way."

The line was silent when he finished talking. For five seconds, then ten. Then twenty.

He turned up the speed of the wipers, but they still barely kept up.

"Are you even still there?" he asked Thomas.

"Yeah, I'm here."

"Okay. And your thoughts are . . . ?"

"I'm not sure about any of what you just said, but I guess it's pretty nice that at least you would call me and say it."

Chapter Twenty-Three

The Things We'll Do to Appease a Ghost

He drove to the house where he'd spent so much time with Madeleine. But as he pulled in, he proceeded cautiously. There might be someone else living there now.

There were no cars in the driveway.

He rang the doorbell, thinking if there was a tenant he could simply ask his or her permission to sit a minute on the grounds.

It was exactly three days short of the six-month anniversary of her death, and the finality of the whole thing was weighing heavily on him. And in three days Patricia would get in touch again. This time he could see it coming, and he had a chance to think about what he might report.

No one answered the door.

He walked around to the patio on the backyard side and looked through the sliding glass window, through the kitchen and into the big living room. The furniture was all covered, the drop cloths layered with dust.

He sat down on the patio, the way they had done together so many times.

The sky was a clear, brilliant blue with a few faint wisps of clouds here and there, like stretched cotton. He half expected Lily the cat to come warbling through the yard to greet him, but of course she was at his house now.

He dropped his head back and closed his eyes.

"I'm only doing this for you," he said in the direction of the sky.

Then he took out his phone and called Caroline.

She picked up on the second ring.

"Caroline?"

"Who's calling, please? I don't know this number. I almost didn't pick up because I didn't recognize your number."

"It's Michael Woodbine."

The statement was met with a brief silence.

"Wait, really? This is not a joke?"

"Why would I joke about a thing like that?"

"I have some friends who would. They're always laughing at me because I talk about you too much. But it's really you?"

"Definitely me," he said.

"I didn't think you'd call. You didn't for months, so I just figured you never would. Did you want to talk to someone about Madeleine?"

"No," he said, and pressed his eyes closed again. "Well. Yes. Maybe. Maybe at some point it would be nice to talk about her, if you're open to that. But that's not why I called. I called to ask you out."

"On a date?"

"Yeah. That kind of out."

"Then you're feeling ready to date again."

"No."

"Oh. I figured if you're asking me out on a date it's because you're feeling a little better about losing Madeleine."

"Not really, no. I'm still having a pretty hard time with it. Okay, here goes. Full disclosure here. Before she died I promised her I would date again. And her sister promised her she would check up on me every three months to make sure I kept my promise. And in three days it will have been six months. Now I'm starting to have to think about what I'm going to tell her this time. I mean, not only is she checking up on me, but in a weird sort of way I feel like Madeleine is too. Despite the fact that I know that's impossible. It just feels that way sometimes. But I totally get that this is all very weird, and if you want nothing to do with any of it I'll understand."

A pause. While he waited, birds sang in the trees. Maybe they'd been singing all along and he had only just snapped into the moment enough to notice. Probably they had been.

"Wait, wait, wait," she said. "Let me see if I have this straight. You want to go out with me one time because it'll get a ghost and her sister off your case."

"No. Not at all. That's not it at all. And it's my own fault, because I'm doing a bad job of explaining myself to you. So let me try again, please. No, I don't want to go out with you only once. I want to take a genuine shot at dating again, even though I don't feel ready. Partly because of something Mr. Dunning said. He said sometimes you have to do a thing called 'fake it till you make it.' He called it a saying for people who like their advice to rhyme. I guess the idea is that if you keep saying or doing something, your subconscious kind of . . . catches up to the idea. And also because I'm not sure how much I still believe in the whole concept of waiting until you're ready to do something. I mean, are we ever really ready? It seems to me that sometimes the only way to do something is just to do it, and the ready comes later. I think a person could waste a whole life waiting until this unfamiliar thing they're afraid of doing feels like a thing they can do. So I'm asking you out. But again, I know it's weird, and if you tell me to go to hell I promise I won't blame you one bit."

A long silence fell. Long enough that he began to be encouraged, simply because she hadn't said no *yet*. He had assumed it would be a quick no.

"You know what?" she said after a time. "I can actually deal with that. I only have one stipulation. No, not even a stipulation. That's too formal and weird. A request. I'd love to go on a date with you, but not to a restaurant. Is that okay?"

"Sure, I guess. I'll think of something else."

"See?" she said, her voice more relaxed now. Almost playful. "I can be weird too."

"At this point," he said, "you're almost obligated to try to keep up with me in that regard."

———

The following day was a Saturday, and he picked her up at eleven thirty in the morning.

"Broad daylight," she said as she got into his car. "Bold choice."

"The things I want to do don't work well in the dark."

"I guess I'm glad to hear that, since we hardly know each other."

He pulled away from the curb, and they drove in silence for a time. A mile maybe.

She was wearing a bright-yellow sweater, and offered him quick smiles that seemed to come naturally—that seemed to spring up and out of her rather than being dredged up on purpose. He wasn't used to that. Madeleine had smiled at him from time to time, usually in a way that had made his bones turn to jelly. But it was never a spontaneous and easy-looking thing like Caroline's smiles.

Then again, Caroline wasn't dealing with having her life prematurely ripped away.

"I *feel* like I know you, though," she said.

"Yeah, that's the weird thing about making a film like the one I made. People feel like they know me inside and out, but at the same time I don't know them at all. Happens all the time. I'm trying to get used to it, but it's still weird."

"Sorry," she said.

"Don't be. No apologies. Mr. Dunning taught me a lot about how to look at situations like that. He told me both parties are just being human. He said something like . . . he wasn't going to step out from under shame or apologies without at least offering an escape path to the other party."

"I like that," she said.

"Help me catch up," he said. "Tell me about you."

"Okay. Let's see. I come from a very big family. Lots of brothers and a sister. I'm in my third year at the state university, and after that I'm hoping to get into law school."

"Ah, a lawyer," he said. "You can make a good living doing that."

"No, not the way I'd be doing it. I don't want to be one of those high-priced attorneys. I want to be one of the ones people can go to when they can't afford the good-living ones. I'll probably never be rich."

"Maybe not financially."

They drove in silence for several minutes, during which he glanced over at her face a couple of times. Because it was a nice face.

"How far are we going?" she asked after a time.

"Maybe another five or ten minutes. I'm taking us to that big park on the other side of town."

"Wait. Don't you live near the college?"

"I do."

"Isn't there a nice little park in your neighborhood? How far do you live from that?"

"Ten blocks."

"Why not that park?"

"Too many trees," he said.

"You don't like trees?"

"I love trees. But kites don't love trees. Trees love kites, but for all the wrong reasons. They like to eat them for lunch."

"Oh, you brought a kite!"

"I brought two kites. That way we not only have to keep them in the air, we have to keep them from getting tangled up with each other. It's more challenging that way."

"I like a good challenge."

"You'd almost have to," he said, "or you never would have said yes to this date after the way I asked you."

———

"This is unbelievable," he said. "I've never seen the weather play a trick anything like this."

He had taken the kites out of the trunk, and by the time he had set them up and attached them to their string reels, the wind had died. Just completely died.

"It *was* pretty sudden," she said.

"Well." Michael dropped both hands—each one containing a kite—to his sides. "I guess we could eat and see if it comes back."

"Oh, there's food."

"Yeah, of course there's food. I wouldn't invite you out right before lunchtime and then not feed you." He put the kites away in the trunk and began to pull out the bag of food. Then he stopped suddenly, bag in midair. "Wait. It's okay if the food is *from* a restaurant, right?"

"Of course. I'm sorry if I was weird."

"No, it's okay. It's good. If you can be, then I can be."

He found them a nice spot on the grass and spread out a plaid blanket. She sat, and he began unpacking the sandwiches.

"That looks like a lot of food," she said.

"I based my choices on what you told me you do and don't like to eat, but then I got insecure about my decisions and I ended up getting four sandwiches, just to make sure we'd end up with something you'd want."

She chose the avocado and tomato with sprouts, and Michael picked the egg salad.

He spread out paper plates and napkins, and for a while they ate without talking.

"You're going to make another film," she said. "Right?"

"Yeah, I guess. I mean, yeah. I am. I pretty much have to. It seems to be what I do now."

"What's the subject matter?"

"I've been getting that question a lot lately," he said. "And unfortunately I have absolutely no idea."

"Oh."

That left things hanging for a minute or two.

"Partly it's because the last one came to me so naturally," he said. "I mean, it was just *there*. And I always knew it was so right. And I'm not sure there's another idea that's such a good fit for me. I just don't know if another one exists. That might have been one of a kind. And, also, I feel like I need to rest from this one. It's been so intense. So much around it that was unexpected."

"Say more about that."

"I guess . . ." he began. "I guess it's hard to put into words. When I made it, I never thought anybody would see it. Of course I didn't. Why would I? It was a beginner film for a college class. And then when I realized people would watch it, I pictured them all being strangers. I didn't think about my mother watching it. I didn't think about people from my past coming out of the woodwork because of it. I didn't think about people like you, who were strangers when they watched it, but maybe wouldn't be strangers later on, and how much they would know about me going in."

She chewed her sandwich and seemed to think about that for a few seconds.

"Maybe the problem," she said, "is thinking the next one has to be just as personal."

"Say more about that," Michael said, borrowing her phrase.

"Well. The documentary filmmaker looks around at the world and finds a subject that needs exposing. Right? Maybe it's something they know from personal experience, but it doesn't have to be."

Oddly, he realized, he had not thought of that. He had pictured another idea wrenched squirming from the depths of his soul or nothing at all.

"It *would* be a relief to make a film about somebody else's situation for a change." He looked up and around at the sky. The clouds were thick and billowing, and intensely white. The wind was absolutely still. "Still not a kite day," he said.

"No. But the clouds are the kind you can stare at until you start to see shapes in them. You did that as a kid, right?"

"Not really."

"Oh, you're in for a treat. As soon as we've put away these sandwiches, I'm going to rock your world. G-rated version."

———

"That one looks like the roadrunner from the cartoons," he said, pointing at the sky.

"It totally does!"

They were lying on their backs on the blanket, side by side, their shoulders a respectful few inches apart. The clouds looked nearly solid, like something you'd be afraid to fly a plane through, and the shapes were endless.

"Look, it even has that weird little topknot on its head," she said. "Or whatever you call that. And the one long, awkward leg sticking out like it's running."

"Actually I think it's called a crest," he said.

"How did you know that?"

"I'm not sure. I must have read it somewhere."

"Can I tell you a story?"

"Of course," he said.

But for a moment she didn't, so he said more.

"A true story? Or a fanciful story about cloud shapes?"

"Oh, definitely a true story," she said.

"Okay. Tell away."

"From the time I was seventeen to the time I was nineteen, I had a boyfriend."

He wasn't going to say anything, for fear of seeming to interrupt her. But then she stalled for so long that he felt he needed to weigh in.

"That's a long relationship at that age. I mean . . . isn't it?"

"Oh, very. It was very unusual. We were talking about our future together. The other girls, you didn't even have time to ask how it was going with their boyfriends because it was already gone. I'd ask them how the guy was and they'd be like, 'Please. That was so last week.' Anyway. His name was Jeremy. I thought he was the one, and that we'd get married and have children and spend our whole lives together. And then on our second Valentine's Day, he took me to this nice restaurant, which was kind of a big deal, because neither of our parents had money. We never went to restaurants with our families, either one of us. I have seven brothers and a sister. We were lucky to be able to afford to eat at home. And we'd never gone to one together. But he had a part-time job, and he saved up to do it. Not a particularly fancy place, but a real restaurant, with nice tablecloths, and candlelight. He had a motorcycle. And after this nice dinner he drove me home on the back of his motorcycle, and he walked me to the front porch and kissed me good night, because my parents were inside keeping an eye on things. And I remember when he got back on the bike he gave me the funniest wave. I can see it in my head when I close my eyes, but I'm not sure I can describe it. It was like this big fancy gesture with his arm like a conductor would do in a cartoon. And I laughed and I laughed, and then I went back in the house. And I never saw Jeremy again."

"He left you?"

"In a manner of speaking. He got seven blocks down my street and was going through an intersection and a guy in a one-ton truck ran a stop sign without even touching the brake. Hit the bike, threw him clear of it. Ran over the bike. And by the time he'd managed to stop the truck he'd run over Jeremy."

She stopped talking, and Michael didn't start for a minute. He had to let her words move into—and through—him, and settle.

"You didn't tell me that when we first met."

"I don't generally tell anybody that the first time I meet them."

"Right, but . . . that was when I told you Madeleine had just died. I would have thought you would have told me as a way of saying you knew how I felt."

"I hated it when people did that to me, though. Everybody was always trying to tell me they knew how I felt. I didn't believe for a second that they did, and even if they did I'm not sure how that was helpful. I mean, does anybody really know how anybody else feels? You have no idea how it felt to me to lose someone in the time it takes to blink. I have no idea how it felt to you to watch the life drain out of somebody you love in dribs and drabs, a little bit more every day. Anyway. I thought if I told you that story it would help you understand some things you might've thought were weird."

They stared up at the clouds together while Michael tried to piece together what he was supposed to understand. When it hit him, it hit him from nowhere, and all at once.

"Oh. I get it. That's why you didn't want to have a date in a restaurant."

"I know it's just a silly superstition. And it's not like something I can't get beyond. It was more like . . . first dates are kind of nerve-racking anyway, especially if it's with someone special. I just figured, why add one more thing to stress about?"

"I'm sorry you had to lose Jeremy."

"I'm sorry you had to lose Madeleine."

They gazed at the clouds for a moment longer. Michael saw one that looked like a turtle, but he didn't say so. It seemed like too frivolous a thing to talk about now.

He felt her slip her hand into his.

"Is this okay?" she asked.

"Yeah. It's okay."

"So, anyway, if we have a second date, we can go to a restaurant. If you want. And I mean, if you even want to have a second date. I don't mean to assume."

"Oh, I definitely think we should have a second date," he said.

Then he pointed out the turtle.

Other cloud shapes followed.

Chapter Twenty-Four

What We Hold in the Palm of Our Hand

Their second date was the following Friday night. Six days later. That put it several days past the dreaded six-month anniversary of his loss. Oddly, Patricia had not texted or called.

Their second date was in a restaurant.

"How are you feeling so far?" he asked her over breadsticks.

"Good."

But she didn't look good.

"Really?"

"No. Actually not great. But I didn't want to say so because I didn't want you to think I was some kind of basket case."

"You shouldn't blame yourself for things like that. It's evolutionary."

"Say more about that."

The waiter arrived, accidentally interrupting the conversation. Michael ordered fettuccine Alfredo. Caroline ordered eggplant parmesan.

"I just read a book about this in the last couple of months," he said when the waiter had left. "Short version—our brains evolved to help us not be eaten by a dinosaur. Let's say we were walking by this particular big rock and a dinosaur jumped out and tried to eat us. If we're lucky enough to survive the experience, our brain is going to go on high alert every time we pass that rock. It's not ideally helpful, because the dinosaur could definitely be behind a different rock next time, but it's there to try to help us. And we all seem to want to beat ourselves up for it, which is silly, because it's just the way all brains work. Here's where I found it really helpful. Mr. Dunning told me not to read the reviews of my film. Good ones or bad ones. He said the good ones would make me think I'm better than I actually am, and the bad ones would make me think I made a bad film, when in fact films are not objectively good or bad. They're a matter of taste."

She paused in the eating of her breadstick, holding it like a magic wand.

"There were bad reviews of your film? How is that even possible?"

"There are bad reviews of everything. There's literally no project in the arts that everyone uniformly agrees is good or bad. Ideally you judge not by each review but by the balance. And my balance was good. Maybe five in a hundred were critical in some way, and sometimes in a pretty small way even then."

"So you read them."

"Yeah. I was weak and I didn't follow the advice. I'd read twenty-five raves and then find one dismissive one, and that one bad one would be all I could think about for days. And then I started getting down on myself for that. Like, 'Oh, I'm such a negative person. Why can't I just let it go?' But it's evolutionary. Our brains evolved to put more weight on the negative, so we could survive. Let's say on the one hand you might have a chance at food, or a chance to mate, and on the other hand you could be eaten by a dinosaur. Our brain weights the negative more heavily, because if we get eaten it's game over, and we'll never get to find food or mate again. That changed my thinking about myself a lot. And now I think it's weird that we're all beating ourselves up for these things that are just literally what every human brain does."

He stopped talking. Took a sip of his water. She was chewing in a distant way, almost dreamily, he thought. She was wearing a deep-blue dress, and he found the color evocative. As though it were pulling some kind of emotion out of him.

"You're different from other guys," she said.

"So I've been told."

"I mean that in a good way, though."

The waiter brought their food. Michael waved away the cracked black pepper from a wooden mill as big as the waiter's arm. Caroline accepted the offer, and Michael was surprised by how long it took her to say "when." It was a lot of pepper.

"Can I tell you another story?" she asked when the waiter peeled away again.

"Of course."

"It's not as sad as the last one."

"Good. For your sake. I'd hate to think anything else that bad happened to you."

"I wanted to tell you this story last time, but it's not first-date material. It's actually not second-date material either, but I feel close to you, and I'm telling it anyway. Especially after what you just said. About how we judge ourselves for pretty normal things."

"Tell away," he said, and started in on his fettuccine.

"On our first Valentine's Day together, Jeremy got me this necklace." She lifted one hand to her collarbone and touched a small pearl pendant hanging there. "I got him a silver ring with a dragon etched on it. He had this thing about dragons. After the accident, his parents sent me the ring, because they thought I'd want to have it. I was going to put it on a chain and wear it around my neck, but first I had to get a chain, so in the meantime I just set the ring on my dresser. I went to bed that night, and when I woke up the next morning the dragon ring was lying in the palm of my hand."

Michael stopped chewing and felt his eyes go wide. He did not immediately comment.

"I was lying on my right side, so my right hand was on the bed, palm up. And the ring was just sitting there in the palm of my hand."

"How do you think that happened?"

"I don't have any way of knowing, and I guess I never will. I don't think it levitated there. I'm a little too down-to-earth for that. I don't think Jeremy's ghost took it off the dresser and set it there. I can think of two possible explanations. One, I got up and got it in my sleep, but I don't remember doing it. Which would be unlike anything I've ever done before. I sleep like the dead. I don't even roll around. And when I'm awake it's sudden and I know it. I'm either a hundred percent awake or a hundred percent asleep. But I can't swear for a fact that there wasn't some odd exception to the rule. Two, I guess maybe the cat could have been playing with it and brought it up onto the bed for some reason. And maybe I rolled over on it, and moved it out from under my hip or something because it was uncomfortable, and then went right back to sleep. But why would the cat care about that ring? There were dozens of little trinkets sitting around on that dresser, and she never showed any interest in any of them."

"Maybe it smelled like him."

"No. It couldn't have. He was wearing it when he had the accident. I don't want to go into too much detail while we're eating, but everything had to be thoroughly cleaned and disinfected before it was returned. I just feel like . . . I hope it doesn't sound silly, but even if there's a perfectly logical explanation for how it got there, it still felt completely significant."

"Like a message," Michael said.

"Right. Exactly. Did you ever feel like you got a message from Madeleine?"

"No. I wish I could say yes, but no. I think I'm not even all that open to it. I know that might sound strange, but I think I still feel a little bitter about losing her. People say to me, 'Oh, in a way she's still with you,' but she's not with me the way she was, the way I want her to be, and so I kind of reject the idea that any other ways count. And then I don't even know if I believe in that. No offense to you and your experience."

"None taken. I'm not even saying you *should* believe it. I didn't believe it either before the thing with the ring, and I'm not positive I believe it now. I get tired of people who tell me how sure they are about things like that—things they can't possibly know. I think the only real answer is just to say we don't know. Maybe it was nothing. Maybe it was something. I've just noticed since then how a lot of people have experiences like that after somebody dies. And a lot of them might have other explanations, like the UFOs that turn out to be weather balloons or swamp gas, but the stories are all so different and fascinating."

"Might even make an interesting documentary," he said.

Her eyes seemed to grow wider and brighter, and quite suddenly.

"You took the words right out of my mouth. But I didn't want to say it, because I think it might subject you to a lot of criticism. Most people would think it's kind of . . . you know. Out there."

"Not necessarily," he said. "I think there could be a right line to walk with it. If I acted like I knew what it all meant, or like I could prove something, I'm sure I'd be criticized. But if the stories were all as interesting as yours . . . I think the key would be to put it out without judgment. Like, 'How do these stories make you feel? What do you believe about it? And does anything feel different when you at least allow for the possibility?'"

They ate quietly for a few minutes. Michael wasn't sure if she seemed okay or not.

"I honestly didn't bring that up as a film idea," she said. "I thought about it, but I wasn't trying to get you to think about it."

"You *didn't* bring it up as a film idea. *I* did. I don't know how it would pan out, but it feels good to at least have an idea for a change."

"It doesn't ruin it that it was sort of my idea?"

"The first one was sort of Mr. Dunning's idea, but I made it my own."

"Yeah you did. You know I've kind of had a crush on you ever since the first time I watched it, right? I hope it's okay to say that. Probably a lot of it was the way I felt when you found out with the camera rolling that Madeleine was dying. I was just far enough out from my own loss that I really felt it with you. But that's not all of it. You were just so honest and vulnerable. And handsome. And you were so worried about the scars on your chest that you didn't even know how handsome you were. And that's such an attractive quality in a guy. Did I say too much?"

"No, it's okay," Michael told her. "You kind of said things before that gave me the general idea. You don't wear that ring."

"The dragon ring?"

"Right. You said you were going to put it on a chain and wear it around your neck."

"Truthfully? It was too heavy. I have it on a string hanging from a lamp over my bed. I don't think the important thing is how I display it. It's just nice having something of his." She took another bite, chewed carefully. Then she added, "Do you have anything of Madeleine's?"

"I have her cat," he said.

"Oh," she said, drawing the word out long. "That's so nice. That's so much better than a piece of jewelry. A real living flesh-and-blood being who knew her and loved her. You're so lucky. I envy that."

"She's a nice cat. She likes to be held tightly, and she purrs."

"Heaven," Caroline said. "Just what a grieving person needs."

They ate quietly for a minute or two.

Then she said, "I'm going to point something out, and I hope you don't mind. I'm not going to press the issue. But you just said you'd never had an experience like that with Madeleine. And I'm not saying that's not true. But when you first called me to ask me out, you said her sister calls to check up on you and you have a weird sense that she's checking up on you too."

"Oh," Michael said. "I guess I did say that, didn't I?"

"It's not a big dramatic experience. But it's something."

"I suppose it is," Michael said.

They drove up to the curb in front of the home where she lived with her parents, and he pulled on the hand brake.

"I'll walk you to your door," he said.

"No!" Her voice came out loud, probably louder than she had meant it to be. Sudden, and distressed. "I'm sorry. I didn't mean to shout like that. But please don't."

"Oh. Right. Jeremy walked you to your door and kissed you good night before he drove away."

"I hope you don't think I'm being ridiculous."

"No, I think you've had trauma. There's a difference. I won't walk you to your door, but can I kiss you good night if I do it here in the car?"

"I'd be *so* disappointed if you didn't," she said.

He leaned toward her and closed his eyes, and their lips touched. Just for a handful of seconds. It wasn't passionate. More soft and serious. There was something comfortable about it. Familiar, almost. But maybe "familiar" wasn't the right word, he thought. Not as though he already knew her somehow, but more as if it was easy to know her. Something he could fall into without much resistance.

He pulled back and opened his eyes, and they smiled at each other. A little shyly.

"Maybe we can do something next weekend," he said.

"That would be nice."

She jumped out and closed his car door. She glanced back at him once on her way to the porch. He waited and watched until she was inside safely, then shifted into gear and drove.

Seven blocks later, his phone rang.

It startled him.

It startled him because, without meaning to, he had been counting the blocks. And a little of the superstition had begun to rub off on him as he got closer to seven.

His heart drumming, he pulled over to the curb and picked up the call.

"Hello?"

"Michael? It's Patricia."

"You're late."

"Yeah, I know I'm late. I figured I'd give you a few more days to get your act together. Except . . . that's a bald-faced lie. I just forgot. So. Seeing anybody?"

While she spoke, he stared through his window at the stop sign on the corner. The seventh corner. He wondered if this was the exact intersection. Possibly not. It might have been seven blocks in the opposite direction.

"Funny you should mention it," he said. "I've just recently started dating a very nice young woman named Caroline."

"Define 'just recently.'"

"Like, within the past week."

"In other words, you made a date with her because you knew I'd be calling."

"Pretty much. Yeah. But I like her. And we've been out twice."

"Oh, what the hell," Patricia said. "That still counts. Now. I'm supposed to ask if she's your age."

"Nope, sorry. She's older."

"Damn it, Michael. You're killing me here. How much older?"

"Almost two months. She turned twenty-one last month, and I don't turn twenty-one till next month."

He could feel a smile tug at the corners of his mouth as he waited for her reaction.

"You enjoy messing with me," Patricia said, "don't you?"

"Little bit, yeah."

"Okay, back to the quiz. Next question. Does she have any reason to doubt her appearance?"

"If there's one thing I've learned in my life so far," Michael said, "it's that just about everybody does."

"You're doing it again. Does she really have an unusual reason?"

"No. She's lovely."

"Great, you passed. And I won't be calling again."

"Wait," Michael said. Quickly, before she could end the call.

"Wait what?"

"Call again. Please. Call in three months and make me take the quiz again."

"Why? You think you'll fall back to being alone?"

"I doubt it."

"Then why would I call and put you through the wringer again?"

"It just makes me feel more connected to her. If that's okay."

Silence.

A large, light-colored bird like an owl swooped down from a tree, through the beam of a streetlight.

"Fine. Talk to you in three months."

"Thanks for understanding," he said.

But she had already ended the call.

Chapter Twenty-Five

Before It All Fades into History

"Thanks for taking the time to sit down with me," Michael said. "Especially since I'm not in your class anymore."

"I'll always think of you as my student," Dunning said. "I'm your mentor, and we're friends. It was never conditional."

They sat on a wrought iron bench outdoors, in a tree-studded area of campus. The grass was a brilliant green, the cloudless sky so blue it was almost navy. It made Michael feel grateful and uplifted in a way he hadn't for a very long time. If he ever had.

"I have two ideas for films, and I wanted to run them by you," he said.

"I have to admit, when you asked to talk to me I was hoping that's what you had on your mind. I know it's easy to get stuck after an early success. Everybody thinks it's so lucky to hit big on your first time out—and it is, in a way. But I've seen some very good filmmakers get mired in what they think people expect of them next."

"I think I'm just coming out of that," Michael said. "Anyway. Here goes. I'm feeling wildly insecure about running this by you all of a sudden, but I didn't bring you here to chicken out. So. Okay."

He took a deep, slightly shaky breath. He honestly hadn't known how much emotional weight this meeting carried until he opened his mouth to share the ideas.

"Idea number one. And you might think this is a little too out there. But it's been brought to my attention lately that a lot of people who've lost a loved one have had experiences that they feel are the person getting in touch in some way. Checking in or sending a message that they're okay. But I'm not thinking about a film delving into the phenomenon itself and whether it is what the people think it is. I was thinking of it as more of a look at the role the experiences play in a person's grief. The stories can be so beautiful and thought-provoking, and I'd just like to get people thinking about what they believe, like if they think their loved one is completely, one hundred percent gone or not. But it may be a little too woo-woo for you. Or for me. Or for everybody. Now that I'm saying it out loud I have some serious doubts."

Dunning shifted on the bench and crossed his legs at the knee. He was wearing old-fashioned-looking wing-tip shoes and argyle socks, and his expression took on a look that was both serious and faraway.

"Just the way you described it, I like it," he said. "The woo-woo would come in if you were trying to convince the viewer that they should believe these were actual paranormal experiences."

"That's exactly what I thought," Michael said. "That's exactly what I told Caroline."

"But I like it as a hook into how individual people are experiencing grief. And since that's a subject you know something about, I think you'd do a sensitive job on it. And it might even help you with your own grief."

"Do you believe in it?"

"I know only that I don't know," Dunning said. "More things in Heaven and Earth, as the saying goes."

"So you don't rule it out."

"I don't completely believe what I can't prove, and I don't completely rule out what I can't disprove."

They sat quietly in the sun for a moment. Dunning was wearing a brimmed hat and dark sunglasses, which spared him most attention from passersby. Michael hadn't thought to bring sunglasses, and he had to squint to see his mentor's face.

"Tell me," Dunning said. "Have you had one of these experiences yourself since losing Madeleine?"

"No. I mean, not to any extent that it fits into the film idea."

"Maybe just as well. It might be a relief to do something less personal next time. Film-wise."

"Amen. Did *you* ever? After your family died?"

"No. I honestly never considered the idea. I guess I thought of my lovely aunts as a way my parents had of helping me from beyond the grave, but there's certainly nothing paranormal about that. What's the second idea?"

"I've been thinking a lot about Rex Aronfeld and his Hitler story. And I've started wondering if there are other people still alive who might have met or talked to him. Or met anybody else who was a significant person in the Third Reich. But maybe there aren't. I mean, Rex would be nearly a hundred and five now. I guess it would have to be people who met him when they were a little kid."

"Not necessarily," Dunning said. "Aronfeld met him in 1936. Hitler was alive until '45, though I expect after the war began he had fewer casual meetings. Still, there were others who were available to be met later in history. Adolf Eichmann comes to mind. He took off to Argentina after the war and was captured by the Israelis and brought back to stand trial in 1961. I'm sure a lot of people met him well after the war."

"I've heard of him, but I guess I don't know as much as I should about him. Was he a key figure?"

"I should say so. He was considered by most to be the chief architect of what the Nazis called the Final Solution. He was hanged in '62. He probably encountered a lot of people in prison in Israel, and in court, not to mention during the previous years in Argentina after the war. It might be interesting to talk to people who knew him in South America but didn't know who he was at the time. But let's say you find a sufficient number to interview. What are you hoping these people will tell you?"

"A couple of things," Michael began. "I wonder if there are more people who have deep regrets about the meeting, the way Rex did—who maybe felt overwhelmed by the person's power and didn't say much, and then kicked themselves for it later. And I wonder—especially if they met someone like that before it was clear what was being done in Nazi Germany, or later when he'd taken on a new identity and they thought he was someone else—what their impression was. Did they feel like they were in the presence of evil, or did the person seem more ordinary? I wonder if it's like those newspaper stories about serial killers. The ones where the reporter talks to the neighbors, and they say the killer was quiet and kept to himself, but that he was always polite and took good care of his mother, and they just can't believe he could have done such monstrous things because he seemed so completely unremarkable. I'm curious as to whether people who could do such vile things could also be ordinary in some ways."

"The banality of evil," Dunning said.

"I'm not sure what that means."

"You've never read any Hannah Arendt?"

"No."

"You must, in my opinion, if you're going to do this. She was a German author. A historian. She was present at a lot of Eichmann's trial, and she wrote a book about it that contained the phrase *The Banality of Evil* in its subtitle. Her proposition was that Eichmann was a joiner, and was never thinking for himself, and that a person could do terribly evil things without starting out with evil intentions. But you're walking a fine line with a project like that as well. Her work was extremely controversial, because it was seen as an apologia. I don't know that she meant it that way, but I do know how much people like their history in bold, unambiguous black and white. I don't mean to sound as though I agree with Arendt. I actually don't. I think that man had a great depth of evil intention, but his life was on the line and he had plenty of reason to try to convince everyone he was dispassionately following orders. I watched his face—his testimony was filmed—and I saw evil in every expression, and I don't know how she missed it. Anyway, watch, read, draw your own conclusions. It's not my role to tell anybody what to think."

"I wasn't thinking so much about exploring whether they were evil or not. To me it seems to go without saying that they were. I was thinking more about whether they *seemed* evil in a casual meeting, or if they just seemed like anybody else you might meet."

"I think it sounds interesting," Dunning said.

"I realize as I hear myself talk about it that it's obvious I haven't done my homework on the subject. But I will. I've been putting it off because I know how hard it'll be to read about. But I promise I will."

"I know you will," Dunning said.

"Which do you think I should do?"

"Which?"

"Yeah. I'm trying to decide."

"You're not only going to make one more film for the whole rest of your life, are you? I certainly hope not."

"I hope not too."

"Then make them both."

"Right. So obvious." Michael smacked himself in the forehead with the heel of his hand. A little harder than he had intended. "Now I just need to decide which to make first."

"Really? This is a problem? Speaking of things that are obvious. One of them has a sell-by date and the other one doesn't."

"Right. Duh. The Nazi one first, because the people I'd be interviewing are getting close to the ends of their lives."

"Which is actually another reason I like the idea. Because there's not much time left to do it, and someone else could have the same or a similar idea in the future, but the moment would have passed. It's very important for a filmmaker to grab hold of events that are about to fade into history. Not that a massive amount of film hasn't already been devoted to the subject, but yours seems to have an unusual slant."

"Thanks. That gives me a lot of direction."

They sat in the sun a moment longer.

Michael knew Dunning would want to go home to his wife soon. In fact, he expected it to be the next words out of his mentor's mouth.

Instead Dunning said, "It's wonderful to see you getting back up on your feet, Michael. Professionally and otherwise. I know it knocked you down flat when Madeleine died."

"It's been hard. Yeah."

"It's supposed to be hard. That's inevitable. But then you got back up anyway, which I think is the only part of the thing that really matters." Then he said the part Michael had been expecting. "Well. I should probably get home to my wife."

He stood and brushed his pant leg clear of something Michael couldn't see.

"Thanks for the advice."

"One more bit of advice," Dunning said before walking away. "Start looking into a few good interpreters. Because the vast majority of people you'll want to interview will speak only German or Spanish. Or possibly Hebrew."

"Crap," Michael said. "Hadn't thought about that at all."

But Dunning was already too far away to hear.

———

He showed up at her house at about six, with a bouquet of flowers he'd bought from the florist at the end of his street.

He hadn't met her parents yet, so he stood on the front porch and texted her.

"I'm here. Can you come out?"

"Here where?"

"Here in front of your door."

A moment later the door opened and she popped out.

"These are for you," he said, and handed her the flowers.

"How sweet."

"I would have knocked, but I haven't met your parents yet . . ."

"And it seems too soon for that, because we've only been on a few dates . . ."

"Right. Exactly. But I have no problem meeting them, anytime you think it feels right. And I want you to meet mine. They never met Madeleine, so they'd like that. Take a walk with me?"

They set off down the street together on foot, Caroline still holding the flowers.

"He liked the idea," Michael said.

"Mr. Dunning?"

"Right."

"My idea? I mean, our idea?"

"He liked them both, actually."

"So which are you going to make?"

"I'm going to make them both."

"Which are you going to make first?"

"See, I made that same mistake. When I was talking to Mr. Dunning. And he set me straight."

"Right. Got it. You have to make the other one first, because the people you'd want to interview are very old now."

"Exactly."

They walked in silence for a time.

There was a playground on her corner, surrounded by a chain-link fence but with its gate standing wide open. It was completely deserted. Apparently all the children were home eating dinner.

He stepped inside, and she followed.

"You know," she said, and then paused. As if unsure about the next part. "You could have made either one of those films even if the ideas hadn't been ones he liked."

"Yeah, I know that," Michael said.

He walked over to the swing set and sat on a swing, allowing it to pivot slightly back and forth around his feet, which were firmly planted on the dirt. She sat in the swing beside his, the flowers in her lap.

"Here's the thing, though," he said. "I just value his opinion so much. He's one of those people . . . I'm not sure how to explain this. It's like, when he tells me what he thinks, I realize it's what I think too. You know. Underneath all the second-guessing and self-doubt and talking myself out of things."

"I get it," she said. "It's good to have somebody like that."

For a few minutes they only swung. Tentatively at first, but gradually putting their body motion into it more and more, so on the upswing they sailed exhilaratingly high.

Then Caroline stopped herself, bracing her feet in the dirt.

"I have to ask this straight out," she said.

Michael stopped his motion the same way, and they sat looking into each other's faces in the fading daylight.

"I think I know the answer to this," she said, "but we haven't exactly said it out loud, and now I need it said out loud."

"Okay. What?"

"You're inviting me to be part of the after-death film?"

"Of course."

"Like . . . on camera."

"Absolutely. You're the key storyteller."

"And will it have some stuff about Jeremy? You know. Some background on his life and all?"

"I think it should."

"So it'll kind of be a tribute to his life. That part of the film, anyway."

"Right," Michael said. "We'll immortalize him. That's exactly how it's supposed to be. That's something a film can do well. It's one reason I like them so much."

They didn't talk much after that, but they swung in silence until they ran out of daylight, and he walked her home.

MICHAEL,
AGE TWENTY-FIVE

Chapter Twenty-Six

When Love Is a Living Thing

Zach Brownstein, the reporter, showed up at Michael and Caroline's house at 10:00 a.m. sharp.

He looked older, more so than four or five years of absence should have justified. He just seemed to have stepped more fully into the role of full-fledged adult.

Then again, Michael thought, he might make the same observation about himself if he hadn't seen himself on every single one of those intervening days.

"You know why I called you this time," Zach said as Michael waved him into the foyer, "right?"

"There was a note on your desk saying to call me?"

He was half kidding in the way he said it.

"No, I've moved up in the world. I leave the notes now. But I wanted to do this interview myself because we have history. I called because you've moved up in your world too."

Michael assumed he was referring to the Tribeca Audience Award, and the honors at Sundance. But before he could open his mouth to say so, Zach set him straight.

"Twenty-something years old and about to receive a LAFCA achievement award? I'd say that's news, especially in LA."

It wasn't that Michael didn't completely agree that being honored by the Los Angeles Film Critics Association was a huge deal, but Michael himself had only heard about it that morning, and he hadn't expected Zach to know.

"I didn't figure you would have heard about that."

"Dude," Zach said. "I'm the media. I knew yesterday. I'm guessing I knew before you did."

———

Michael led him out to a redwood deck overlooking a small forest.

"Wow, you're right at the edge of civilization here," Zach said.

"We like it that way. I hope you don't mind talking outside. Caroline is just finally getting the baby down for a nap, and I don't want to make that job any harder than it needs to be."

"Not a problem at all. It's tradition, actually."

He wasn't carrying a miniature tape recorder anymore. Instead he set his phone to record their conversation, placing it on the glass table between them.

"How old is your daughter?"

"Nineteen months."

"Is she talking?"

"A better question would be does she ever stop talking, and I mean even to take a breath."

"Walking?"

"Running. Everywhere. She's incredibly fast, and at the same time extremely prone to getting out over her own feet and falling. There's pretty much no such thing as taking your eyes off her, even for a split second. When she goes down for a nap, the silence is just stunning, and when she gets up, the whole house revolves around her. This tiny little person who barely comes up above my knees, and she literally sucks every ounce of attention and energy out of everybody in the room. It's amazing. And that's not a complaint. I adore her, and I wouldn't trade having her for anything, but I honestly didn't know, going in, what a task this was going to be."

"Nobody knows," Zach said. "Until they know. What's her name?"

"Rose."

"Rose," Zach repeated. "That's nice. I like that. If you don't mind, can I ask about the house? Really nice house. Big. Remote. Seems to be on a lot of land. How big is the lot?"

"A little over four acres."

"And here comes the nosy question. Do you own it, or is it a rental?"

"We own it. Well. The bank owns most of it, but someday we might be able to flip over to holding a controlling share. Decades from now, most likely."

"Then you're doing well with your films."

Michael snorted out a laugh. He couldn't help it.

"Critically? Yeah. Very well. Financially? Oh hell no. You don't get rich doing independent documentaries. I was able to buy the house because I have a job as a sound mixer with a television-production company."

"In LA?"

"Aren't they all?"

"It's quite a commute."

"I almost never have to go in, though. That's the great thing about modern tech jobs. If you've got high-speed internet you're as good as in the office. It's a great job for me. Gives me time to do my own work on the side, and I've had a chance to make a lot of connections in the industry."

Lily the cat jumped up onto the deck and warbled her way over to Michael, casting a cautious side-eye toward the visitor. She jumped onto Michael's lap and walked back and forth, rubbing and purring.

"So you're busy," Zach said.

"You could say that. I'm also trying my hand as an actor."

"Acting. That's new."

"Not really. It's actually old. It was the first thing I ever wanted to be. But I'd completely convinced myself that I couldn't do it, because sooner or later someone would ask me to do a shirtless scene. Or a nude scene. But most of the time nobody does. And besides, everybody pretty much knows that about me going in. I'm not completely knocking it out of the park as an actor, but I'm not sure I need to. I mostly just wanted to prove to myself that I can. I had three lines on that new NBC show with Clark Fischer. We'll see if I get any further than that. At this point the thing is pretty much its own reward."

The sliding glass door to the deck rolled back and Caroline stuck her head out.

"I finally got her down for a nap," she said. "You must be Zach."

She moved smoothly across the deck with her hand out, and he rose and shook it.

"No, don't get up," she said. "You don't have to stand on ceremony here. I just wanted to meet you. I'm sure you know Michael gives you a world of credit for the success of *Here I Am*."

"We actually hadn't gotten to the part about my credit yet," Zach said, and sat down.

There was a slight teasing tone in his voice, as if playfully challenging Michael for not yet delivering the appreciation.

"I was getting there very soon," Michael said.

"Oops," Caroline said. "My bad."

"It's okay," Michael said. "We just got caught up talking about other things. Yeah, when *Here I Am* first went up on Netflix, I figured nobody would watch it. A documentary short that started out as a student film? It's not like it was about to trend on the service or end up as a suggestion on the home page. But then a stunning number of people actually sat down and watched the thing, and I'm sure it was because reading the story made them want to see the film."

"Hmm," Zach said. "Films need publicity. Not exactly breaking news. But I'm glad I could help."

"You two need anything?" Caroline asked. "Coffee?"

"You need to go sit down and rest," Michael said. "You've had a tough morning looking after Rose. I can get Zach some coffee or something."

"Nothing at all for me," Zach said. "I already drank way too much coffee on the drive up."

"Nice meeting you, Zach," Caroline said. "But Michael is right. I need to go get horizontal. They always say sleep when the baby is sleeping. You know. If you ever want to sleep again."

———

After she left, he and Zach sat staring out over the forest for what struck Michael as a surprising length of time. Somehow he hadn't expected that. He'd figured it was all about words with Zach, at least in a professional setting. He toyed with the idea that the bucolic neighborhood had as much of a calming effect on Zach as it did on him, and on Caroline.

Michael only stroked the cat's back and waited.

Zach seemed to visibly rouse himself after a time.

"Okay, getting back to it. You've made not one but two more films since I last saw you. And one of them won awards at both Tribeca and Sundance, not to mention a bunch of smaller festivals."

"Actually they both did well at the smaller festivals."

"But with this LAFCA announcement, one of them can definitely be considered a breakout."

"And it's not the one anybody expected," Michael said.

"Really? Do you feel that way? I saw them both and I wasn't that surprised. You thought *An Unremarkable Man* would be the one to break out? I'm not at all surprised that it was *The Dragon Ring*. Don't get me wrong. Both excellent films. But go ahead, tell me why you said what you just said."

"I guess I just felt like *Unremarkable* spoke to a more serious subject. More significant and important. Of course, it's a subject that's been spoken to an awful lot."

"Yours was different, though."

"I hope so," Michael said. "That's sure what I was going for."

"You want to know why I wasn't surprised that *Dragon Ring* broke through instead? Because *An Unremarkable Man* was a deep dive into evil, and *The Dragon Ring* was a deep dive into love."

"Interesting," Michael said. "I never looked at it quite that way, but then I'm not exactly in a position to be objective. I'm probably the last person who can accurately judge the films, not to mention compare them to each other. I guess it's like the old joke about being a painter on a scaffold—the problem is you can't step back and get any perspective on your work. But of course it did occur to me that taking a deep dive into human evil would be unsettling to a lot of people."

"Some people like that, though, which is why we have horror movies. But here's the thing about *Dragon Ring*, and this is purely my opinion. You made love into a living thing. I don't mean you *made* it that, exactly. You didn't change love. You're not that powerful. Who is? But what I got out of the film was not so much about whether a deceased person still has any kind of presence in our world, but more that the love two people share has a life of its own. That when two people love each other and one of them dies, the love goes on living. And that's a powerful message. People are going to respond to that at a deep level."

"Interesting," Michael said.

"You can't tell me you didn't know you accomplished that."

"I guess . . . more that I never thought to frame it quite that way."

———

"One more question before I wrap up," Zach said.

It was nearly an hour later. They had spent the hour talking mostly about the aftermath to *Here I Am*. The people from Michael's past who had come out of the woodwork, and what resolution had resulted.

Losing Madeleine. And, of course, how that first film had led him directly into getting married, settling down, and starting a family.

"Okay . . ."

"In your opinion, is there a common theme that runs through all three films? They're each so different, but there must be something that interests you about the human condition that drew you to all three subjects."

"It's a good question," Michael said. "Nobody's ever asked before. And I guess I'd have to think about it. I mean . . . I know, on a feeling level. But it might take me a minute to wrap it up in words."

They stared over the forest for a moment more. The clouds had taken on that popcorn appearance, covering nearly the entire sky with their bumpy pattern. Where the sun shone behind them, its light burst through in iridescent color.

"It has something to do with going through our lives apologizing. I think that was most obvious in my first film, because it was literally about being completely unapologetic about my appearance. About everybody's appearance. But then Rex got me thinking, because he had this huge life regret over shaking Hitler's hand. And, really, why should he regret it? He was a fifteen-year-old boy, and, besides, millions of people didn't die *because of* the handshake. And they still would have died if Rex had spit on him. That got me thinking about people who might have encountered that same evil in their lives and now they feel apologetic because they feel like there was some magical, nonexistent thing they could have done to stop the tragedies. But there was nothing they could have done. Don't get me wrong. If we've hurt somebody or behaved badly, I'm all for apologies. But I just keep seeing how we go through our lives apologizing for things that either aren't wrong at all or are totally out of our control."

"I like it," Zach said. "But I'm having trouble extending it to *The Dragon Ring*."

"Really? Seems like an easy connection to me. I made the film to try to bring experiences like that out into the light, because they were mostly kept quiet. Why were they ever in darkness? Why would a person have an experience like that and hold it as a secret? Because they're made to feel apologetic for believing something that can't be proved in any scientific way, and that other people don't believe."

"So, life without apologies is the theme."

"Unless you actually owe one, yeah."

Zach reached over and touched his phone to end the recording.

"I like that a lot," he said. "And I totally have all I need. I'll send you a link to the piece when it goes live. And I'll see you at the LAFCA ceremony. I'm covering it, so I'll be in the audience cheering your achievement."

———

Rose came barreling into the foyer, Caroline and the cat following close behind, just as Zach was saying goodbye at the door.

"Daddy, Daddy, Daddy, I woke up!"

Then she stopped dead when she saw a stranger in the house. Her eyes, always huge, grew inexplicably wider. She fell silent, and stood spraddle-legged and slightly wobbly, tugging at the saggy behind of her pull-up diaper.

"You don't have to be afraid, Rose. This is Zach. He's a friend."

"Friend?" she said, her voice uncharacteristically tiny.

"Hey," Zach said. "Can I get a picture of the three of you?"

"Now?" Caroline asked, sounding exasperated. "She's a mess. I'm a mess. I'd have to put on makeup and change my clothes, and change her clothes, and . . ."

"How about faces only?" Zach asked. "Natural light. You don't need makeup. You look great."

"I do not look great."

"Wife of mine," Michael said, striking a friendly and partly joking tone, "why are you apologizing for your appearance? What do you think it's supposed to be that it's not? And who do you owe it to, to look some special way? You're beautiful."

"Okay, point taken, but at least let me brush my hair and brush the baby's hair. Are you in a hurry?"

"Not *that* much of one," Zach said.

She scooped up the baby and hurried upstairs.

"I'm glad you were the one to say that," Zach said, "so I didn't have to."

"It's a hard habit to break."

"You still have trouble with it sometimes?"

"Doesn't everybody? But I catch myself. Usually."

Caroline came back with freshly combed hair, holding their daughter, also with freshly combed hair. They all stepped out into the front yard together.

And that was how Michael and his beautiful family ended up on the front page of the Arts section of the *Los Angeles Times*.

Chapter Twenty-Seven

A Rock, a Crown Jewel, and an Idea

"I need your advice on something," Michael said.

It was a handful of weeks later, and he was standing in front of their full-length bedroom mirror, trying to choose his clothing for the awards ceremony. Caroline was standing behind him. He could see her face near the reflection of his own shoulder.

"Okay, sure," she said. "What is it? I love the jacket. I hope you're not having second thoughts about the jacket."

He had bought it only two days earlier, and it had stretched their budget. But how often does one take the stage to be honored at a significant awards ceremony?

"No, the jacket is a definite, and it's perfect with these pants. I have about three shirts that would be great, but I don't think the shirt is all that important. Here's the issue. Here's what I'm going back and forth about. The idea was to button the shirt up to my throat and wear it with this thin black tie. But now I'm thinking of doing something bold, and I want you to tell me if I'm making a mistake."

He loosened the tie and pulled it free. As he stood looking at them both in the mirror, he reached up and undid his collar button, and the two buttons below it. It left his shirt just enough open at the neck that a couple of inches of his scarring was visible.

"It's not enough that it would be a total distraction," he said. "It's not like it'll be all anybody will see."

"But it's enough that you're making a strong statement that you don't need to hide it."

"Exactly."

"You definitely should do it."

"That's what I thought." He opened his hand and let the tie fall to the floor. "I just needed to hear you tell me you backed me up on that."

———

When Michael's mother arrived to look after the baby, she made a beeline for Michael, staring directly at his open collar. Both of her hands came up, as if she would pull the top of the shirt together. As if she would button it for him.

Then her hands froze in the air for a moment, and she dropped them to her sides.

"Good choice," she said. "Very admirable and brave. I support you."

"Thank you, Mom. I know stuff like that is hard for you, so that means a lot. And thanks for staying with Rose."

"A long evening with the light of my life," she said. "I think I'll manage."

———

They stood together in front of the theater, before a white backdrop printed with the stylized LAFCA logo, while a team of photographers all took their picture at once.

Michael tried to smile, but he was deeply nervous, and a little overwhelmed, and whatever his face was doing didn't feel like a natural smile.

He could feel himself obsessively touching the folded sheet of paper in his jacket pocket—the notes for his brief speech—as if the written words might have flown away and left him rudderless and without the thoughts he would so desperately need.

In time they moved inside and sat, and Michael pulled his phone out of his pocket and stared at it closely in the dim light.

"Shouldn't you turn that off?" Caroline whispered in his ear.

"I have it on silent," he whispered back.

He had been hoping all day for a text or email from Mr. Dunning, but so far had not received one. However, he was surprised to see an email from Jonah Levy, the generous man who had helped him edit his first film and submit it to Netflix.

"We take no credit whatsoever for your talent," it said, "but still Dennis and I are overflowing with pride for your success, and we honestly couldn't be happier for you."

He wanted to send something in return, but a heart emoji seemed too corny, and the words would not come. He would have to save his reply for a moment when his brain was working properly.

He slipped the phone back into his pocket and tried to breathe steadily until it was time to take the stage.

———

When his award was announced, Michael heard it as if from far away. As if he'd been at thousands of feet of altitude, and his ears just would not pop.

He stood, and Caroline stood, and he hugged her tightly and kissed her on the cheek as the audience applauded distantly in his ears.

"Couldn't have done it without you," he said.

"In this case, true," she said.

Michael took the stage.

The presenter handed him his plaque and stepped away, and he stood alone at the podium, staring into lights that seemed to blind him. Lights that made the audience disappear.

He left the notes in his pocket, because he was suddenly sure he knew them by heart. He knew exactly what he wanted to say.

"I'm so, so grateful for this honor," he said. "I'm not sure there's any way to convey that as strongly as I feel it. I want to thank my beautiful wife, Caroline, because she supports me a hundred percent, always, and my parents for the same reason. And I want to thank my mentor and teacher, Robert Dunning. You're my rock, and what I learned from you is everything. And not just about film, either. I learned how to be a person from watching you do it so well.

"The *LA Times* reporter Zach Brownstein told me he thought the reason this film resonated with viewers is because it's a deep dive into love. Because it holds up love as a living thing, a real entity that lives on when one of the two lovers—romantic or not—dies. So, related to that idea, I'd like to thank two people who are no longer with us. I'd like to thank Madeleine Greenhaven-Shaver for taking good care of me until I met Caroline, and I want to thank Jeremy Bloom for taking good care of Caroline until she met me.

"One more thing, and then I promise to give you your stage back. This is not in my notes, and I hadn't planned to say it, but I want to thank my birth parents for giving me away to the Woodbines, where I could thrive. There was a lot I wanted you to do that you didn't do, or didn't do well, but you got that part right.

"I realize that might sound weirdly personal for an acceptance speech, but face it—that's kind of my professional wheelhouse at this point."

From the white wilderness on the other side of the lights he heard a light rumble of laughter and a smattering of applause.

"Thank you so much for this," he said, holding up the plaque.

As he left the stage and returned to Caroline, the audience applause no longer sounded distant. It was thunderous in his ears.

It was something he knew he would hear as he was going to sleep that night. It was something he felt he could draw back to himself— draw upon—for encouragement, anytime it was needed.

It just wasn't one of those things a person could ever possibly forget.

———

They posed for more pictures with the plaque.

They said no to the after-parties because they had a baby at home.

As they waited for the valet to bring their car around, Michael slipped his phone out of his pocket. This time there was a text from Dunning.

"Michael, you are my crowning achievement as a teacher," it said. "The jewel in the center of that crown. Watching you practice being a person inspires me, and apparently it inspires countless others as well. Enjoy tonight—you earned it."

"What?" Caroline said.

He could only imagine she was asking as a reaction to the expression on his face.

He handed her the phone and let her read it for herself, because speaking was something that felt out of his reach for a moment.

When he looked up again, Zach was standing in front of him.

"I thought I wasn't going to get a chance to talk to you," Zach said.

"I'm sorry. We need to get home to the baby. She's a lot for my mom to handle. Wait. Did I just apologize for having a baby who needs us?"

"You kind of did," Zach said.

"Yeah, I heard it too," Caroline added.

"I take it back, then," Michael said. "She's our priority, and that's exactly as it should be. No apologies."

"Fair enough. But before you go, though, Michael. Real quick, and this is on the record. What's up next for you, film-wise?"

"I have absolutely no idea," Michael said. "But the right idea will come along. It always does."

Caroline drove on the way home, because Michael was utterly wrung out.

He sat in the passenger seat—head leaned back on the headrest, eyes half open—and watched the world flash by the window. A three-quarter moon hung over the mountains to the east, and seemed to be racing with them, keeping up as they sped along.

"Being around a lot of people takes it out of you," she said, "doesn't it?"

"I used to think it was about the nature of the appearance, but yeah. I'm beginning to think so."

"I didn't know you were going to mention Jeremy in your speech."

"Is it okay that I did?"

"It's wonderful. I was just surprised."

"Seemed like the least I could do. Without him there would never have been this film, and I wouldn't have just gotten an award."

They drove for several miles without talking.

The Southern California sprawl faded as they got closer to home, until soon only the moon remained, racing alongside them over dark fields. Or seeming to, in any case.

"I was just thinking," she said. "I was thinking about how sure I was that he was the one. And now I'm starting to think maybe there are people in our lives who aren't just 'the one.' Maybe that's oversimplifying life. Maybe sometimes a person is more like the one who takes you to where you need to be next and then jumps off there. Not necessarily by jumping off the planet. You know. But just jumping out of your life in one way or another."

"That's a nice idea," Michael said. "That's such a nice idea it could almost be a film. I'll have to think about that."

Illuminated only by the moonlight and their headlights, they drove the dark highway—thinking—all the way back home.

BOOK CLUB QUESTIONS

1. Michael decides to live his life without apologies, ultimately deciding that is the only way he will be free. How would Michael's life have been different if he hadn't met Professor Dunning? Have you ever met a person in your life who had a strong impact on you in the same way?

2. When Michael speaks with his father about making the film, and how it might upset his mother if he follows through with it, Michael's father says, "But that's not a proper way to go through life, holding off doing the things you want to do because it might upset someone else." Why do you think his father gave him this advice, and do you believe this was the right thing to tell his son?

3. At the filming of his segment, Tim McDonnell, the janitor, discusses how being "stick-thin" is interpreted differently when you're a man than when you're a woman. Do you agree societal pressures are different for men and women? If so, in what ways beyond body image?

4. When 103-year-old Rex shows up for his filming slot with Michael, he notes how the word "old" often comes with a negative connotation in today's society. He gives the example: "Let's say you had a blind date and someone asks you how it was. You say, 'He was old.' And that means it was terrible . . ." Have you ever seen or heard the word "old" be used as a derogatory term, and why do you think this is?

5. Michael has spent most of his life keeping his scars a secret. By having the courage to accept his body and let his insecurities go, he was able to help not only himself but other people as well. By taking the risks to be our true selves, do we also encourage others to do the same? Was it worth the risk for Michael, and why might people be averse to doing the same?

6. When Michael meets up with his birth parents, Miles and Livie, their reaction to seeing him in the film rubs Michael the wrong way. But Miles tries to shut down Michael's feelings by telling him he's being too sensitive. Michael's reply is "Whenever I hear anybody tell anybody else they're too sensitive, all I hear is 'I want to feel free to say offensive things to you and it really inconveniences me when you mind.'" Do you agree with Michael's interpretation, and did he respond appropriately in this situation?

7. After Madeleine's death, Michael struggles to get back up on his feet, both professionally and personally. He tells Professor Dunning that one of the hardest things for him is other people claiming they know how he feels, when that isn't helpful at all because no one really knows how another person feels. Why might it be so difficult to say the right thing when someone has experienced a loss? If you've dealt with grief before, was there anything that helped you, or have you found ways to help others?

8. Toward the end of the book, Michael and the reporter, Zach, are discussing the last two films Michael has released. Zach notes that *The Dragon Ring* is so successful because it is a deep dive into love. He mentions Michael and Madeleine's relationship and goes on to tell him, "When two people love each other and one of them dies, the love goes on living." Do you believe this statement to be true? Have you had any experiences that reinforce this idea in your own life?

ABOUT THE AUTHOR

Photo © 2019 Douglas Sonders

Catherine Ryan Hyde is the *New York Times, Wall Street Journal,* and #1 Amazon Charts bestselling author of nearly fifty books and counting. An avid traveler, equestrian, and amateur photographer, she shares her astrophotography with readers on her website.

Her novel *Pay It Forward* was adapted into a major motion picture, chosen by the American Library Association (ALA) for its Best Books for Young Adults list and translated into more than twenty-three languages for distribution in over thirty countries. Both *Becoming Chloe* and *Jumpstart the World* were included on the ALA's Rainbow Book List, and *Jumpstart the World* was a finalist for two Lambda Literary Awards. *Where We Belong* won two Rainbow Awards in 2013, and *The Language of Hoofbeats* won a Rainbow Award in 2015.

More than fifty of her short stories have been published in the *Antioch Review, Michigan Quarterly Review, Virginia Quarterly*

Review, *Ploughshares*, *Glimmer Train*, and many other journals; in the anthologies *Santa Barbara Stories* and *California Shorts*; and in the bestselling anthology *Dog Is My Co-Pilot*. Her stories have been honored by the Raymond Carver Short Story Contest and the Tobias Wolff Award and have been nominated for *The Best American Short Stories*, the O. Henry Award, and the Pushcart Prize. Three have been cited in the annual *Best American Short Stories* anthology.

As a professional public speaker, she has addressed the National Conference on Education, twice spoken at Cornell University, met with AmeriCorps members at the White House, and shared a dais with Bill Clinton.

For more information, please visit the author at www. catherineryanhyde.com.